TIMOTHY R. BALDWIN

Shadows of Deceit

A Cassie Maddox Mystery, Book 1

INDIES UNITED PUBLISHING HOUSE, LLC

Library of Congress Control Number: 2025902007

First edition

ISBN (paperback): 978-1-64456-792-0
ISBN (hardcover): 978-1-64456-839-2

This book was professionally typeset on Reedsy.
Find out more at reedsy.com

Praise for Shadows of Deceit

"Shadows of Deceit had me on the edge of my seat from start to finish."
— **Readers' Favorite**

"Reminiscent of John Grisham's The Firm, Shadows of Deceit kept me in its grip from the first to the last page."
— **Readers' Favorite**

"A compelling introduction to a relentless and relatable private investigator. The hard-edged first-person narrative and fast-moving plot give this noir-inspired novel a gritty sense of momentum."
— **Self-Publishing Review**

* * *

"A classic, fast-moving private-eye mystery."
— **Reedsy Discovery**

"This book comes out swinging from the first page and does not let up at all."
— **BookSirens Reviewer**

* * *

"An edge-of-your-seat thriller with sharp dialogue, tight pacing, and a mystery that unravels brilliantly. I devoured it in days and can't wait for the sequel."
— **Robert Plant**, author of *Dark Matter*

“A fast-paced tale of corruption, danger, and compelling characters. Baldwin delivers tangled alliances, escalating stakes, and a promising start to a standout series.”
— **Max Hiller**, author of A ‘Cadillac’ Holland Mystery series

“A sharp cat-and-mouse thriller with youthful energy, family tension, and rising stakes. Cassie Maddox is a fresh, engaging PI you’ll want to follow into the next case.”
— **Jennie Rosenblum**, Editor, Indies United Publishing House

Also by Timothy R. Baldwin

A Shot at Mercy (2019, 2021)
A Crock of Sundries, Volume 1 (2021)
Chemical Burns (2022)
The Unwanted Guest and Other Short Thrillers (2024)

A Kahale and Claude Mystery Series
Book 1: Camp Lenape (2019)
Book 2: Shadows of Doubt (2020)
Book 2.5: A Bazaar Christmas (2020)
Book 3: Operation Varsity Blues (2020)

These and more at
https://www.indiesunited.net/timothy-baldwin

Welcome to Lenape City

Lenape City has a memory. The streets remember secrets, the skyline bears witness to corruption, and the shadows have their own loyalties.

At the heart of it all is Cassie Maddox—a rookie private investigator with a sealed juvenile record, a reluctant badge of legacy, and a stubborn moral compass. By day, she runs background checks out of her mother's attic. By night, she follows trails no one else dares, with nothing but a secondhand camera, a burning need for justice, and a few too many people underestimating her.

Shadows of Deceit introduces readers to a noir-tinged cityscape where the truth is always buried beneath layers of power, privilege, and well-tailored lies.

Coming Soon to the Series

Book 2: Dynasty of Deceit

Book 3: Behind the Ivy

Book 4: The Tarnished Band

1

Assignment

Light snowflakes whisk over the windshield of my mid-90s Cadillac DeVille as it hits another pothole, jolting me and the camera next to me. I cringe. Six months into moonlighting as a PI while I support myself as a paralegal proves difficult.

Still, this is the most exciting case yet! Gregory Hunter is a cheating husband.

Up ahead, Mr. Hunter careens in a late 90s Toyota Sedan straight into Lenape City, a town large enough to get lost in but not so large the locals wouldn't notice when a newcomer moves into town.

Several car lengths ahead, the Toyota hooks a right on Broadway. Its driver, Gregory Hunter, has done this more than once since I started following him this afternoon when he left his offices at Lenape Savings and Loans, a few miles from the home he shares in the suburbs with his wife, Trudy Hunter.

Maybe he's on to me, or perhaps he's just paranoid. It's too early in my investigation, but I've followed him long enough to understand his driving habits. I hit my right signal and ease into the turn, wincing as the passenger side wheel grinds against the wheel well, and my unsecured camera shifts in the front passenger seat.

My father, the great Detective Dylan Maddox, gave me this twenty-year-old white Cadillac DeVille car. "Cassie," he said when he tossed me the keys on my twentieth birthday. "You'll need a car if you're going to work at that law firm. You remember Ol' Bess. She's a real looker."

That was five years ago, and one of his many not-so-subtle hints that he wouldn't forget about my now sealed juvenile record, which comprises a series of petty thefts, one breaking and entering, and a night of joyriding with this old Cadillac when I was fifteen. All this embarrassed him and won me a reputation with the Lenape City Police Department.

As the Cadillac straightens onto Broadway, I rest my hand on the camera to keep it from sliding further. Gently used and recently purchased, this is a necessary expense, especially if I want to catch Mr. Hunter "in the act," as Mrs. Hunter called it when she hired me.

* * *

I sat across from her at an obscure diner. Trudy Hunter leaned in, eyeing me coyly. "You know, Cassie, that's what you PI types do? Catch cheating husbands in the act." A stray lock of graying hair fell over her right eye. She swiped at it, waiting for my reply.

I shifted in my seat as I put down my mug. "Mrs. Hunter, I want you to understand I've only been at this for six months. There are plenty of others who have far more experience—"

Trudy waved a hand as she cut me off. "I know that, dear. But the others are too well-known and too expensive. My husband won't recognize you."

I took a sip from my mug before responding. "Okay. But I'm not likely to capture photos of your husband bare-assed and rolling in the sack with some hot secretary. This isn't the movies."

Trudy laughed. "I understand. You'll follow him and take photos. That's what you do. Capture photos of cheating husbands with their mistresses."

* * *

If my dad had been present, he'd have laughed and told her to bugger off. But she kept her doe-eyed gaze locked on me. I could've refused, but I needed the cash, the experience, and the reference if I ever planned to go solo. Until then, my current employer, Sampson & Sampson, sponsored my license while I worked under their lead investigator. I've done plenty of investigative work, including background checks, interviews, and research. I gained limited surveillance experience, assisting a lead investigator as we followed a disgruntled ex-employee suspected of damaging property in revenge for his termination.

Conducting surveillance on a spouse suspected of infidelity is new for me. Still, it was only a matter of time before something like this would come up. That was all the excuse I needed to spend a few hundred bucks on a better zoom lens for my camera and a couple of optical attachments for my phone. When I agreed to take on the case, Trudy squealed with delight, like I'd surprised her with an early Christmas present.

If my father knew I'd accepted this job and spent a few hundred bucks on new equipment, he'd have a fit, which was one of many reasons I wouldn't let him in on my little business. He'd micromanage and criticize everything, even the things that weren't his business. I obtained my PI license a little over six months ago. I moonlighted as an independent investigator out of the finished attic of my mom's house, paying her what I could afford until I got the investigative service off the ground. Dad joked that he'd join me when he retired.

* * *

Gregory Hunter takes a left two blocks ahead. He nearly escapes, but I keep up with him. I turn left at the next street, hoping to spot him on a cross street. He drives erratically through the industrial part of the city. Still, I have seen nothing that suggests he's cheating. Maybe he is a liar, especially since this 6 p.m. outing takes him miles away from his usual route between home and work.

I doubt he's having an affair. But it's only my second day tailing him, and I haven't yet received a full background check from my best friend, Rafi Alvi.

I glance down one cross street, then another until I catch sight of the rusty rear of an old Toyota bouncing over every pothole in its path. If I turn now, he'll surely see me, and that's the last thing I want. I take the next turn, relieved that the road is smooth and my ancient car won't rattle and give me away.

My phone rings through the car speakers, thanks to Rafi, who installed a Bluetooth system for me. I activate the talk mode.

"Cassie Maddox, Private Investigative Services," I say with forced cheerfulness.

"Cassie, it's your mom," Julia Maddox says as if I wouldn't recognize her voice.

I swallow back the disappointment. "Hey, Mom. Busy right now."

"How busy can you be, Cass? You just got off work, didn't you?" Julia asks.

"No, Mom, I'm working right now," I say. "I have this case and—"

"Since you're out," Julia interrupts me. "Can you pick up some cheese and a fruit platter? I'm running around like a madwoman trying to get ready for —"

"Sure, mom," I say, cutting her off.

"Thanks, hon," Mom says. "What time do you think you'll be home?"

I turn down another street where boutique shops and ancient architecture clash with a stray warehouse better suited two blocks away in the industrial district. I spot Hunter's car parked outside the Genesee Country Club.

"Sorry, Mom! Gotta go."

I hang up just as she adds more items to the grocery list. In a sense, my mom is right. I am not currently conducting research for Sampson & Sampson. But that's only because she doesn't see Cassie Maddox, Private Investigator, as a proper job. That is one thing my parents agree upon. I sigh as I bring the Cadillac to a slow roll, searching for a parking space big enough to dock the old boat.

The Genesee Country Club is on one of Lenape City's main streets, in the heart of downtown, right on the edge of the historic district. At three stories high, the Romanesque building competes with City Hall as the tallest building in a town that is no larger than twenty-two square miles, with each square mile occupied by some three thousand people. It's not so big that the neighborhood busybody couldn't keep tabs on the out-of-towner.

I spot a parking space and squeeze in, facing the Genesee Country Club. I grab my camera and focus on the country club, zooming in on the familiar marble steps. In high school, I worked here as a server under my uncle, Alfred Maddox. I cut ties with him after he insisted he could get me on a scholarship in one of my first-pick schools. Like my dad, Uncle Alfred is well-connected, but it didn't sit well with me when I got accepted into Dartmouth. Soon thereafter, I dropped out. My uncle insisted my rejection of his offer was a personal affront to his character, and we haven't spoken since. Seeing no activity on the Genesee's steps, I set my camera down and scan the neighboring buildings.

Boutique shops and restaurants border the country club. Since I didn't see Gregory Hunter step into the country club, I can't conclude that this excursion into the city has anything to do with my uncle's business. Grabbing my phone and camera, I get out of the car, slinging the camera over my shoulder. It's time to hunker down for a stake-out in this historic town, and I know just the place.

2

Shadowy Meeting

2Beans Cafe is a geometrically shaped boutique shop serving coffee and small fare. Its pentagon shape allows me to position myself at any table and do some people-watching while I sip coffee. Plus, my childhood best friend, Lila Baker, works here.

The front door chimes as I walk into the shop and take in the nostalgic decor integrated with a modern design. At just after 6 p.m., two customers sit in leather chairs, immersed in their phones, each with a cup of coffee by their side. Behind the counter where she prepares an order, Lila glances up. She wears dark eyeliner and a streak of purple colors her layered pixie cut.

She grins and draws out her greeting, "Hey, Cassandra."

"Hey, girl," I say, dropping my things at a table catty-corner from two of the windows. I turn on my camera. Aiming it out the window while zooming in on the country club, I snap a few photos of people too busy to enter the building. Zooming out, I scan the rest of the area.

Lila plops herself in the chair across from me. She eyes the camera as I set it down. "Oh! You've gone legit? Not just background checks?"

I nod with excitement. "Plus, the new client paid in advance."

"And one step closer to your own office," Lila says.

"Maybe," I say.

"Well," Lila says, quickly glancing around and leaning in. "Guess who might be able to help you with that?"

"Really?" I say. "You got the accounting job at—"

I pause as one of Lila's coworkers glares at me.

Lila giggles. "Don't worry about her. She already knows. I start tomorrow at The Peterson Group."

I touch her streak of purple. "And this? Are they going to make you go all professional?"

Lila shrugs. "They didn't say anything. But, seriously, get your own office, or maybe we could get an apartment together."

This isn't the first time Lila mentioned rooming together.

"And don't say I'll think about it," Lila adds.

I laugh. "Yes!"

Lila's eyes widen. "Really?"

"If not now, then when?" I ask.

Lila narrows her eyes as she stands. "Girl, I'm gonna hold you to that." Her face softens. "Let me get you your coffee, Cassandra Maddox."

"Thanks," I say, glancing out the window.

Lila is the only person besides my mother who can get away with calling me Cassandra. Sometime around the age of twelve, I adopted the shorter form. But Lila knew me way before that. She is also right about my tendency to procrastinate, just as she is right when she says official police work isn't quite my thing. Somehow, though, the investigative services do suit me. Maybe it's independence that I crave.

Lila brings me the coffee. "I'd hang with you, but..." she says, nodding at a few customers coming in from the cold.

"No problem," I say, holding up my camera.

"Yeah," Lila says. "Before I go, there's this new club, Phantom Beats. We totally have to go this week to celebrate."

I grin. "This weekend?"

"Definitely," Lila says. "But we'll have to go shopping first. How about Thursday night?"

"Five-thirty?" I ask.

"See you then!" Lila says, bouncing up from her seat and returning to her post just as the door chimes to the tune of a small group of suits — men and women.

I turn my attention to my camera and the sites, zooming in on the sidewalk and scanning the area around Gregory Hunter's car. A mix of pedestrians in jeans and winter coats and others in business attire pass by, mingling with those who exit shops or businesses.

My heart skips a beat when I spot Gregory Hunter two blocks away, passing under a red awning with Chinese characters. Even though he wears a hoodie and keeps his head down, I don't miss his thick mustache and tall, athletic frame.

I gather my things and stand. "Lila, catch up with ya later!"

"For sure," she calls out as I exit.

Shouldering my way through dawdling pedestrians, I close the distance between myself and Hunter. For an athletic guy, he doesn't move fast. A block away, he turns down an alleyway. I pick up my pace and ignore the complaints of a young couple who gape at a storefront window.

I duck into the alleyway. Nearly week-old garbage immediately bombards my senses. The alleyway is the length of two city blocks, with two buildings built against each other with side rather than rear exits. Though security lights line the tops of some buildings, they create deeper and darker shadows, shrouding who knows what. I notice smashed security lights mounted on the corners of some buildings.

My heart races as I listen for signs of company—whispered voices or the splash of footsteps in day-old puddles.

Careful not to trip over a trash can lid or step in broken glass, I plod ahead, ever closer to the narrow intersection. Making myself as small as possible, I place my back against the wall and inch myself forward until I can peek around the corner. When I do, my breath catches in my chest.

Forty feet away, shrouded in the shadows of the next back alley intersection, Gregory Hunter stands, his hands shoved in his pockets. He shuffles his feet as he paces. Then, a woman, tall and lean and dressed in black, appears from his left.

My chest tightens. She could've entered this rendezvous point from any direction—hell! She could've entered from right behind me. In my haste to catch up with Hunter, I'd been careless. If my father knew, he'd surely lecture me, but that doesn't matter now. Gregory removes his hands from his pockets and faces her. The woman approaches him with ease while Gregory shifts his weight. As they speak in hushed voices, I catch an occasional snippet of their conversation: *we have little time... contractors are threatening to pull out...*

This isn't a meeting between lovers. From where I take up position, I strain to catch snippets of their hushed conversations. I have to get closer.

3

Eavesdropping

My heart pounds in my chest as I cautiously crawl towards the edge of the building. Peeking around the corner, I duck behind a stack of crates and listen to the hushed conversation between Gregory Hunter and the woman several yards away. Their words cut through the still night air like shards of glass.

"I need those records. My employer will pull out if they don't see where the money is going," the woman demands with sharp impatience.

Gregory's voice trembles as he replies, "I understand, but if Peterson finds out I'm leaking information, I'm as good as dead."

My mind races as I realize this is more than just a simple investigation into a husband's alleged infidelity. Instead, the woman's words hint at accounting fraud, and the tremble in Gregory's voice implies more than simple hyperbole.

I discreetly adjust my camera and snap a few photos, hoping they will step out of the shadows and into the dim light where I can get a better angle of the woman. The woman's whispers hiss through the dark alleyway.

"This mess has pulled us both in too deep. The kickbacks could sink us. Just get us what we need or risk being shut out." She takes a step forward, backing Gregory against the wall. "Do you understand?"

I snap a few photos, hoping to catch a clear image of her profile in the dim light.

Gregory's back hugs the wall. "I... understand."

My chest tightens at the mention of kickbacks. They aren't the only players in this complex financial plot. But they are pawns directed by those who would risk the lives of others for monetary gain.

At best, I've landed in the middle of a financial plot. Stuck in the shadows, crouched behind a pile of old crates, while cold, damp air seeps through my jacket. Despite my instincts to end this stakeout rather than risk getting caught, I am stuck here until Gregory and this mysterious woman end their conversation.

At Hunter's mention of the name Peterson, I wonder about the connection between The Peterson Group and Lenape Savings & Loans. I'll have to ask Trudy Hunter if Gregory mentioned working with The Peterson Group.

I shift my position and freeze at Hunter's voice.

"Someone's been snooping around. If they catch wind of this..."

My breathing quickens. The woman's cold voice cuts in.

"Make sure they don't catch wind of this. We're too close to get caught. Just do your job and keep your mouth shut."

I know I've stumbled upon something big. This isn't just a case of infidelity; it's a dangerous game of deception and greed.

Glass shatters in the distance, causing me to freeze behind the crates. Instinctively, I reach for my 9mm, a Sig, safely concealed beneath my jacket. I hold my breath, listening.

I imagine Gregory and the woman glancing in my direction while I attempt to make myself smaller. High-heeled footsteps approach.

"What is it?" Gregory asks.

The footsteps halt.

I press myself further into the shadows.

Did they hear me?

I control my breathing, knowing the slightest sound will give me away.

"We should probably call it a night," Gregory mutters, but I can hear the tension in his voice.

The woman hushes him. "Are you positive nobody followed you?"

I curse myself for not being more careful. *Amateur move, Cassie.*

"Positive," Gregory replies, with a tremor in his voice. "Look, can we wrap this up? The longer we wait here—"

"You'll leave when I say you can," the woman snaps. "About those records…"

I risk a peek around the edge of the crate.

The woman's back is to me, and I glimpse the tension in Gregory's face.

"You'll have them by the end of the week," Gregory says. "Then I'm out."

She steps towards him.

A cat screeches down another alleyway while trash cans clatter. The woman turns away from Gregory and marches down the opposite alleyway. Once alone, Gregory slips his hand into his pocket and pulls out his phone. After dialing, he puts his phone to his ear and says, "She's getting too close."

He waits.

"I understand."

Stuffing the phone back in his pocket, he heads in my direction, his eyes focusing ahead. Somehow, despite passing by just feet away, he doesn't notice me in the shadows.

I wait until a few minutes after Hunter's footsteps vanish, then I slip away. As I walk towards the streets, my mind races with the implications of what I have just witnessed. The woman in the meeting clearly presented herself as having the upper hand, yet Gregory's last phone call suggested he is merely playing the part of the woman's timid and unequal counterpart in this financial scheme.

Though my mind races with the implications of what I have just witnessed. I must be careful. I must never allow myself to be cornered like that again. Something other than an alleycat spooked the woman, and that something had an equal effect on me. Though I carry my gun most times, pulling it out in the alleyway could have had fatal consequences. But for whom?

Dad always taught me never to point a gun at a target I don't intend to destroy. Neither Hunter nor the woman presented a threat. If the woman had discovered me, I would have blown my cover, jeopardizing this case and possibly my career.

Rookie move, Cassie.

This case isn't just about catching a cheating spouse anymore—it's about blowing wide open a corrupt financial scheme right here in Lenape City. As a private investigator, I have no business pulling on this thread of corruption. I can turn this over to any detective, including my father, Detective Dylan Maddox. That would be the right move.

Besides, Trudy Hunter only needs to know that her husband is not guilty of marital infidelity. And the police need to know what I just witnessed. But will a handful of shaky pictures taken in dim lighting be enough? My limited training tells me that the police need more credible evidence before taking over the case.

4

Allies

I park my car outside R.A. Pharmacy, a few miles away from my mother's house, feeling hopeful that the photos on my camera will sufficiently interest the police in opening an investigation. I pull out the SD card and transfer the pictures to my laptop before entering the pharmacy. Ritvik Alvi, the owner, greets me in his usual heavy accent.

"Cassie, Beta, how are you today?" he asks. "Rafi will be out soon. Can I get you anything?"

I force a smile, trying to hide the lingering tension. "Actually, this is business-related." I hold up the SD card. "And my mom wants a cheese and fruit platter."

Ritvik points. "Cheese and fruit are down aisle five," he says. He leans in closer. "How's your case going?"

"I wouldn't exactly call it a success," I reply, holding up the SD card. "I might even drop the case once these are developed."

"Too complicated?" Ritvik asks.

I let out a sigh. I've known Ritvik and his son my whole life. He is like an uncle to me, his house a haven before my parents separated. I can't lie to him. "It might be too risky."

Ritvik waves at a few customers who enter the store. "Is the payoff worth it, though?"

"I can't say for sure," I say, anticipating Ritvik's response.

"You're a smart girl," he says sincerely. "And your father can help, you know. You don't have to do this alone."

Just then, Rafi appears from behind a shelf carrying restocking items, which he sets on the counter.

"Rafi," Ritvik gestures towards me. "Cassie is here."

Rafi spins around, flashing that charming smile I used to fall for. His ebony skin matches his father's, and my heart aches at the familiar sight. "I have something for you," he says, gesturing for me to follow him to the photo center. I give his father a wave as we pass by.

As Rafi disappears behind the counter, my heart flutters with anticipation. Moments later, he reappears, holding a thin envelope in his hand. Part of me wants it to contain something meaningful, a sign that we still have hope.

"Is that it?" I ask, trying to conceal my vulnerability.

"What can I say?" he replies with a grin. "It seems your guy is clean."

I furrow my brows, unsure if I want to believe it. But I know I need to see the photos taken earlier. I hand Rafi the SD card.

"These are mostly architecture photos and people staring at their phones as they walk through town," I explain as he inserts the card into the computer. "This case isn't about catching a cheating husband. It's—" I hesitate, not wanting to reveal too much.

But Rafi's eyes light up with curiosity. "Do you need surveillance or digital tracking? You know I can do more than assist with background checks." My heart swells at the thought of working closely with Rafi.

"I know you can," I tease. "Let's see what these photos reveal. Can you have them developed by tomorrow?"

Just then, Ritvik calls for Rafi's help with a broken register. Rafi reluctantly hands over the SD card.

"I've copied the photos onto the computer. The prints will be ready tomorrow morning," Rafi promises before rushing to assist Ritvik.

A graduate of the School of Engineering, Rafi is overqualified but more than capable of fixing things in the store when they go haywire. I've worked with him several times on background checks when my caseload backed up, but that type of work pales compared to my current case.

As realistic as I am about the investigative service industry, I know being hired to follow a man suspected of infidelity is the most exciting thing that could happen. However, this case exceeds my expectations with potential corporate sabotage and a threat to my client's husband's life.

Heading down aisle five, I pass a few moderately irate customers grumbling about equipment issues. I grab a bag of cheese and another bag of mixed fruit. That will suffice for whatever my mother is planning at the house.

The two customers ahead of me pay in cash, a habit any frequenter of this store has picked up.

After paying for my things, I say, "See you soon." As much as I try to act professional, seeing Rafi always brings back a rush of old memories and feelings that I thought were long buried.

"Wait," Ritvik interrupts. "Have you heard about the new development project? I heard they're offering a space for startup businesses."

I nod absentmindedly, my thoughts still lingering on Rafi.

"Stop by tomorrow," Rafi says as he fiddles with the register. "We can catch up."

But I can't help but imagine us working together on this case. It's what we planned when we were dating - me in the field, him providing support. And now, landing such a big case so early in my career is beyond what I could have imagined.

* * *

Reality sets in as I walk back to my car. Whoever that woman is, Gregory Hunter's life is in danger. My training and studies scream to pass this on to people more qualified than me. But what would I be passing on? A retelling of a conversation I overheard isn't hard evidence, nor are photos of a clandestine meeting in a cold, dark alleyway.

I sit in my car in the parking lot, staring at my camera's viewfinder while I scroll through the photos on the SD card. These will not be enough to build a solid case against anyone, especially not against Gregory Hunter.

I need more evidence, concrete proof that his life is truly in danger and that he is indeed being targeted by someone.

But how am I supposed to gather that? I can't follow him around 24/7 or install hidden cameras in his home. Asking him directly about the woman will only reveal my involvement in this investigation.

Leaning back in my seat, I let out a heavy sigh. This simple case is more complicated than I thought. I can feel a headache coming on and rub my temples, hoping to stave it off.

I glance down at the viewfinder again, this time studying each photo more closely. There has to be some clue or detail that can lead me to more information. But all I can see are two shadowy figures meeting in an alleyway, their faces obscured by shadows.

I zoom in on the woman. Even in the shadows, the camera catches a scarf around her neck. With a few adjustments on my laptop back in my office attic, I can lighten the image and perhaps remove enough shadows to make out any unique markers one of the boutique shops in town can identify. I don't know how that will help, but it's a start, and it gives me hope—hope that I can do this alone with a little help from Rafi, of course.

With that bit of hope, I head home. Upon arrival, I bypass my mother, who is reading in the living room, and head upstairs.

* * *

As I climb the narrow stairs to my attic office, the old wood creaks under my feet, echoing my growing unease. The space is small but cozy, filled with the soft glow of my desk lamp and the familiar scent of old books and coffee. I settle into my chair, the leather worn smooth from countless work hours, and boot up my computer.

The photos load slowly, each pixelated image a reminder of the gravity of what I've stumbled upon. I zoom in on the woman's scarf, adjusting the contrast and sharpness. As the image clears, I can make out a distinct pattern—intricate swirls of gold and red on a deep blue background.

My heart races. I recognize that design. It's from Lenape City's most exclusive boutique, Gilded Threads. Gilded Threads makes only a handful of those scarves each season, numbering each one. I know this because Lila and I regularly browse the store, though she and I know we can never afford such an item on our meager incomes.

I lean back in my chair, the weight of this new information settling over me. The scarf is a lead but a tenuous one at best. Gilded Threads is known for its discretion as much as its luxury goods. The likelihood of them divulging customer information, even for a numbered, limited edition item, is slim to none.

Still, I can't shake the feeling that this is important. I search the boutique's website on my laptop, scrolling through their current collection. There it is—the Midnight Whisper scarf, a stunning piece with intricate gold and red swirls on deep blue silk. Gilded Threads made ten this season, each priced at a staggering amount that makes my eyes water.

I chew on my lower lip, a habit I've never managed to break. The boutique opens at 10 a.m. tomorrow.

I glance at my watch. It's already past midnight. I have been so caught up in my investigation that I've lost track of time. The house is quiet now; my mother is likely asleep downstairs.

I lean back in my chair, stretching my arms above my head, attempting to relieve the tension in my muscles. The soft glow of my desk lamp casts long shadows across the room, making the stacks of case files and books loom larger than life. Outside, the wind whispers through the trees, a gentle reminder of the world beyond my little attic sanctuary.

My mind races with possibilities. Who is this woman in the expensive scarf? How is she connected to Gregory Hunter? And most importantly, what kind of danger is he in?

I pull out my phone, hesitating for a moment before texting Lila. *Are you up for some undercover shopping tomorrow?*

Her response comes almost immediately. *Always!* Her quick reply brings a smile to my face. Lila's enthusiasm is infectious, even through a simple text message. I can already picture her excitement at the prospect of our "undercover shopping" expedition.

Awesome! We'll go to The Gilded Threads at 10 a.m.

I place my phone down and turn back to my computer, determined to squeeze every detail from the photos before calling it a night. As I zoom in and out, adjusting contrast and shadows, the image of the alleyway takes on an almost surreal quality. The brick walls seem to pulse with hidden secrets, the shadows dancing at the edges of my vision like they are trying to tell me something. My phone dings, letting me know Lila has received and replied to my message. But that will have to wait. I lean in, knowing I am onto something.

In the corner of one frame, I notice a glint of metal. Enhancing the area reveals a partial license plate on a sleek black car parked not quite out of view. It isn't much but another breadcrumb on this increasingly complex trail. As I zoom in further, I mentally kick myself for not seeing the vehicle. Tailing Hunter and straining to hear every word between him and the woman had absorbed me too much.

"Keep your head on a swivel, Cass," I whisper while squinting at the partial license plate.

The first numbers, still hidden in the shadows and graininess of the photo, are enough to begin my search. I scribble the numbers and letters onto a nearby notepad, my handwriting messy in my haste.

The clock on my computer screen blinks at 1:30 a.m. I rub my eyes, feeling the strain of hours spent staring at the screen. But I can't stop now, not when I'm this close to… something.

I pull up the DMV database. While using the DMV for personal investigations isn't strictly legal, I have access through my PI license. Whether this is personal or professional is a grey area. However, this is about protecting someone's life—at least, that's what I tell myself as I input the partial plate number.

The search returns hundreds of results. I groan, leaning back in my chair. It's a start, but without the make and model of the vehicle or three more numbers, I see myself at a dead-end, at least for the night.

5

Gilded Threads

The chime above the door heralds our entry into Gilded Threads at the stroke of 10 am, a sound that resonates with our bubbling excitement. I shoot Lila a grin as the boutique unfolds before us like a treasure trove, the air thick with the scent of luxury— leather, perfume, and something else. Maybe it's just the smell of money.

"When was the last time we were here?" Lila's voice dips and rises with a musical lilt. "It's been what? Four months?"

"Something like that," I reply, my gaze sweeping over the gleaming displays. "Will you look at these?"

We pause at a rack of dresses, each an intricate work of art, their price tags intentionally discreet.

Lila reaches out, her fingertips brushing a gown's delicate beading. She laughs with a twinkle in her eye. "This would be perfect for our Thursday night out at Phantom Beats, don't you think?"

"Perfect and entirely out of budget," I say, but there's no missing the longing in my voice. We're two kids from Lenape City who've seen the rough edges of life; such opulence isn't meant for us, or so some would have us believe.

"Never hurts to try them on, Cassie," she teases, nudging me towards a dress with a plunging neckline and shimmering sequins. "Live a little."

"Imagine showing up to a stakeout in one of these," I muse, running a hand down a rich velvet blazer, its texture whisper-soft beneath my fingers. "Would certainly throw them off the scent."

"Or get you on the best-dressed investigators list," Lila chuckles, her warm and genuine laughter echoing in the vaulted space.

"Is there even such a thing?" I ask, mock seriousness masking the real threads of curiosity weaving through my mind.

"First time for everything," Lila replies, giving me an impish wink before drifting towards a display of handbags, each more exquisite than the last.

"Look at these," she calls. She gazes at various watches, each glinting under the soft lighting. "For when you finally make it big, huh?"

"Right," I laugh, though the idea invokes a pulse of pride. One day, I'll get there. One day, my father's shadow won't loom so large, either.

"Let's just enjoy the view for now," I suggest, the double weight of my aspirations and my mission here at Gilded Threads settling comfortably upon me.

"Best view in Lenape City," Lila agrees, her arm looping through mine as we explore, our reflections dancing in the polished glass and chrome. Moments like these—simple, shared—remind me why I do what I do. For the truth, yes. But also to protect the relationships that matter most.

I weave through the aisles of Gilded Threads, each step bringing me closer to my true mark within the silk and sequins.

"Keep your eyes open for a scarf known as Midnight Whisper," I tell Lila. "It's gold and red—"

"With swirls that dance on deep blue silk," Lila finishes. "Seriously, what's with the scarf obsession?"

"Trust me, it's more than just a pretty piece of fabric," I say, focusing my watchful gaze on each display. "It's the centerpiece of design and elegance."

I'm determined to find it, not for fashion, but because it holds answers—answers worth far more than the staggering price tag dangling from its hem.

"Ooh, look at you, all detective mode," she teases, but her smile fades as I remain locked in my search. "You'll find it, Cass. If it's here, you'll spot it in no time."

"Thanks," I reply, though my gut churns with the fear that we might be too late.

As we round another immaculate corner lined with mannequins dressed in the latest Lenape City chic, Lila's sharp intake of breath catches my attention. She clutches my arm, her grip tight.

"Isn't that Dan Lutman?" Her whisper slices through the boutique's hushed ambiance, laced with an excitement I haven't heard since our high school days.

Following her gaze, I lock eyes with the familiar figure browsing a rack of designer suits. In casual clothes that do little to hide his new athletic build, Dan looks different from the lanky teenager we once knew.

"Wow, it is him," I acknowledge, surprised at how the sight of an old classmate can momentarily eclipse my single-minded pursuit. "Didn't expect to see him in a place like this."

"Let's go say hi!" Lila urges, already taking a step forward before I can react.

"Wait," I hesitate, the investigator in me whispering caution, but Lila's enthusiasm is a force unto itself. With one last glance at the surrounding finery, I let her pull me toward a past that seems both distant and suddenly present.

Stepping through the boutique's curated landscape, I trail Lila with a reluctant curiosity. She moves with a bounce in her step, and I can't help but admire her ability to draw me into this spontaneous reunion.

"Dan?" she calls out, her voice a melody of cheer.

He turns, his face lighting up with recognition. "Lila? Cassie? No way!" The surprise in his tone is genuine, a stark contrast to the calculated calmness of this place.

"How long has it been?" I ask, my voice steady but warm.

"Five, maybe six years," Dan's smile is easy and open. It's funny how time can layer someone you used to know with a veneer of unfamiliarity. "Too long. What brings you two here?"

"Shopping for a party," Lila answers, her hands flitting towards a sequined dress nearby. "And Cassie's on a mission to find some elusive scarf."

"Ah, the thrill of the hunt," he teases, crossing his arms.

"Something like that," I admit, my eyes catching a flash of deep blue silk from the corner of my eye—maybe the Midnight Whisper. But I push the thought aside, focusing on the now. "How about you? Never pegged you as the Gilded Threads type."

"Ah, well," he rubs the back of his neck, looking slightly embarrassed. "I'm on the hunt for a gift. My sister's birthday is coming up."

"Gift, you say?" Lila's eyebrows arch in surprise as she glances at Dan, her tone laced with playful incredulity. "That's quite the shopping list for a Tuesday."

"Yep," Dan agrees, scratching the back of his neck with a sheepish grin. "Got a couple of birthdays coming up in the family, and my sister always had a thing for fancy scarves. Thought I'd try my luck here."

I bite my lip, stifling a smirk. Gilded Threads isn't your run-of-the-mill gift shop. Dan's casual attire seems almost defiant against the luxurious backdrop surrounding us. It's odd that he's here, but then again, life after high school takes people on paths as unpredictable as Lenape City's winding streets.

"Of course," I nod, remembering how Dan's sister, even in high school, seemed to have a scarf for every day of the week. "So, what are you up to these days?"

"I joined the LCPD last year." Dan brushes a hand over his hair, a touch of pride in his stance.

"Wow, really?" Lila says, leaning in closer. "That's amazing!"

"Thanks." He nods, the corners of his eyes crinkling. "It's been quite the ride."

The LCPD—Lenape City Police Department. Surprise crashes over me, mingling with a sense of inevitability. "That's...unexpected," I manage, tucking a strand of hair behind my ear. "Have you ever run into my dad, then?"

"Your dad?" He pauses, considering. "Detective Dylan Maddox, right? Yeah, I've heard a lot about him around the precinct. Legendary status and all that. Haven't had the pleasure personally, though."

My lips curve into a half-smile, a strange cocktail of pride and distance swirling within me. "Yeah, that sounds about right."

"How about you, Cassie? What are you up to?" Dan asks.

"Private investigation," I say.

"Must be cool, following in his footsteps, sort of," Dan muses, his gaze flickering between us.

"Sort of," I say, the words tasting bittersweet.

"Anyway, I should probably get back to it. Great seeing you both," Dan says with a nod, his attention already drifting toward a colorful display of fabrics across the room.

"Likewise," I reply, while Lila waves him off with promises to catch up soon.

We watch him disappear between the racks, and for a moment, the air feels lighter, less laden with untold stories and unasked questions. Then, returning to our own search, we blend again into the silk, lace, and sequins surrounding us.

Lila's elbow nudges mine, a silent signal that draws my gaze from Dan's retreating form to the space he once occupied. "You never told me there was a history there," she whispers with a conspiratorial glint in her eye.

"History is overstating it." The words tumble out, light and dismissive. Yet, I can't help but think back to the lingering looks and hesitant invitations from Dan that had punctuated our final year of high school. A time when Rafi and I were an 'us,' and Dan's quiet interest in me became just another background hum in the cacophony of teenage drama.

"Rafi always seemed like your perfect match anyway," Lila muses. "Why'd it end? You never told me?"

I shrug. What can I say? We were immature kids who needed time. Then again, did Rafi and I ever really end? Feeling a swelling within me, I clear my throat.

"We're still friends," I say.

"Friends, huh?" Lila nudges me. "Cassandra Maddox, you still have feelings for Rafi, right?"

Heat rushes to my face, but before I respond, a presence cuts through our reminiscing. A woman approaches, her poise and appearance embodying Gilded Threads' elegance—silver hair coiffed into a flawless chignon, a tailored suit hugging her frame with bespoke assurance, and eyes that command attention. Her presence is inseparable from the threads of fabric woven into the tapestry of this boutique.

"May I assist you, ladies?" Her smooth voice wraps around us like silk. Her name tag, discreet yet distinct against her lapel, reads "Eleanor."

"Actually, Eleanor, yes," I say, my tone matching her professionalism as I let instinct guide the conversation. "I've been tracking down a scarf—the Midnight Whisper. I heard it's exclusive to this store."

"Ah, yes, the Midnight Whisper." Eleanor's lips curl into a knowing smile as if mentioning the scarf conjures an image worthy of the piece's dramatic name. "It has been quite popular among our discerning clientele."

"Discerning, yeah..." I murmur, my thoughts racing. This isn't just about fabric and threads—it's about identifying a woman potentially putting my client's husband in jeopardy.

"Is there one available?" Lila chimes in, her voice laced with the same urgency I feel pulsing in my veins. She's more than just my wingwoman; she's my partner in crime-solving.

Eleanor inclines her head, considering us for a moment. "I believe we may have one left in stock. If you'll follow me, please."

"Thank you," I breathe out, relief mingling with anticipation. As we trail behind Eleanor, I share a look with Lila—one that says we're onto something big. And as for Dan, his presence here today is another puzzle piece waiting to be placed. But for now, I focus on the path ahead, each step bringing me closer to discovering the name of last night's mystery woman wearing the elusive Midnight Whisper.

We glide through the maze of Gilded Threads' luxury, Eleanor leading us with the poise of a queen in her court. The Midnight Whisper scarf hovers in my mind, its secrets wrapped in silken folds.

"Actually," I interject casually, "a friend of mine recently bought one of these scarves. It looked absolutely stunning on her—especially with her red hair."

Eleanor pauses and turns, a spark of recognition flitting across her features. "Ah, yes, Shayan. Her hair is distinctive, and her timeless beauty harmonizes effortlessly with our pieces' refined elegance."

"That definitely sounds like Shayan," I nod, allowing her name to sink in, engraving it into my memory. Lila catches the weight of the moment, her gaze locking onto mine. That's our lead—Shayan's not just another affluent shopper; she possesses answers about Gregory Hunter.

Eleanor pauses at a rack, her fingers sifting through silk and wool, pausing on intricate patterns woven into shades of blue, purple, and red. She frowns. "It seems we sold the last Midnight Whisper. Can I interest you in Sunrise Echo?" Eleanor displays a vibrant scarf featuring soft pastels with peach, gold, and sky blue hues. She waves her hand over the scarf. "These delicate patterns evoke the first light of dawn, perfect for the coming spring. Would you like to try it on?"

Lila and I exchange a glance. She shakes her head, and I look at the woman poised with anticipation.

"No, thank you," I tell the woman, offering a warm smile. "We appreciate your help. I really had my heart set on the Midnight Whisper."

As we exit Gilded Threads, the cold winter air contrasts with the controlled warmth and elegance we leave behind.

"So, you've got a name. But did you see anything you liked?" Lila asks.

"Not really," I say, giving Lila a knowing glance. "I'm thinking something more within our price range?"

"Luna Chic Boutique," Lila exclaims, her excitement infectious.

"Definitely," I agree, matching her enthusiasm. "But what to wear to Phantom Beats? I'm sure you spotted a few items that would look killer on you."

"I only spotted a pair of heels that would make you look like a femme fatale straight out of a spy movie," she teases, nudging me playfully.

"Definitely not my style," I say with a laugh. Our Thursday girls' night out promises more than revelry; it's an opportunity to blend into the vibrant tapestry of Lenape City's nightlife, where secrets might slip as easily as cocktails from a bartender's hand.

Weaving through the midmorning crowd, Lila can't shake off her astonishment. "Cass, how do you do it? You didn't just get her talking; you practically turned her into your informant." Her voice carries a familiar blend of awe and amusement.

"Guess it's all in the approach," I say, shrugging nonchalantly even though my heart swells with pride.

"Seriously, you have this…this way of making people want to tell you everything," she continues, looping her arm through mine. "They don't teach that in PI school, do they?"

"PI school" has been a running joke between us ever since I started Maddox Investigative Services. There's no real academy for private eyes—at least not one I attended. Still, Lila thinks of my on-the-job learning as a covert training program.

"Maybe it's a talent passed down from Dad, or maybe it's just a lot of practice," I admit with a grin. "You know, the Maddox charm."

"Whatever it is, it works. And hey, if this detective gig doesn't pan out, you'd make a great saleswoman."

"Ha! Let's hope it doesn't come to that," I reply, bumping her shoulder lightly as we dodge a cyclist zooming past.

"Promise me you'll never waste that gift on something like selling used cars."

"Wouldn't even dream of it," I say.

We laugh together, a moment that stitches the fabric of our friendship tighter. These times, when Lila's laughter rings free and my guard drops, I remember why we're not just friends but sisters.

"Hey, Cassie, Lila." Dan's voice rolls over us like an unexpected wave as we approach the corner. We turn to find him leaning against a lamppost, his casual stance belying the sharpness in his eyes. Eyes that follow me more closely than I'm used to.

"Dan," I acknowledge with a nod, wondering what brought him back around. Maybe it's just coincidence, or perhaps it's the investigator in him, too—curiosity weaving its threads.

He pushes off from the post, falling in step beside us, hands tucked in his pockets. "I gotta say, I'm impressed," he starts, his gaze fixed on me now. The intensity of it sends a current down my spine, alerting every instinct I have. "Few could've gotten a name out of that clerk so smoothly."

"It's just a first name," I respond, keeping my tone even despite the flutter in my chest. It's not every day a Lenape City PD officer gives you a nod of respect.

"Clearly, you've got a knack for it," Dan says, and there's a sincerity in his tone that feels like sunlight breaking through clouds. "If you ever decide to trade the shadows for a badge, let me know."

"Thanks, Dan, but I'm pretty set on my path," I smile. "Besides, I've attempted that once, and it didn't go well."

"Fair enough," he concedes, but I catch the hint of admiration that lingers before he turns away. "Well, take care, you two. Stay sharp."

"Always do," I call after him. Still, my thoughts are already racing ahead. With a partial plate and a partial name in the bag, the lines of this investigation are already forming around what I've yet to determine.

"See?" Lila nudges me, a knowing smirk playing on her lips. "Even the cops see it."

"Let's just hope they can keep up," I quip back, feeling the weight of anticipation settle over me like a second skin. Determining the rest of the license plate and the last name of this Shayan is only one part of a story yet to unfold.

6

An Unexpected Partnership

I wake up as the first light of dawn filters through my bedroom curtains, heralding the start of another busy day. My phone buzzes incessantly on the nightstand, its screen illuminating with emails and appointment reminders. I rub my eyes and swing out of bed, ready to dive into the day's chaos.

After a quick shower and much-needed coffee, I settle into my desk, flipping open my laptop. Though cramped, the attic office is mine, and right now, I have work to do. The usual mix of updates, appointment reminders, and spam floods my inbox until one subject line jumps out at me.

URGENT: New Assignment – Shayan Easton

I freeze. The name hits me like a jolt of static electricity. Shayan Easton. I just heard the name Shayan at Gilded Threads, tied to the scarf—Midnight Whisper.

You are not such a talented investigator, after all. Are you Cassie? I kick myself for not getting Shayan's last name from Eleanor.

Clicking the email open, I scan the details. Sampson & Sampson has assigned me to investigate Shayan Easton, an employee of Shenandoah Partners, who is suspected of financial misconduct. The firm wants to know if she's been funneling company funds or passing sensitive information to competitors.

I exhale slowly, my mind racing. Is this the same Shayan who met with Gregory Hunter two nights ago? The timing is too coincidental. I need to dig deeper.

I open a browser and pull up Shenandoah Partners' website. Their latest projects—Heritage Commons, Old Town Plaza, and Historic Harmony— plaster across the sleek homepage. I click the link for Old Town Plaza, revealing a mixed-use development set to open in a few months. Incubator spaces for small businesses. The kind of place that could be a front for something bigger, or the perfect place to open up an office space easily accessible to the public. Lila and I could even lease one apartment in the development, putting me right above the office. In a few months, I'll have enough to secure half of the deposit. Having clients to support the venture is entirely different.

I tap my fingers against the desk, staring at the screen.

Assuming Shayan Easton is the same person I'm looking for, what were she and Hunter discussing two nights ago? Her demand for financial records from Peterson and her fear of being compromised come back to my mind. The employer she is referring to is either Shenandoah Partners or an enigmatic third party. Either way, she's a thread in a much bigger tapestry—and I need to find out where it leads.

I check the time. I have a lot of time before my 1 p.m. meeting with Thomas Pence, the C.E.O. of Shenandoah Partners.

Closing the browser, I click on the folder containing the photographs from the previous night's meeting.

As I told Rafi, most photos are of pedestrians and historic architecture. Scrolling past these, I come to the first of Gregory Hunter as he approaches the alleyway. The street lamps illuminate the photograph, which I zoom in on. Another man stands with his back against a storefront window. Nothing about him screams "person of note," though his gaze does appear to land on Gregory. He is people-watching, waiting outside the store for his significant other, or following Gregory. I think back to the previous night and recall the glass breaking. This man could have followed behind me and knocked over a glass bottle, or it could have been a coincidence.

I zoom in closer to see the man's profile, but the photo is too grainy to reveal any clear features. Frustrated, I drag the image into my case files on Gregory Hunter and move on to the next set of photos—the meeting between Gregory and Shayan.

My breath catches as I study the images. Even in profile, even under the dim alleyway light, there's no mistaking the striking red hair peeking out from beneath the woman's beanie cap. And then, there's the scarf—the same deep blue silk adorned with gold and red swirls.

I sit back and crack a knuckle. This isn't just some woman in a shady deal—this is likely the same Shayan Easton who is now the target of my investigation.

I flick through more images. Shayan's face remains mostly turned away, and her features are obscured by the winter coat's high collar. But it's her— the woman who warned Gregory Hunter he didn't get to decide when he was done.

I exhale slowly and drag the images into my files. This isn't a coincidence. Not by a long shot.

I open a Word Document and begin typing a report for Trudy Hunter, detailing my following him into town. Then, I come to the conversation I overheard. How much does Trudy need to know at this point? I am obligated to report everything I observe. Then again, if this becomes a police matter, this report would be part of an ongoing investigation.

I rapidly click on the keyboard and transcribe the conversation from memory. When the conversation ends, I reread it, then stand and stretch. Speculation aside, Hunter and this woman are involved in a financial kickback scheme that involves at least two parties. It isn't clear who they represent or whether there is a connection between The Peterson Group and Shenandoah Partners.

After finishing my report for Trudy, I open my email and type a greeting. As I prepare to attach the file, my phone rings.

The caller ID displays "Lenape City Police."

I clench my teeth, a bad habit I've picked up from Dad.

"What does he want?" I grumble as I pick up the phone.

On the third ring, I try to lighten my mood with a smile and answer, "Morning, Dad."

"Good morning, Ms. Maddox," a voice that doesn't belong to my father replies. "This is Chief Burgess. I apologize for calling you so early."

"Chief Burgess," I reply, then swallow back my embarrassment. "Good morning. What can I do for you?"

"I'd like you to come to the station and discuss a case you're working on."

My stomach tightens. "Which case is this?"

"I'll explain everything when you arrive," Chief Burgess says. "What time can you get here?"

I glance at the unfinished email to Trudy. "I was headed that way for a 1 p.m. appointment. I can stop by before then."

"I'll see you then," Chief Burgess says. "And Cassie, it's very important that you don't tell your father about this."

"Understood, Chief."

Upon hanging up the phone, I recall the last time I sat alone in the same room with the police chief. Back then, Chief Burgess was still a detective while I was fifteen. He had me seated in a dimly lit interrogation room. The cold metal chair felt more like a punishment than a place to sit. I had committed a series of petty thefts around the neighborhood. When arrested, my father correctly decided I should accept responsibility, leaving Detective Burgess to handle it; Burgess seemed more disheartened than angry, emphasizing my squandered potential. His remarks invoked equal parts of shame and defiance in me. The ordeal also resulted in being let off with a stern warning and a promise to my father to stay out of trouble. The memory of the whole experience remains a stinging reminder of the pressure of living up to my father's legacy and not disappointing the entire police force in the process.

I turn back to the computer and sigh as I hit save on the email to Trudy. I wonder which case Chief Burgess wants to speak to me about. Aside from Trudy Hunter and me, no one knows about Gregory Hunter. This leaves me wondering if the case in question is another assigned by Sampson & Sampson.

One thing for sure, if Dad had called, I would have told him to bugger off. But since it's the Chief, I'll have to see what's on his mind and comply with his unnecessary orders to keep my father in the dark.

* * *

I gather my things and leave my mother's house, making a quick stop at R.A. Pharmacy for the photographs Rafi promised me.

As usual, Ritvik waves at me from behind the counter. "Cassie, good morning."

"Good morning! Rafi said the photos would be ready." I smile.

"Oh, yes," Ritvik says as he ducks behind the counter to grab an envelope. "Rafi mentioned you'd be stopping by. He had a job interview this morning."

"Oh!" I exclaim as he hands me the envelope. "He didn't mention anything about it."

Ritvik winks at me. "It was supposed to be a surprise, so don't let on that you already know."

"I won't," I laugh. "Have a great day!"

* * *

I easily navigate the busy streets of Lenape City until I reach the Police Precinct. This familiar safe haven brings order to my chaotic life. As I enter the station, my shoulders tense up. Dad sits at his desk speaking on the phone on the far left, surrounded by stacks of paperwork and the glow of his computer screen. At another desk, a detective talks intensely with some young women. Five other desks remain empty and organized.

I zip down the far right side of the cluster of desks towards Chief Burgess' office. My dad notices my movements and gives me a slight nod, to which I respond with a brief smile before knocking on the Chief's open door.

He looks up from his work and signals for me to come in, motioning for me to close the door behind me. I do as instructed, setting my bag down beside me as I sit.

"How have you been, Chief?" I ask.

"Great!" He leans forward, looking pleased. "And I'm glad to see you sitting across from me on the right side of the law this time."

I shift in my seat. "I thought you'd bring that up."

He folds his hands in front of him. "Let's get straight to it, then. Your case seems to intersect with one of ours."

"Which case?" I inquire.

He pulls out a manila envelope and slides it over to me. As I cautiously open it, my throat tightens at the sight of myself crouched in a grainy black-and-white alleyway, eavesdropping on a conversation I probably had no business overhearing. In the blurred background of the photo stand Gregory Hunter and Shayan.

"What did you hear or see between that man and woman?" Chief Burgess asks.

I take out my collection of photographs and hand them over to him. He flips through them while I explain. "The man is Gregory Hunter. His wife hired me to gather evidence of an adulterous affair. So far, I've only caught him in the alleyway with that woman."

Chief Burgess nods, listening intently as I recount what I overheard two nights ago in the alleyway, letting him know I transcribed the conversation from memory. I stick to the facts, holding back any speculations.

"Impressive," he says when I finish. "I'm proud of how much you've grown. Who would've thought you'd be working with the police?"

My face flushes at the praise. "Working with the police?"

Chief Burgess nods, adding, "Your case and ours are currently overlapping. We typically require a PI to hand over all their findings. However, you are uniquely positioned to investigate a new angle we may have missed."

"But I'm still new at this," I protest. "There must be others more qualified for this job than me."

"Cassie, don't underestimate yourself," Chief Burgess insists, holding up my photographs. "You possess the skills we need. This is a high-profile case, and discretion is crucial."

My stomach flutters nervously. "High profile?"

"Oh yes," Chief Burgess confirms. "And if your work leads to an arrest, Cassie Maddox Investigative Services will gain significant credibility by working with us."

"You've convinced me, Chief. What exactly do you need me to do?"

"Find out everything about Gregory Hunter and his involvement with this woman," he instructs.

"Consider it done," I say confidently, reaching for my bag and pulling out a contract.

Chief Burgess waves it away. "No need for that, Cassie. We anticipated you'd say yes and have already drawn up our contract."

He hands me the document. As I skim through it, I see that it outlines over one hundred hours of work in one month with a payment of five thousand dollars upon completion. Naturally, I'll be reporting directly to Chief Burgess. The contract also includes standard legal terms regarding liability and confidentiality.

I quickly sign the contract and place it back on the desk. "Should I end my contract with Trudy Hunter with something like, 'Good news! Your husband isn't cheating on you'?"

Chief Burgess asks, "Have you found conclusive evidence proving he isn't cheating on her?"

I admit, "I suppose not."

"Continue to report Gregory Hunter's activity to his wife, but delay sending out the specifics of what you witnessed Monday night," Chief Burgess says.

"That seems duplicitous," I say. "What if Mrs. Hunter finds out I withheld information?"

"Right now, all you know is that Gregory Hunter met with a woman in an alleyway. They exchanged a few words and parted ways."

I protest, "But their lives could be in danger."

Chief Burgess raises his hand. "When you get a chance, send over your incident report." He picks up the photographs. "Do you mind if I keep these?"

I stand. "Of course. Those photos are now the property of Lenape City Police anyway."

Chief Burgess adds, locking the photographs in a drawer, "You'll do great, Cassie. Trust your instincts and stick to the reporting plan."

As I turn to leave, Dad approaches with fiery intensity. Though I quicken my steps, he catches up with me within several feet of the exit.

"Cassie," he says, his voice low and stern. "What are you doing here? Why didn't you stop to say hi?"

"We acknowledged each other," I reply, trying to keep my voice steady. "Besides, I wasn't here for a social visit. Chief Burgess wanted to see me."

"See you?" Dad asks, his eyes searching my own. "For what?"

I step away. "I'm on a case, Dad."

"On a case?" Dad's gaze wanders before settling back on me. "Cassie, that's great news! But why didn't you tell me? You know I could help."

"Because the Chief has instructed me not to loop you into the case," I say firmly. "Besides, I need to do this alone. You've always overshadowed me, and I need to prove that I can handle things myself."

As Dad fumbles for a reply, Chief Burgess steps out of his office.

"Detective Maddox," he says, "can I see you for a moment?"

Dad glances between us, his jaw tightening. "This isn't over, Cassie," he says before following Chief Burgess.

"Good luck," Chief Burgess says to me, giving me a supportive nod as he leads Dad into his office.

With the door closing, I turn away with a grin. Chief Burgess believes in me and trusts me to handle something this big. Yet, a familiar knot forms in my stomach. Dad wouldn't see this as a win for me. Somehow, he'd find a way to insert himself into my investigation.

Straightening my shoulders, I head toward the precinct exit, claiming the case assigned to me alone while steeling myself for a meeting with one of Lenape City's most influential business leaders.

7

Shenandoah Partners

At 12:45, I enter Shenandoah Partners' sleek, modern office building. It stands out from the aging buildings in this part of Lenape City. I pause in the polished lobby, admiring a tabletop three-dimensional rendering of the developer's projects. Heritage Commons for the North Side, Old Town Plaza for the East Side, and Historic Harmony for the city center.

As I look around, I wonder if other developers have partnered with Shenandoah or if Shenandoah is financing all three projects at once. My eyes drift to the abstract art on the walls - one trying to imitate Edvard Munch's "The Scream" and a large structure in the center that leaves me feeling hollow.

"Ms. Maddox?" A voice interrupts my thoughts. Jenna, the receptionist, directs me to a spacious corner office.

Thomas Pence, CEO of Shenandoah Partners, stands up to greet me. He's tall and confident, wearing a sharp suit.

"Ms. Maddox, welcome," he says as we shake hands. "Please, have a seat."

I thank him and take the offered chair.

"Are you familiar with our work at Shenandoah Partners?" he asks.

"I did a little research," I reply. "And I saw the scale models in the lobby when I arrived."

"Great!" Pence grins, showing off his unnaturally white teeth. "Let me fill you in on anything you may have missed."

Sitting, Pence taps the top of his desk. The lights in his office dim, and a bird's-eye view of Lenape City fades in on the walls to my left and right and on the wall right behind Pence.

Thomas Pence winks and, with practiced ease, offers a history of Lenape City's architectural developments over the last hundred years. The history lesson segues into a flashy and unnecessary pitch of how Shenandoah's latest projects will bring a modern feel to the aging city's landscape while boosting the city's plummeting economy by attracting new businesses and residents who will more than willingly pay the high prices necessary to support the amenities these projects offer. As his pitch continues, images and videos sync with each of his points.

"...and so you see, these projects will guarantee this city's success and economic and population growth for decades to come."

The lights come up suddenly, causing me to blink until my eyes adjust to the sudden change. Thomas Pence remains standing behind his desk, grinning.

"Ms. Maddox," he says. "What do you think?"

"It's all," I clear my throat. "Very impressive. I read online that Old Town Plaza will feature incubator spaces for startups and small businesses."

The smile fades from his eyes. "Yes, but we're smoothing out some bumps we've hit."

Nodding, I wait for him to explain.

"We're scheduled to finish in three months," he says, leaning forward. "Were you interested in leasing one of those spaces?"

"Yes. I'm looking to open up office space and—"

"You should also check out the properties of our competitors," Pence interrupts.

Though put off by his interruption, I ask. "Are you not the only developer with major projects in the city?"

Pence let out a deep, rumbling chuckle as he settles into his seat. His eyes glimmer with amusement as he leans in close. "Have you heard of Hathaway Realty and The Peterson Group?"

The mention of The Peterson Group sends alarm bells ringing in my head. Memories of past conversations and encounters flood my mind, all tied to the name Peterson—Lila Baker's new job, Gregory Hunter's mysterious evening rendezvous with Shayan.

My curiosity piqued, I ask cautiously, "Do they offer similar incubator space as yours?"

Pence flashes his signature two-thousand-dollar smile and gives a knowing wink. "You should check them out."

A door on the right wall opens as if on cue, and a woman enters, carrying a manila envelope.

"Right on time," Pence remarks, gesturing towards the woman. "Ms. Maddox, meet Lisa Chenoweth - my interim assistant while Shayan Easton is away."

Lisa hands me the manila envelope as Pence continues. "Shayan hasn't shown up for work in almost a week now."

"Has it really been that long?" Pence muses before shifting his gaze to me with a hint of tension. "Last week, she accessed and downloaded confidential information–financial records, investment properties–without authorization."

Lisa chimes in, her voice carrying a slight strain: "We're not sure what's going on with her, but we need your help to get to the bottom of it."

I flip through the file Lisa gave me, noting Shayan's impressive track record as an employee. When I reach a page with her photo, I shift uncomfortably in my seat. Her red hair is unmistakable, and her features are classically stunning. There's little doubt that this Shayan Easton is the same woman from Hunter's mysterious encounter two nights ago—the same woman Eleanor referenced at Gilded Threads.

Pence's voice interrupts my thoughts. "Unsettling, isn't it?"

"What is, sir?" I ask.

"That an otherwise loyal employee could suddenly turn on you."

"It is," I say, closing the folder and filing it into my bag. "I'll look into Shayan's disappearance. May I ask another question?"

"Anything," Pence says.

"Why not involve the police?"

Pence gives me a tight smile. "Sampson & Sampson assured complete discretion in this matter, Ms. Maddox. We're concerned about the integrity of our operations."

Leaving Shenandoah Partners with more questions than answers, I suspect Thomas Pence is hiding vital information. Even with my prior knowledge of Shayan, it's too soon to draw conclusions or make accusations—neither of which is my job. I only need to report my findings to my employer, who will then report them to Shenandoah.

I now have three clients—Trudy Hunter, Lenape City Police, and Shenandoah Partners. The odds of this overlap are low, but not impossible. My job is to report the facts, but balancing three cases centered on the same person is bound to get messy.

I've been tracking Gregory Hunter for four days, but both Shenandoah Partners and the police hired me today. Shayan Easton is at the center of all three cases—suspected of theft by her employer, tied to Hunter through that alleyway meeting, and now flagged in a police investigation I don't yet have all the details on. The timing alone makes my skin itch.

I don't know if the cases truly intersect or if I'm just seeing patterns because I expect to find them. But if Shayan *is* Gregory Hunter's mystery woman, things will get complicated fast. If that link proves true, it could mean walking away from one of my clients—likely Shenandoah Partners—depending on where my findings lead.

For now, I need to stick to what I *know*, keep my reports factual, and follow the evidence, not my gut. But the longer I sit with this, the harder it is to ignore the feeling that I've stepped into something much bigger than just a cheating husband or a missing employee.

I return to the car and reflect on the meeting with Thomas Pence and Lisa, his interim assistant. The whole encounter feels as polished and rehearsed as the multimedia presentation. Lisa's perfectly timed entrance with Shayan Easton's file and Pence's apparent eagerness to direct me to other developers reinforce the feeling of inauthenticity. Shayan Easton's apparent connection bothers me, though not enough to consider this coincidence a trend.

The encounter with Dad also bothers me. Involving him in my work will involve one part interference, one part overprotection, and a full part suffocation. Since becoming a PI six months ago, the tension in our relationship has grown. He has wanted me to follow in his footsteps, but I have something to prove to myself - I can handle myself without Dad's guidance. With its complex connections, this high-stakes case could be my chance to do just that. I key the ignition, grateful to Chief Burgess for this opportunity and for pulling Dad off my back in the precinct.

Driving away from Shenandoah Partners, I remind myself to stay neutral and objective. My job is to follow the evidence, not my instincts. But the lines between my clients are already blurring, and the truth—whatever it is—won't stay buried forever. I don't owe Shenandoah Partners anything beyond the facts, and if those facts lead where I suspect they might, my real obligations will be to Trudy Hunter, Chief Burgess, and the law firm that trusted me with this case.

8

Seeking Help

As I drive, the unanswered questions from the meeting with Thomas Pence weigh heavily on my mind. When he hired Sampson & Sampson, did he specifically request me as the investigator, or was that a coincidence? Though this case may need discretion, some more experienced investigators could handle this task. And why did he redirect the conversation to Old Town Plaza's incubator space? What is he not telling me?

I record my thoughts and speculations on my phone as I continue driving. I will report back to Chief Burgess and Sampson & Sampson once I have gathered enough details to eliminate any room for speculation. With over ninety hours left on this LCPD investigation, I still need help. Despite my father's eagerness to help, I don't want his involvement, and the Chief made it very clear he didn't want my father's involvement either. That leaves only one other person with the resources and willingness to assist - Rafi Alvi.

After a twenty-minute drive and easy navigation through the city, I arrive at R.A. Pharmacy. Seeing the familiar neon sign brings little comfort amidst all the chaos. The Alvis have always been a source of unwavering support and friendship, especially during my parents' separation. They became like a second family to me, providing an anchor during life's most turbulent storms.

The door chimes as I enter the pharmacy. Rafi assists a customer with his usual charm, but his face lights up with a smile when he sees me.

"Cassie, what's up?" he asks once the customer is gone.

I give him a quick once-over and can't help but smirk. "You look good!"

Rafi blushes slightly. "Thanks! I had a job interview."

"Your father told me," I say. "How did it go?"

Rafi grins and nods. "Good, good! Did he tell you where?"

"He just said you had an interview," I reply.

He leans in closer. "With Lenape City Police Department."

I am surprised by this news and struggle to contain my shock. "Really? With your skills —"

Rafi laughs. "Not as an officer. In their I.T. Department."

"I'm at a loss for words," I admit.

He shrugs casually. "They haven't offered me the job yet."

"I'm sure they will," I reassure him, then add, "Speaking of jobs...I need your help."

"Give me a minute," he says.

I step aside while he helps another customer, using the time to gather my thoughts on what exactly I need him to look into. After the customer leaves, Rafi turns to me. "Okay, shoot!"

I fill him in on my strange encounter with Thomas Pence and then make my request. "Can you check out the properties they handle? Especially Old Town Plaza. I want to know if anything suspicious is going on there. I would do it myself, but Pence has shut me out of investigating Old Town Plaza. He'll probably hear about it if I show up at their sales office."

Rafi glances down at his suit thoughtfully. "Do you think this outfit will work as a disguise?"

I chuckle. "Of course."

His expression turns serious. "I'll see what I can find out. Give me a day or two."

"Thanks, Rafi. I owe you one."

"Just the usual fee," he says with a hint of amusement. "Until...you know."

* * *

As I bid him farewell, I exit the store and pull up the map app on my phone. My next stop is Hathaway Properties' offices. Since I'm already in the city, I head toward the three Shenandoah properties on my list. As I drive through Lenape City, I can't help but think about how Maddox and Alvi Investigative Services would sound as a business name. But then again, Rafi might prefer his name first on the sign.

I take a detour to Heritage Commons and then Heritage Plaza. Both developments live up to Pence's promises and their impressive multimedia presentations and renderings. Despite still being under construction, the buildings seamlessly blend with the city's historic brick structures. And as I gaze upon them, my heart feels a pang at the thought of Rafi standing by my side, admiring them with me.

Twenty minutes later, I park my car across from Old Town Plaza and grab my camera. I zoom in on the final stages of construction and snap a few photos. A foreman speaks to a couple of crew members. Others work on installing windows. The more expansive windows on the lower levels suggest retail space. In contrast, the upper windows give off an office-space vibe. Nestled next to a park, this space promises to attract businesses that are more likely to launch an economic boom in Lenape City.

Flashing lights—the old cherries and berries—catch my attention.

I glance in the rear-view mirror. A patrol car pulls up behind me and parks. My heart sinks as a uniformed male officer exits the vehicle and saunters toward me. As he comes into view, I do a double-take. Dan Lutman? What's he doing here?

I roll down the window, and a gust of cold, damp air assaults the warmth of my car. Dan peers in.

"Cassie?" His wide eyes and the lilt in his voice express shock.

"The one and only," I say. "A second meeting in two days; that's quite the coincidence."

He flashes a grin, but it's too quick and practiced. "Another meeting like this, and we might start calling it a pattern."

I raise an eyebrow. "Sure, I might call that a pattern."

Dan glances across the street, tapping his notebook with an irregular rhythm before he pulls it out. "What brings you to this side of town?"

"Sightseeing," I say, holding up my camera. "Am I double-parked?"

"No, ma'am," he says, nodding toward Old Town Plaza. "Foreman over there spotted some loitering and described a white Cadillac."

I doubt his story, but I go along with it. "I'm investigating on behalf of Mr. Pence, the property owner. Would you like to see the contract?"

Dan leans in a little too close, the smell of his cologne mixing with the cold air. He whispers. "I believe you, Cassie. But just be careful poking around in this town. Some locals don't take kindly to outsiders."

I narrow my eyes, a knot forming in my stomach. Something's off, but I can't place it. "Dan, are you following me on the Chief's orders, or someone else's?"

His fingers tighten around the notebook. He avoids my gaze, glancing over his shoulder. "Just doing my rounds," he says, his voice too steady, too rehearsed. He rips a page from his notebook and hands it to me. "In case you need anything. Drive safe."

I glance down—a phone number. No name, no explanation.

"Thanks," I say, but Dan has already started his trek back toward the patrol car.

Frustration and determination bubble within me as I drive away. Was Dan really just following up on a call, or did someone send him to check in on me?

At the next red light, I pull out the crumpled note and enter the number into my phone, saving it under Dan Lutman—or Watchdog? My thumb hovers over the call button for half a second before I lock the screen and toss my phone onto the passenger seat.

I have no choice but to continue blindly, ignoring Dan's warning and parking the Cadillac in one of Hathaway Properties' visitor spots before heading inside.

While Shenandoah Properties exudes glamour, Hathaway Properties' lobby has a charming old-town feel. Warm lights and 18th-century paintings adorn the walls, depicting the area's past as a rural landscape.

The receptionist looks up and smiles warmly at me. "Can I assist you?"

Glancing at the paintings behind her, I approach her desk. "I'm here to see Rhonda Hathaway."

She clicks on her keyboard. "And your name?"

"Cassandra Maddox," I reply. "I don't have an appointment, but Thomas Pence from Shenandoah Properties referred me."

Her smile becomes stiff. "What is the purpose of your visit?"

"I'm interested in leasing office space."

"Unfortunately, appointments are required. We have availability tomorrow at 2 p.m.. Does that work for you?"

"Yes," I agree.

She adds the appointment to her calendar and hands me a business card. "See you tomorrow, Ms. Maddox."

"Thank you," I say before leaving the lobby. Glancing back, I notice the receptionist immediately makes a phone call. I chide myself for mentioning Thomas Pence's name, but tell myself it's just paranoia. Either way, I secured an appointment.

Stay calm, Cass, I remind myself.

* * *

After returning to my car, I quickly check my phone for any new messages. One is from Dad, expressing his pride in me. The other is from Mom, reminding me to grab some groceries on my way home. She has even sent me a list of items she needs. I reply with a thumbs-up emoji, letting her know I got the message.

Another message is from Trudy Hunter: *I haven't seen Gregory in over 24 hrs. I hope he's okay. Have you found anything out? I was reviewing some of our banking records and found something funny. Can we meet tomorrow? Someplace remote but open.*

I reply: *Let's meet at Heritage Park. Does 8 a.m. work for you?*

I set my phone down and drive to my final destination–the grocery store. Once there, I put the items from Mom's list into the cart and head to the pharmacy to pick up her prescription. While waiting for the pharmacist, my attention wanders as I gaze at mothers with small children in the check-out line or individuals lost in their little worlds as they impatiently wait in line.

My heart skips a beat when I catch Shayan Easton's profile as she darts toward the exit with a few plastic bags. Leaving my cart at the pharmacist, I excuse myself and hurry toward the exit. When I reach the parking lot, Shayan Easton is already getting into her car - a silver Camry.

"Ms. Easton," I call out. "Shayan!"

Shayan slams the car door without acknowledging me.

"Dammit!" I say as I watch her drive away.

Turning with a sigh, I return to the pharmacy counter and collect Mom's prescription and the cart I had abandoned.

Back at the house, I hand Mom the bag of groceries and the prescription. She thanks me with a weary smile. "You've had a long day, Cassie. You should rest."

"I will, Mom," I assure her, though my mind is far from ready to rest. I retreat to the attic, my thoughts swirling with everything I have uncovered.

Hours later, after taking care of a few items for Sampson & Sampson, I write a formal draft of my investigative report. That's when exhaustion threatens to overtake me. That's also when my phone chimes with a welcomed ping from my friend Lila.

Hey girl! Quick reminder! We're meeting at Luna Chic Boutique at 5:30 p.m. tomorrow! Can't wait to shop with you! See you there!

I smile and text her back.

Got it! Super excited!

As I welcome the brief reprieve of Lila's text, the weight of the investigation remains heavy on my shoulders. Thursday night, Lila and I will party at Phantom Beat. I can't deny that I'm looking forward to a break.

As I prepare for bed, my phone rings. The number isn't familiar, but I answer it.

"Cassie Maddox."

There is a pause before a woman's voice responds. "You were following me."

"Is this—"

"No names," the woman interrupts. "But yes, at the grocery store."

Adrenaline takes over, and my exhaustion fades as my throat tightens. "But how did you get my number?"

"Let's just say I still have access even if I'm not in the office," she says. "And you're not as invisible as you need to be in your line of work."

"One could say the same about you," I say, reaching for the bag where I stored her employee file.

"Tomorrow," she says. "Meadow Brook Homestead, 6 a.m."

She hangs up before I can respond. Flopping onto my bed, I open my phone's browser and search for Meadow Brook Homestead. An address pops up with farm-related images and rolling fields of wheat and corn being plowed by horse-powered tractors driven by Amish men and women.

"Great!" I sigh. "A field trip!"

I flip off the light and lie in bed, my mind racing with thoughts. Downstairs, I hear Mom clanking dishes in the kitchen while the wind whistles through the trees outside. If Mom knew about the mysterious call, she would have urged me to be careful, and Dad would have insisted on joining me.

They both would be right. I should be cautious, but also not go alone. Fidgeting in bed, I reach for my phone and dial Rafi's number. He answers immediately.

"Cassie! Is everything okay?"

"I'm not sure," I say. "I have a 6 a.m. meeting 50 miles away from town. Can you ride with me?"

"Of course," Rafi replies without hesitation. "When and where should we meet?"

"4:30 at my house."

With that settled, I try to fall asleep, but my restless mind keeps me up all night.

9

New Connections

The sun peeks over the horizon as snow flurries fall. I sit in the driver's seat while Rafi, beside me, takes in the changing scenery from suburbs to rolling hills.

"Are you sure about this, Cassie?" he asks. "Does Shayan know about your plus one?"

His words land heavier than they should, stirring something in my chest I'm not ready to name. A plus one. A casual label, but not when it's him. Not when it drags up the history between us—late-night confessions that never quite turned into commitments, the space we keep between us that's always felt like a question neither of us has answered.

I sip my coffee, using the warmth to steady myself. "She'll have to deal with it. And she never specified coming alone." My voice is even and casual. But inside, I wonder if Rafi hears what I'm really saying.

We pass by Amish farms and weathered barns, admiring the picturesque landscape before us. As we approach Meadow Brook Homestead, a thought crosses my mind. "What do you think is Shayan's connection to the Amish?"

Rafi shrugs and sips his coffee while glancing at the GPS map. "Your guess is as good as mine. Looks like we're almost there, though."

The GPS announces our arrival at a dilapidated barn. Winter storms and summer sun have damaged the peeling white paint. Shayan, dressed in a chic parka, appears by the entrance and motions for us to drive forward. I exchange a look with Rafi, both of us unsure of what awaits us on this uncharted journey.

I navigate the vintage DeVille up the steep driveway, feeling the crunch of gravel beneath the tires. Shayan leads me into a rundown barn, motioning for me to stop. My heart races as I shift into park and roll down the window.

"Ms. Easton?" I call out, trying to maintain composure in front of this mysterious woman in her stylish attire.

She approaches my car and reaches into her pocket. My pulse spikes and my fingers twitch toward the ignition key, ready to bolt if necessary. But she catches the movement and holds up her hands in a slow, deliberate sign of surrender.

"I'm not here to hurt you, Cassie," she says. "I'm here because you need to know the truth."

The weight of her words presses against my ribs. How does she know Shenandoah hired me to find her? More importantly, why is she coming to *me*?

She exhales, glancing over her shoulder at the stretch of land behind her as if expecting someone to emerge from the quiet expanse of the farm. "Shenandoah isn't what it seems," she says. "Their projects? The numbers don't add up. Old Town Plaza, Historic Harmony—they're making *far* more money than they should be. More than what's on the books."

The words settle like a stone in my stomach. *Money off the books.* I stay quiet, letting her fill the silence.

"As Thomas's assistant, I oversaw the financial records. At first, it was just small inconsistencies—unexplained funds moving between accounts, payments with no clear invoice." She folds her arms against the chill. "But then I found something bigger—money flowing into companies that don't exist. Or at least, they *shouldn't* exist."

My mind races. Shell companies. Fake expenses. Kickbacks. Classic money laundering techniques.

"Why tell me this?" I ask.

Her lips press together before she answers. "Because I saw something I wasn't supposed to. And now, they're making me out to be the bad guy—someone who stole trade secrets from Shenandoah Partners."

I tense up. *Did she?*

Before I can ask, she looks toward the barn, her expression unreadable. "It's peaceful out here, isn't it?" she murmurs. "Hard to believe that just a few miles away, people are playing a game where the only rule is—don't get caught."

I swallow hard. The air feels heavier, thick with something unspoken. Whatever Shayan knows, it's enough to make her run. And if I'm not careful, I might be next.

"Why are you telling me?" I ask.

Shayan looks away, crossing her arms across her chest. "I couldn't go to the police," she admits, trembling. "You're the next best thing."

Shayan slips her hand into her pocket and pulls out a thumb drive. "This has all of Shenandoah's financial records and commercial contracts. You'll know who to give this to when the time is right. Opening it yourselves will trigger an alert to Shenandoah's cybersecurity team."

"Why not go to the FBI with this?"

"No Feds!" Shayan shoves the thumb drive toward me. "Please... just trust me. This information is way too dangerous."

Despite what feels like a major conflict of interest, I pocket the drive. "Anything else?"

Shayan avoids my gaze. "Request a tour of Old Town Plaza. You and your friend can go together. Pretend you're looking for an apartment. That's where you need to look."

Her evasiveness triggers a thought in my mind. A tour of Old Town Plaza could be a suitable cover for further investigation. I nod. "What do you know about Gregory Hunter?"

"Not here," Shayan says, pressing her lips together and backing away. "Just be careful."

With that, she turns and disappears into the barn's darkness. I watch for further movement from her.

Rafi shifts in his seat. "That is weird."

"You got that right," I say.

As we return to the road and head back into the city, the peaceful Amish farmlands blur as the sun rises, casting a pale glow over the snow-covered fields. Meanwhile, my thoughts shift toward exploring Old Town Plaza. Public and real estate records can only show so much without getting onto the premises. Rafi's voice shatters my focus.

"Cassie, what will you do with the thumb drive?"

"We have to find out what's on it," I respond.

"No offense," Rafi says, "but if it's as dangerous as Shayan claims, maybe we shouldn't risk opening it and alerting Shenandoah's cybersecurity team."

I chew on my bottom lip, processing his words. "You're right. We should hand the drive over to the authorities as soon as possible."

"But..." Rafi trails off, sensing my hesitation.

My grip tightens on the steering wheel. "It's not that simple. My dad and I... we don't see eye to eye. He has this compulsion to protect me at all costs, and it wouldn't surprise me if he's having Dan Lutman follow me. If I give up the drive now, the department will shut me down before making any progress."

Rafi, understanding the gravity of my situation, nods.

"And Shayan also mentioned not being ready to go to the police yet," I continue. "If we turn it over now, the Chief will be bound by bureaucratic red tape that could hinder us or even tip off the perpetrators. This case is becoming more complex by the minute, and the Chief entrusted me with it under the agreement that I report my progress. I need leeway to do that."

I pause as Rafi gazes out the window at the passing scenery. "Rafi, I've spent too long in Dad's shadow, not quite measuring up to his legacy," I say. "I'll piece this case together on my terms and prove that I - WE are more than capable of this work."

Rafi turns his gaze toward me and gives a slight nod. "I get it, Cassie. Just... this is much bigger than you thought. Just be careful, okay?"

"I will, Rafi. Thanks for understanding." I manage a weak smile. "Do you think you can get past the firewall on that drive while staying under the radar?"

He grins, leaning back with an easy confidence. "For now, yeah. I'll do what I can while I still *can*." He shrugs, but there's something behind his eyes—anticipation, maybe even hesitation. "Word is, my application got bumped up. If that turns into something real, I won't be able to pull this kind of thing anymore."

I pause, absorbing what he's just told me. "That's great news, Rafi." And it *is*. But it also means my best tech guy might be out of reach soon.

He smirks. "Don't get all sentimental on me. You've still got me—for now."

I shake my head with a soft laugh. "Then let's make it count."

* * *

Later, I meet Trudy in Heritage Park. The manicured park, covered in untouched snow, contrasts with the turmoil Trudy is likely experiencing. As I approach her, I notice she sits alone while an elderly couple walks the paved pathway around the park.

I sit beside Trudy, noting how she clutches an envelope and creases its corners. "Trudy, what's going on?"

She hands me the envelope. With her hand now free, she loosens the scarf around her neck as she speaks. "Gregory isn't working where he claimed. I found out when I checked our joint account and saw cash transactions instead of direct deposits from Lenape Savings and Loan. This goes back over two years."

I frown, open the envelope, and scan the top document for a visual. Red ink marks a series of cash deposits—irregular amounts just under ten thousand dollars. Flipping through the pages shows more red marks, noting deposits made weeks apart over the last two years. A pattern like this wouldn't just raise Trudy's suspicions—it could trigger a red flag at the bank and land Gregory in the IRS's crosshairs. "Why did you just find this out now?"

Trudy sighs. "He takes care of all the finances. I only checked because a biller called today. We missed one of our payments."

Leaning back, I consider the implication. "I have ways of looking into

Gregory's employment with Lenape Savings and Loan. I'll sort this out."

As I return to my car, I piece together what I already know, which isn't much. Shayan's thumb drive and her warning only suggest corruption. Shayan might be a disgruntled employee retaliating against her boss. Perhaps she conspired with Gregory Hunter to profit from Shenandoah's secrets, and her meeting with me was just smoke. But that doesn't explain what is up with Gregory Hunter's financial records.

For two-plus years, an unknown party provided Gregory with cash payments. Shayan's knowledge of those cash payments to Gregory will give the context for their nighttime meeting. Unfortunately, she clammed up when I mentioned Gregory Hunter's name.

There is only one way to rule out Shenandoah Partners as Gregory's source of cash: getting past the firewall undetected. Then, we'll see what Shayan saw and determine when to pass the USB off to Chief Burgess. Either way, today's events paint a picture of a web of deception and corruption that goes deeper than I expected.

10

Suspicious Activity

Trudy and I go our separate ways at the entrance to Heritage Park, her in her car and me in the Cadillac. I turn on the ignition, the roar of the engine filling my ears as I jot down quick, frantic notes about Gregory Hunter from my conversation with Trudy.

Gregory's cash deposits into his and Trudy's joint bank account show a recklessness that could trigger suspicion and bring federal agencies knocking. I suspect Gregory's recent meeting with Shayan showed him just how dangerous this game is.

With my appointment at Hathaway Properties coming up, I ease out of the parking space in the Cadillac. As I do so, I catch sight of Trudy's car idling in my rearview mirror. Then, a tall man in a dark suit approaches her vehicle, his presence feeling out of place in the empty park. My instincts scream at me—a lone man in a suit here? Something doesn't add up.

I make a U-turn and pull up next to him, my heart racing as I roll down the window. His eyes widen in surprise, a flash of panic crossing his face before he composes himself with a strained smile.

"Hi!" I say, keeping my voice light and breezy.

He brushes off beads of water from his suit jacket. "Can I help you?"

"Yeah," I reply, injecting embarrassment into my tone. "I'm lost, and my GPS isn't working. Can you point me towards the nearest gas station?"

As Trudy's car drives past us, the man's shoulders tense and his eyes follow her departure. He checks his watch, then meets my gaze.

"Turn left," he says. "You won't miss the Speedway or the Turkey Hill."

"Of course," I say with a giggle. "Stay dry."

He grunts and flips up his collar as I roll up the window. In the rearview mirror, I catch him pulling out a phone. His gaze flickers back to me as he speaks. A knot forms in my gut.

As I turn toward Hathaway Properties, my heart pounds. The weight of dread presses into my shoulders. That man's call was about me. I cut him off before he could reach his mark. But who is he? A private investigator? A cop? Or something much more sinister?

* * *

The snow falls in thick sheets, shrouding the city streets as I pull into the parking lot of the two-story office building. My stomach churns at the sight of two unmarked police cars with discreet lights sitting out front.

Inside, the secretary greets me with a forced warmth. "It's nice to see you, Ms. Maddox."

"I'm here for my two o'clock with Rhonda Hathaway," I say, trying to keep my voice steady.

She glances at her screen and then back at me. "Ms. Hathaway is busy at the moment."

"Not a problem," I say, placing my hands on the counter. "I can wait."

But her eyes dart away, and her lips tighten. "It's best to reschedule. She'll be unavailable all day."

I nod toward the parking lot. "Is that because of the police cars parked out front?"

The secretary's swivel chair squeaks as she shifts her weight. "I cannot comment on that." Her eyes flicker toward an empty desk nearby.

Suspicious, I press her. "Tomorrow, then?"

She glances at her screen and taps a few keys before answering. "Tomorrow won't be possible either. I can work you into next week's schedule."

I survey the empty lobby chairs, then lean toward her. "Are your phones on silent?" My mind races with possibilities of why they might avoid calls and meetings.

The secretary's brow furrows and her eyes narrow. "I'm not sure what you mean."

"Just thinking aloud," I say, tapping my fingers on the counter. As I push back, I sense a rise in tension. "I'll call to reschedule."

"Of course," she replies with a lilt in her voice. "Have a good day. I'll give Ms. Hathaway your regards."

"Thanks," I mutter under my breath, my frustration boiling over as I storm out of the building. "For nothing."

For an hour, I sit in my car outside Hathaway Properties, watching the front entrance. My nerves fray as I try to figure out what is happening. The police cruisers parked outside only add to the sense of foreboding, as if guarding a dark secret within the building's walls.

I drive around back where I spot a familiar figure slipping out the door—Gregory Hunter. With no time to waste, I park and snap photos of him before he can disappear into his beat-up Toyota. When Hunter keys the ignition, the engine whines and coughs to life. I snap a few more photos as he backs the car out with a squeal, then points the grill in my direction. Crouching low in my seat, I wait as the vehicle approaches and passes with a tired whir. When the engine pops in the distance and the clanking fades, I pull out and follow Hunter.

As we weave through the city streets, we pass through Victorian outskirts and into the aging business district. Neon signs flicker in the afternoon gloom as we pass by retail spaces and rundown buildings—evidence of a failed attempt at revitalization. But it's where Gregory stops that catches my attention.

He parallel parks in front of a black-and-white building with a faux marble veneer. The engine shuts off with a jolt, and Gregory steps out, keeping his back toward the car while he eyes the streets. My gut tells me he suspects a tail, though he has yet to spot them.

When Gregory enters the building, I pass by, my eyes catching the sign above the glass entrance: The Peterson Group: *A Better Building, A Better Business.* The slogan lingers in my mind as I park down the street and scribble a note: We need to talk. Contact me as soon as possible—Cassie Maddox.

I slip out of my car and enter The Peterson Group's lobby. The receptionist speaks with someone on the phone while tapping away at her keyboard. With her attention focused elsewhere, I grab an envelope from a stack sitting on her desk.

"I'm sorry," the receptionist says. "Can I help you?"

"Please give this to the man who just walked in," I say, enclosing the note and addressing it to Gregory Hunter.

"If you want to wait, he should be–"

"Thanks for your help," I say, turning toward the door.

The receptionist makes a comment, but I don't stay long enough to catch what she says.

As I reach my car, my phone buzzes and I pull it out of my pocket. "This is Cassie."

"Cassie, it's your mother."

"Hi," I say. "Do you need me to pick up anything?"

"That's so kind, but no. Your father's coming over for dinner at seven tonight. You're expected to be there."

I bite my lip. "I'll be there."

"You're the best," Mom says, her voice warm.

I hang up before she can launch into a grocery list or more instructions. The last thing I want is to see my father, especially knowing the barrage of questions he'll have regarding the case Chief Burgess has assigned me.

Back in the Cadillac, I adjust the passenger mirror, watching for Gregory while making one more call.

Lila answers on the first ring. "Cassandra! You're not canceling, are you?"

"About that," I say, scanning the street for any sign of Gregory. "My mother arranged this big dinner with my dad and insisted I be there. Can we meet at four?"

"I'll be cutting it close," Lila replies, "but anything for you."

"You're the best!" I echo, cringing as the words leave my mouth, realizing

I've just parroted my mother. Hopefully, Lila doesn't notice.

Half an hour later, Gregory emerges from The Peterson Group, pausing on the sidewalk. He clutches a small envelope—the one I left for him. After a glance up and down the street, he stuffs the envelope into his coat pocket and returns to his car.

I wait until he's out of sight before pulling out of the parking spot and heading toward the shopping district. With over an hour before seeing Lila, a coffee shop break near Luna Chic Boutique would be the perfect place to catch up on some work. The coffee break will also provide some needed downtime before dodging Mom's questions about relationships and "real" jobs and Dad's inevitable grilling about the case. But for now, I have more immediate concerns, like shopping with Lila for the perfect Phantom Beats outfit for tonight. Gregory Hunter and his secrets can wait.

11

Reflections

I cozy into the shadows of the cafe, my laptop open and my back pressed against the wall. It's easy to watch the bustling store across the street from this vantage point—a habit I learned from my father. While out on family dinners, he always insisted, "Know your exits."

Some habits just won't die. Despite my best efforts to distance myself from my father, I can't deny that there are parts of him within me.

A sigh escapes my lips as I type up a report for Chief Burgess. The names Gregory Hunter, Shayan Easton, and Thomas Pence stare back at me from the screen. I hesitate before leaning back to sip my coffee. Pence hired me with minimal references and no hesitation. I thought little of it, but now I realize that both Burgess and Pence had chosen me for one simple reason: discretion.

Both men have something to hide, and they want someone who can keep their secrets safe. Why choose me? Why bother hiring someone inconspicuous? My mind races with possibilities that include corruption within the police force. Corruption could explain why Burgess stressed discretion.

My thoughts drift to Shayan Easton, who knew I was following her as soon as I left Shenandoah Partners. She handed over what she claimed to be stolen financial information like it was nothing, with only a warning that its contents could be dangerous. And then she disappeared into thin air.

And let's not forget Gregory Hunter. His wife found his enormous sums of cash deposits in their account only after she received notification of a billing error. If my note to Gregory has its desired effect, he'll be reaching out to me soon, desperate to unburden his conscience. I am banking on the likelihood that he would rather talk to me than involve the police.

This investigation seems all too convenient. It's almost as if someone wanted me to follow this specific trail and no others. But why? What's the bigger picture here? Is there something more significant at play? I can't shake off the feeling that I'm being set up. But by whom, and for what purpose? Could there be even deeper corruption going on than I suspected? These questions plague my mind as I finish the report and consider the next stage in my investigation, unsure of who I can trust.

My mind drifts to my father and to Chief Burgess. Despite the history between my father and me, I know I can trust him. I can't say the same thing about my father's boss. With the report for the Chief completed, I copy the details about Shayan Easton and draft a report for Thomas Pence. I include the details surrounding our meeting and the handoff of the thumb drive. Then, I hesitate. Letting Burgess and Pence know I possess the USB containing the alleged financial records means handing the evidence over as well. I recall Ms. Easton's remark: *You'll know who to give this to when the time is right.* Though I can't explain why, now doesn't seem to be the right time.

I open the messenger app on my computer and text Rafi. *How is our project coming?*

His message pops up. *I'll finish it by the end of the business day.*

As I reply, the door to the cafe swings open, the bells jingling. Along with the cold air, Lila Baker breezes in with a grin. Her voice cuts through the background noise. "Who's ready to go shopping?"

I force a smile and text Rafi about meeting up later.

"I'm in," I say to Lila. "Let me just gather up my things."

"Take your time," Lila says, plopping into the chair across from me. "So, ask me about my new job."

"How is the new job?" I ask, saving the reports and securing my laptop in my bag.

As she chatters about how new hire orientation drones on, I determine to involve her in my case. She could keep her eyes out for Gregory Hunter.

I swing my bag over my shoulder and stand. "What department are you in?"

Taking my cue, Lila stands. "The riveting world of finance."

I chuckle at her sarcasm as we head across the street to Luna Chic Boutique, a sleek, upscale shop with gold-accented signage. In its expansive glass windows, stylish mannequins pose in the latest fashion trends. A subtle charm announces our entrance and a young woman behind the counter greets us. The interior exudes sophistication—dark wood floors, minimalist gold clothing racks, and a celestial mural spanning one wall. The air carries a faint hint of jasmine and vanilla, adding to the boutique's allure.

Despite the boutique's allure, my mind lingers on the case. If Shenandoah Partners and The Peterson Group are connected, Lila will soon discover how exciting finance can be. She will also be in the perfect position to cross paths with Gregory Hunter.

The thought barely settles before Lila holds up a hanger with an attention-hungry dress, the kind designed to stop conversations.

I run my fingers over the slinky material and shake my head. "Not enough fabric."

"Please," Lila teases, nudging me with her elbow. "If you got it, flaunt it, Cass. Maybe it'll attract a cute guy at the club."

I roll my eyes but smile. "I doubt it; this outfit isn't designed to attract just any cute guy."

Lila oohs and nudges me. "How about a guy like Rafi?"

A slight blush creeps up my neck. Averting my eyes, I feign interest in a rack of dresses to my right. "Rafi and I tried that once, back when we were kids," I mumble. "It's ancient history."

"Ancient history, huh?" Lila arches an eyebrow.

My fingers linger on the soft fabric of a dress as my thoughts drift to Rafi. Lila's right, of course. While our little romantic stint had been in high school,

I still have feelings for Rafi. Aside from Lila, he's my best friend, but I long for something more.

"Earth to Cassie!" Lila calls, snapping me out of my thoughts.

I turn back to Lila, who is now holding up an outfit that is more my style—a sleek, sleeveless black top with thin shoulder straps and a low neckline paired with high-waisted black pants with a tailored, wide-leg fit. The entire ensemble possesses a modern edge—stylish but not too revealing.

"Maybe," I grin, taking the outfit from her. "I'll try this one on."

"That's more like it," Lila beams as I head to the changing rooms.

Inside, I strip out of my usual jeans, t-shirt, and leather jacket, feeling the cool, smooth fabric of the new outfit as I pull it on. The pants hug my waist, while the wide legs create a graceful silhouette. The top draws attention to my shoulders and collarbone, hinting at curves without showing too much.

While gazing at myself in the mirror, thoughts of a conversation I planned to have with Lila cross my mind.

"Hey, what do you think about checking out Old Town Plaza tomorrow?" I ask, raising my voice so she can hear me through the thin wall between our dressing rooms. "I'm considering a move closer to work. Are you free to go apartment hunting tomorrow?"

Lila squeals with excitement. "Yes! I don't go to work until noon on Fridays! We could grab brunch at that cute little bistro afterward, too."

I smile, imagining us both sitting in a cozy corner of some bistro, slurping down soup and making plans. "Sounds perfect."

"By the way, I'm ready! You?"

"All set," I reply.

We step out of our respective dressing rooms, and I can't help but chuckle when I see Lila's outfit. She's gone for something different—a colorful, form-fitting mini dress that hugs her curves in all the right places. The vibrant abstract print draws the eye, and the three keyhole cutouts in the front add a flirty touch. She pairs it with oversized hoop earrings, layered gold necklaces, and those signature black sunglasses that make her look glamorous and mysterious.

She twirls in front of the mirror. "What do you think?"

"You look incredible, Lila," I say. "That outfit is bold and daring—going to turn heads."

"And you look sleek and elegant," she counters, giving me a once-over. "Classic Cassie. We will be the most stylish duo at the club tonight."

I grin and turn to the mirror, admiring how the outfit flatters my figure. "You think so?"

She stands next to me and gives me a nudge. "Absolutely."

While admiring our reflection, something outside catches my eye.

I freeze.

My smile fades as I spot a sleek black sedan creeping by the boutique. The car lingers just a little too long in front of the shop, its tinted windows hiding any sign of its occupants. My heart races as the vehicle turns a corner, its license plate flashing for a moment before disappearing from sight. I catch the make and model, a Lincoln Town Car, and I strain to read the numbers, glimpsing the letters *ADF* before the rest becomes a blur. Could this be the same car from that fateful night when I was watching Gregory Hunter and Shayan Easton in the alley? Panic sets in as I realize that someone else may have been following them...and now they might be watching me. The walls feel like they're closing in, suffocating me as the once fun and carefree moment dissipates into dread and fear.

Lila notices the shift in my mood. "Cass, what's wrong?"

I force a smile, trying to shake off the unease. "Nothing. Something I need to take care of."

She narrows her eyes. "Are you sure?"

"I'm certain!" I say, inflecting cheer into my voice.

After changing, we walk to the register. While Lila stops a few times to admire scarves and hats, I piece together the plate number: *ADF-105*. One number remains if that was, indeed, the same car. For now, I push it out of my mind. A quick DMV search will determine if it's the same car, leading to the question: Who is following us, and why?

As Lila and I part ways, she flashes me one last look of concern before heading out the door. Meanwhile, I stay behind and peer out the boutique's bay windows. Though the cruiser no longer lingers in the open-air shopping center, my unease remains.

Swinging my bag over my shoulder and gripping my new outfit, I exit the boutique. Despite pulling my leather jacket tighter around me against the early evening air, I can't shake the icy dread creeping over me. Maybe these feelings come from the looming family dinner, or perhaps there is something else hiding in the shadows.

12

Family Dinner

The drive from Chic Boutique to my mother's house is only half an hour, but that's not enough time for me to prepare mentally for dinner. Lila's comment about meeting a cute guy at the club tonight lingers in my mind, despite my attempts to ignore it. I don't just want any cute guy - intelligence, stability, and kindness are top qualities for me. I highly doubt that going out to Phantom Beats with Lila will attract the guy I'm looking for.

As I pull into the driveway, I see my dad's car already parked there - his trusty silver sedan he's had for years. He's actually early for once. With a sigh, the excitement from my shopping trip with Lila fades. I was hoping to sneak past my mom and go straight upstairs without being bombarded with her usual questions - what's in the bag, if I bought groceries, and when will I finally get a "real job." It only makes me more eager to move out of my mom's house and get a place with Lila.

But instead of my mom's usual cheerful greeting, I hear low voices coming from the kitchen as soon as I enter the house. I recognize my dad's voice - a tone he uses during negotiations. "It'll be different this time, I promise. Now that Cassie's an adult..."

Hearing my name mentioned, I hurriedly make my way upstairs, ignoring their conversation. In my room, I take out the sleeveless top and high-waisted pants that Lila helped me pick out. As I hold up the top to my torso, I glimpse myself in the mirror. Not too revealing but still classy - Lila's words echo in my head: "If you've got it, flaunt it." Maybe I should take a break from jeans and t-shirts more often.

As I admire the sleek lines of the top against my figure, my mind wanders to Rafi. What would he think of this outfit? I can almost picture his warm, expressive eyes widening slightly, a mix of surprise and appreciation flickering across his face. He's always seen me in my work attire - practical, no-nonsense outfits suited for long stakeouts and impromptu chases. This... this is different.

I smooth the fabric down, feeling a flutter of nerves in my stomach. It's silly, really. As I told Lila, dating Rafi is ancient history. Now, he's my closest friend, my colleague and my tech guru. He's seen me at my best and my worst, covered in mud after a rainy surveillance job, or wired on too much coffee during an all-night data crunch. But somehow, the thought of him seeing me like this, dressed up and ready for a night out, makes my cheeks warm.

A soft knock on my door interrupts my thoughts. "Cassie, dinner's ready," my mom calls.

"Just finishing up some notes," I reply automatically, then cringe at how teenager-ish that sounded. But I am an adult now, I remind myself. Why can't I just move out and be independent?

Downstairs, my dad scrolls through his phone at one end of the table, already set for three. He looks up as I sit down and nods. "Cassie."

"Dad," I say with a forced smile.

My mom brings over a serving bowl and sets it on the table, her gaze shifting between us. "How was work today, Cassie?"

"Fine," I reply simply.

My dad leans forward, his expression intense. "How's your latest case going?"

I try to keep my tone neutral, not wanting to reveal too much information. "I have a few leads."

Dad nods, but continues to press me for more details. "Chief Burgess hasn't told me squat. So spill it. What kind of case is it? Financial? Domestic?"

I grip my fork tightly, trying not to roll my eyes in frustration. "It's a bit of both."

"Do you have any suspects?" he presses further, his gaze sharpening.

I start to answer, but he cuts me off with advice about being patient and persistent and not underestimating a suspect's motivations.

"Yes, Dad," I say curtly. "I know."

My mom intervenes with a gentle nudge. "Cassie's handling it just fine, Dylan."

There's an awkward silence around the table before Dad finally changes the subject. "Have you heard about those teenagers who uncovered a drug ring at Camp Lenape?"

My mom looks unimpressed. "That's old news, Dylan."

Dad ignores her. "One camper, a little girl, stumbled onto the ring and got herself kidnapped. And it turns out one suspect has ties to a human trafficking operation."

I brace myself, knowing where he's going with this. Sure enough, he turns his attention to me, his voice heavy with admiration. "These kids, just high schoolers, are barely sixteen. If they stay on track, they could go far. Maybe even into law enforcement."

I force a smile, feeling like his praise is for someone else entirely. "Thanks for sharing, Dad," I mutter and set down my fork.

Before I can make my escape, he places a hand on mine, his gaze solemn. "Just...be careful out there, Cassie. There's a drug ring we're investigating that's tied to what happened at Camp Lenape. It's bigger than you realize."

I swallow the retort bubbling up inside me and keep my voice neutral. "I'll keep that in mind, Dad. Is there anywhere specific you think I should avoid?"

His gaze darkens slightly, the detective's instinct kicking in. "Just keep your wits about you, Cassie. Like I taught you."

The rest of the dinner goes by in relative silence. I can feel the weight of Dad's presence, his watchful eyes, even as he finally relents from his questions. It's clear he wants to know more, to probe further, but I'm not ready to open up.

Not yet.

As we clear the table, my phone buzzes in my pocket. Seizing the excuse, I step back, glancing at the screen. Rafi's name lights up, and I feel a rush of relief. "I have to take this," I tell Mom, who waves me off with an understanding smile.

"Cassie!" Rafi's voice sounds both excited and nervous. "You will not believe what I found."

My pulse quickens. "You got through the firewall?"

"Cracked it and disarmed the alerts. You will not believe what I uncovered." His tone is thick with urgency. "Shenandoah Partners isn't just fudging numbers, Cassie. They're laundering money. Massive sums moving through shell companies—this is way bigger than Shayan suggested."

I bite my lip, glancing toward the dining room where Dad's voice still rumbles. "When can I see it?"

"How about tonight?" he replies, his excitement barely contained. "I'll print out the financials and make a backup. You'll want to see it all on paper."

"Perfect," I say, adrenaline surging. But I temper my enthusiasm, remembering tonight's plans. "Look, Rafi... I can't come by tonight. I promised Lila I'd go out with her."

There was a pause. "Sure, I get it," he replies, though I can hear the hint of disappointment. "Just be careful. Shenandoah's not playing around. If they find out we're digging this deep..."

"I know," I reply, my voice barely a whisper. "I'll see you first thing tomorrow."

"Alright," he says, and then, more warmly, "Have fun tonight, Cass. You deserve a break."

We end the call and I tuck my phone into my pocket, feeling my heart still racing. The excitement of discovery mixes with dread as I contemplate what tomorrow may bring. I'm deeper than I thought, and this is no longer a simple case of catching a cheater.

Back at the table, my dad's gaze meets mine, studying me with his usual mix of concern and suspicion. I consider telling him everything - about Shenandoah, about the disk from Shayan Easton, about Rafi's findings. But I held back, knowing he would try to take over the case if I did.

"Is everything okay?" he asks.

I force a smile. "Just a friend," I say nonchalantly, avoiding his probing eyes.

My mom clears her throat, breaking the tension. "Cassie, your father is proud of you. We both are."

I nod, but deep down I know they're only proud if I follow their approved path.

Mom gathers the plates, and I slip away, my mind racing. I need to focus on tonight, to unwind with Lila before everything with Shenandoah Partners pulls me further into its orbit.

Upstairs in my room, I pull the sleeveless top and pants from my bag, imagining the way they will look in the dim lights of Phantom Beats. I catch my reflection in the mirror, seeing someone who is both eager and uncertain. This is my life now—balancing the thrill of independence with the heavy expectations of my family.

A text from Lila pops up on my phone, the screen lighting up with a photo of her in her new outfit. The caption reads, *Ready to hit the town, Cass?*

I tap the image, shaking my head with a grin. Lila's skirt is even shorter than I remembered, the abstract swirls of orange, green, and white practically glowing in the dim lighting of her bedroom. The daring cutouts held together by metal rings scream *bold and fearless*—classic Lila. I can already imagine her strutting into Phantom Beats, drawing every eye in the room.

I type back: *Just hoping the club can handle us*, then glance over at my reflection. Compared to Lila's unapologetic statement, my sleek black ensemble feels like a whisper next to her shout. Still, I can't help but admire how effortlessly she pulls it off.

Tonight, I'll put Shenandoah Partners and Gregory Hunter out of my mind. Tomorrow, everything will come back into focus. But for tonight, I'll be Cassie Maddox, out to dance and laugh with her best friend, free from the watchful eyes of her father and the weight of a case that is quickly consuming me.

As I leave the house, I hear Dad call out, "Be careful, Cassie."

His words echo in my mind as I head out, wondering if he'll ever really see me for who I am—and if I'll ever fully escape his shadow.

71

13

Phantom Beats

The bass reverberates through my bones as Lila and I push through the entrance of Phantom Beats. A sea of writhing bodies fills the dance floor, bathed in pulsing neon lights that paint everything in surreal hues. The air is thick with the scent of sweat and sweet cocktails.

"Come on, Cass!" Lila shouts over the music, tugging my arm. Her purple-streaked pixie cut glows electric under the black lights. "Let's dance!"

Lila grabs my hand, her laugh ringing out over the pulsing bass as she pulls me deeper into the crowd. The tailored, wide-legged pants I chose flow against my legs as I move, their sleek black fabric catching the occasional glint of the club's strobe lights. My sleeveless top, with its low neckline and thin straps, feels like armor—a polished, understated look that makes me feel more in control, even here.

In stark contrast, Lila's outfit is impossible to ignore. Her colorful mini-dress hugs her figure, the bold swirls of orange, green, and white illuminated by the ever-changing lights. The keyhole cutouts, held together by gleaming metal rings, flash tantalizing glimpses of skin with every spin of her hips. Heads turn as she weaves through the crowd, her confidence magnetic.

I try to lose myself in the rhythm, closing my eyes and swaying to the beat. The tension in my shoulders refuses to melt away completely, stubbornly clinging like a shadow. Snippets of the case file flash through my mind—bank statements, property deeds, Gregory Hunter's smug face.

Beside me, Lila twirls, her laughter contagious as more eyes drift toward her. I let out a small breath, reminding myself that this night is for forgetting, not analyzing. But the case lingers at the edges of my thoughts, an unwelcome guest at the party.

"You're thinking too hard!" Lila yells, giving me a playful shove. "Forget work for one night!"

I force a smile. "I'm trying!"

We weave deeper into the throng of dancers. That's when I see him - a man at the bar, watching me intently. My steps falter as our eyes lock. There's something familiar about him, but I can't place it. Despite the heat of the club, goosebumps form on my bare arms.

"What's wrong?" Lila asks, noticing my distraction.

I lean in close to her ear. "That guy at the bar - I think I've seen him before."

She glances over casually. "Hot! Go talk to him."

I shake my head. "No, it's not like that. I just can't shake the feeling that I know him from somewhere."

My mind races, trying to place his face. A witness? A suspect? The unease grows as I realize he's still staring, unabashed.

"Maybe we should go," I murmur to Lila.

She frowns. "Already? We just got here."

I force myself to look away from the stranger, plastering on a smile. "You're right. I'm being paranoid. Let's just dance."

But as the beat drops and the crowd surges around us, I can't shake the crawling sensation between my shoulder blades. Who is he? And why can't I place where I've seen him before? The case has me jumping at shadows, but my instincts scream that something isn't right. I just hope I'm wrong.

Lila's hand on my arm snaps me out of my spiraling thoughts. She furrows her brow, concern etched across her face. "Cass, you're a million miles away. What's going on?"

I sigh, shoulders sagging. "Sorry, Li. I can't seem to shut off the investigator's brain tonight."

She nods, understanding flickering in her eyes. "Let's take a breather, yeah? I spotted a cozy corner earlier."

Relief washes over me as Lila gently guides me through the pulsing crowd. We weave past gyrating bodies; the bass thrumming through my bones. I'm grateful for her perceptiveness, for knowing exactly what I need without me having to voice it.

We settle into a dimly lit alcove, the music slightly muffled here. I lean back against the plush velvet seat, scanning the room out of habit. My gaze inevitably lands on the mysterious man at the bar.

"There's something about him," I mutter, more to myself than to Lila.

"The hottie you were eyeing earlier?" Lila teases, but her tone is gentle.

I shake my head, pieces clicking into place. "No, I've definitely seen him before. At Heritage Park, I think."

"The new park in Lenape City?" Lila's eyebrows shoot up. "What would Mr. Mysterious be doing out there?"

I lean in, lowering my voice. "I'm not sure, but I have a hunch it connects to the case.

Lila's eyes widen. "Cass, you don't think—"

"I don't know what to think," I interrupt, frustration coloring my words. "But my gut tells me he's involved somehow. I just don't know how."

As I watch, the man slides off his barstool, moving with purpose towards the exit. My heart races. Do I follow him? Confront him? The investigator in me itches to chase down this lead, but the rational part of my brain warns me against rash decisions.

I turn to Lila, conflict written all over my face. "What do I do?"

A shadow falls across our table, and I instinctively tense. The mysterious man from the bar stands before us, his smile confident and disarming. Up close, I can see the sharp cut of his jawline and the expensive fabric of his tailored suit.

"Ladies," he says, his voice smooth as aged whiskey. "I couldn't help but notice you from across the room. Mind if I join you?"

I force a polite smile, every instinct screaming caution. "Actually, we were about to—"

"Oh, come on, Cass," Lila interjects, her eyes twinkling with mischief. "One drink won't hurt. I'm Lila, and this is Cassie."

The man's gaze locks onto mine, and I feel a chill run down my spine. "Cassie," he repeats, as if savoring the name. "I'm Stanton. It's a pleasure."

I glance at Lila. "Stanton, huh? You think this guy has a first name?"

Lila suddenly stands, fishing her phone from her purse. "Speaking of drinks, I should grab us another round. Stanton, what's your poison?"

Before I can protest, Lila's weaving through the crowd towards the bar, leaving me alone with Stanton. He slides into the vacant seat, his knee brushing mine under the table. I shift away, trying to maintain some distance.

"So, Cassie," Stanton leans in, his cologne mingling with the scent of leather and something I can't quite place. "What brings a woman like you to a place like this?"

I keep my face neutral, mind racing. Is this a chance encounter or something more deliberate? "Just blowing off some steam after work," I reply vaguely. "How about you?"

Stanton's smile doesn't quite reach his eyes. "Oh, you know how it is. Sometimes you need to step away from the office to... see things more clearly."

My pulse quickens. There's a weight to his words, a hidden meaning I can't decipher. I scan his face, searching for any tell that might betray his true intentions. But Stanton's expression remains unreadable, a polished mask of charm.

As the silence stretches between us, the bass from the speakers seems to grow louder, matching the pounding of my heart. I shift away as Stanton leans closer, his cologne heavy in the air.

His voice drops to a near-whisper. "It's good to see you again, Cassie, but I'll cut to the chase. I'm not just some guy looking for a good time. I'm working undercover at Shenandoah Partners." He hands me his card.

My body tenses as I read it over.

U.S. Treasury Department, Internal Revenue Services, Criminal Investigation, James Stanton, Special Agent.

I slip the card into my bag and take a sip from my glass. I savor the smooth, rich flavors of whisky and sweetened bitters before swallowing.

I arch an eyebrow, keeping my voice level. "So, Agent Stanton, what brings a guy like you into an establishment like this?"

He smirks, clearly picking up on my skepticism. "Because I know you're investigating Gregory Hunter. And I think we can help each other."

I lean back, crossing my arms. "That's quite an assumption. What makes you think I'm investigating anyone?"

"Let's just say I have my sources," Stanton replies smoothly. "Hunter and Easton stole some very sensitive information from Shenandoah. Information that could implicate a lot of powerful people."

My mind races, weighing his words against what I already suspected, but had yet to prove. Part of me wants to hear more, to dive deeper into this potential goldmine of information. But the cautious voice in my head, the one that sounds suspiciously like my father, urges restraint.

"And what exactly would this... collaboration entail?" I ask, careful to keep my tone neutral.

Stanton's eyes gleam. "We pool our resources. Share what we know. Together, we can bring Hunter and Easton down and expose whatever they're involved in."

I study his face, searching for any sign of deception. The offer is tempting—access to insider information could blow this case wide open. But can I trust him? Or am I walking into a trap?

"That's quite a proposition," I say. "But how do I know you're not feeding me a line? For all I know, you could work for Hunter or Easton."

Stanton chuckles, but there's an edge to it. "Smart girl. Trust me, if I were working for either of those two, this conversation would go differently."

I open my mouth to respond, but before I can, I spot Lila making her way back through the crowd. Time's running out. I need to decide, and fast.

Stanton leans in closer, his voice dropping even lower. "Look, the information they stole... it's not just financial records or client lists. We're talking about evidence of systematic corruption at the highest levels of Shenandoah Partners."

My eyes narrow. Something doesn't add up. "If it's that sensitive, why would an undercover operative be discussing it in a nightclub?"

A flicker of... something... passes across Stanton's face. Annoyance? Concern? It's gone before I can place it. "Sometimes unconventional methods are necessary when dealing with unconventional threats," he says smoothly.

I nod, but my gut is screaming at me. His story, way too polished, sets my teeth on edge.

"Let's say I believe you," I counter, observing his body language. "What makes you think Hunter or Easton would risk stealing such explosive information?"

Stanton's jaw tightens almost imperceptibly. "That's what we need to find out. But time is running out."

I'm about to press further when Lila appears, drinks in hand. "Sorry that took so long!" she chirps. "The bartender was—"

"No worries," Stanton interrupts, rising smoothly. "I was just leaving." He fixes me with an intense stare. "Remember what I said, Ms. Maddox. Discretion is key. Lives could depend on it."

As he turns to go, I glimpse something in his ear–an earpiece. My suspicion ratchets up another notch as I watch him weave through the crowd, speaking in low tones to someone we can't see.

"What was that all about?" Lila asks, sliding into the booth beside me.

I take a long sip of my drink, buying time to sort through the tangled web of information and half-truths. "I'm not entirely sure," I admit. "But I think I just got pulled even deeper into this mess."

Lila's brow furrows as she studies my face. Her usual playful demeanor fades, replaced by genuine concern. "Cass, you look like you've seen a ghost. Maybe we should call it a night?"

I nod, grateful for her perceptiveness. "Yeah, I think that's a good idea. This music's giving me a headache anyway."

As we stand, Lila loops her arm through mine, her purple-streaked pixie cut catching the pulsing lights. "I've got your back, you know that, right?"

"Always," I say, managing a small smile. But my mind is racing, replaying every word of Stanton's proposition. What if he's telling the truth? What if he isn't? The stakes feel impossibly high.

We weave through the packed dance floor, the bass thumping in my chest. I can't shake the feeling of eyes on me, wondering if Stanton is still watching from some hidden vantage point.

"Earth to Cassie," Lila says, giving my arm a gentle squeeze as we step out into the cool night air. "Want to talk about it?"

I take a deep breath, the crisp breeze clearing some of the club's haze from my head. "It's complicated, Li. I just... I need to be careful."

My eyes scan the street, cataloging details out of habit. A couple arguing by a lamppost. A group of laughing twenty-somethings stumbling towards the next bar. And there, halfway down the block behind us, an unmarked sedan with tinted windows.

"Lila," I say quietly, "don't look now, but I think we're being followed."

Her eyes widen, but to her credit, she doesn't turn around. "What do we do?"

I guide us towards a busier intersection, my protective instincts kicking into overdrive. "Act natural. We're just two friends heading home after a night out."

But my heart is pounding. Who's in that car? Stanton? Someone from Shenandoah? Or is it all just paranoia born from too many late nights chasing leads?

One thing's for certain—this case is about to get a lot more dangerous.

As we weave through the late-night crowd, I can't shake the swirling thoughts in my head. The weight of the investigation presses down on me, each development adding another layer of complexity.

"You know," Lila says, her voice low, "whatever's going on, you don't have to face it alone."

I force a smile, grateful for her presence. "I know. It's just... there's so much at stake."

We turn down a side street, and I use the reflection in a storefront window to check behind us. The sedan is still there, keeping its distance but unmistakably tailing us.

"Lila," I whisper, "when we reach the corner, I want you to hail a cab and go straight home. Don't look back, don't stop for anything."

Her brow furrows with concern. "What about you?"

"I'll be fine," I assure her, even as doubt gnaws at me. "I need to figure out who's following us and why."

As we approach the intersection, my mind races. Stanton's proposition, the stolen information, the web of connections between Shenandoah Partners and the Gregory Hunter case—it's all connected, but how?

"Promise me you'll be careful," Lila says, squeezing my hand before stepping to the curb to wave down a taxi.

I nod, watching her climb into the cab. As it pulls away, I take a deep breath and turn to face the approaching sedan. My hand instinctively reaches for the pepper spray in my purse.

The sedan glides to a stop, its engine purring in the night air. My heart pounds as I watch the tinted window lower with agonizing slowness. The streetlight casts a golden glow across the vehicle's sleek black exterior, making it shimmer like an oil slick. I tense, ready to bolt if necessary. My fingers curl around the pepper spray canister.

A figure emerges from the tinted windows, unfolding like a dark apparition. The street lights paint harsh angles across a face I know all too well. My breath catches in my throat.

"Dad?" I whisper, disbelief coloring my voice.

Detective Dylon Maddox steps onto the sidewalk, his salt-and-pepper hair ruffled by the night breeze. The lines in his face reflect worry as he buttons his favorite threadbare jacket against the cold.

"Cassie," he says, reaching for an embrace.

I back away. "Are you following me?"

"Not at all," he says. "Before leaving your mother's house, I received a call to a crime scene."

I feel a surge of conflicting emotions—relief that it's not an immediate threat, anger at my father's unexpected appearance, and a gnawing worry about what this "crime scene" could mean for my investigation.

"What crime scene?" I ask, my voice tight. "And how did you know where to find me?"

My father's expression darkens. "Gregory Hunter is dead."

The world seems to tilt on its axis. I steady myself against a nearby lamppost, my mind reeling. "What? How?"

"Found outside an abandoned warehouse," Dad says, his detective voice taking over. "Apparent suicide, but..." He trails off, his eyes searching my face. "Look, I know you've been digging into this case. I need to know what you've uncovered."

I shake my head, trying to process this bombshell. The night air feels colder, seeping into my bones. I wrap my arms around myself, staring at my father as the implications of Gregory Hunter's death crash over me.

"Get in the car, Cassie," Dad says, his tone softening. "We need to talk, and this isn't the place for it."

I hesitate, years of striving for independence warring with the part of me that still sees safety in my father's presence. The street lights flicker, casting elongated shadows across the pavement. In the distance, a siren wails, a mournful cry that seems to echo my inner turmoil.

I nod and slide into the passenger seat. The faint scent of pine air freshener mingles with the familiar smell of Dad's cigars.

As the car pulls away from the curb, the city lights blur into a kaleidoscope of color outside the window. The silence between us is heavy, charged with unspoken questions and long-standing tensions. I can feel my father's eyes on me, concern radiating off him in waves.

"Cassie," he begins, his voice gruff but gentle. "I know you want to handle this on your own, but—"

"Dad," I interrupt, my voice above a whisper. "I can't... I can't process all of this right now. Just take me home."

As Dad drives, the weight of Gregory Hunter's death presses down on me, my mind racing through every interaction, every lead, every suspicion I've had over the past week. The neon signs of late-night diners and dive bars flash by, their garish colors a stark contrast to the somber mood in the car.

14

Threads of Deception

The alarm blares, jarring me awake. I bolt upright, my heart racing as images from last night flood back—the pulsing lights of Phantom Beats, Dad's gut-wrenching news of Gregory Hunter's death. A slight hangover. I take a shaky breath, willing my hands to stop trembling.

No time for this. I have work to do.

I swing my legs over the side of the bed, my bare feet hitting the cool hardwood floor. The sensation grounds me, pulling me back to the present. Walking downstairs to the kitchen to make coffee, I file through the case details.

Gregory Hunter. Dead. Possible corruption at Shenandoah Partners. A flash drive with encrypted files.

The coffee maker gurgles to life as I lean against the counter, rubbing the sleep from my eyes. "Focus, Cassie," I mutter to myself. "One step at a time."

My phone buzzes on the counter. A new email from a potential client requesting a background check. Perfect timing—I need to keep up appearances as a run-of-the-mill PI while I dig deeper into Gregory's death.

I fire off a quick response: "Thank you for reaching out. Turnaround time is two to five business days. Let's set up a call to discuss details."

Multitasking engaged, I down a glass of water, pull up my client management software and start sorting through open cases, updating each case as needed and following up on case related emails. All the while, my thoughts circle back to Gregory Hunter and the tangled web I'm unraveling.

The coffee finishes brewing. I pour a steaming mug and take a long sip, savoring the bitter taste. It clears the last sleep induced cobwebs, sharpening my focus.

"Alright, Cassie," I say aloud. "Time to get to work."

I head back upstairs with coffee in one hand and my phone in the other as I thumb through more emails—additional requests for work and an email from Chief Burgess requesting updated case files on the Gregory Hunter Case.

As I pass the second floor, Mom greets me. "Good morning, Cassie. You came in late."

"Morning, Mom," I say without glancing her way. "Catch up with you later."

She mentions making breakfast, to which I tell her I'll grab something on the way. She wants to say more, perhaps about her and Dad getting back together or rattle off a shopping list. I don't wait to entertain a conversation.

I settle at my desk, fingers flying across the keyboard as I dig into financials and property records. Trudy Hunter allowed full access to Gregory's activities, though where those activities lead eludes me. The familiar thrill of the hunt courses through me, pushing aside the nagging doubts and fears.

My phone rings—likely the potential client. Slipping into my professional PI persona, I answer the phone.

"Maddox Investigative Services. Cassie speaking."

As I discuss the details of the background check, part of my mind churns over the investigation into the Gregory Hunter Case—the corruption angle, the flash drive Rafi decrypted, the meeting at Shenandoah Partners.

I end the call telling them I'll begin the search once I receive the completed form 86. As I dive into my next routine task, my determination burns bright. I'm not convinced Gregory's death was a suicide, and I intend to connect it to whatever is going on in this city.

The shrill ring of my phone pierces the air, startling me from my work. Trudy Hunter's name flashes on the screen, and my stomach tightens. I take a calming breath before answering.

"Mrs. Hunter, how are you holding up?" I ask, my voice softening.

A choked sob comes through the line. "Oh, Cassie, it's... it's awful. I can't believe Gregory's gone."

I close my eyes, picturing Trudy's tear-stained face. My chest aches with empathy, but I force myself to maintain emotional distance. This is still a case, and she is still my client, I remind myself.

"I'm so sorry for your loss," I say. "What can I do to help?"

Trudy's voice wavers as she speaks. "That's... that's why I'm calling. The police, they're saying it was just a terrible accident, but I can't shake this feeling that there's more to it."

My pulse quickens. An accident? My father told me it was a suicide. And hearing Trudy confirm my suspicions adds another layer to the investigation.

"What makes you think there's more to it?" I probe, not wanting to lead her.

"It's just... Gregory had been so secretive. Nervous. And all that money came from..." Trudy trails off, uncertainty coloring her words.

I lean forward in my chair, mind racing. "Mrs. Hunter, are you asking me to look into Gregory's death?"

There's a pause, then Trudy's voice comes back stronger. "Yes. Yes, I am. I know it's not your usual case, but please, Cassie. I need to know the truth."

I chew my lip, weighing the risks. This could be dangerous, especially given what I know. But the need to uncover the truth burns within me, impossible to ignore.

"Alright," I say. "I'll do it. But you need to understand, Mrs. Hunter, that I can't promise what we'll find. And if I uncover illegal activity, I'll have to report it to the authorities."

"Of course," Trudy agrees. "Dig as deep as you have to. I just want answers."

"Answers," I echo. "I'll continue my investigation and send you an updated contract."

As I hang up, a mix of excitement and trepidation courses through me. I'm diving deeper into treacherous waters, but there's no turning back now. Gregory Hunter's death is my case, and I won't rest until I've uncovered every secret.

I pause, my fingers hovering over my laptop's keyboard. The conversation with Trudy Hunter still echoes in my mind, but I need to focus. Time to cast a wider net.

Subject: Inquiry regarding urban development opportunities

I address the email to The Peterson Group's general inquiries. My heart races as I craft the message.

To whom it may concern,

I represent a group of investors interested in potential collaborations within Lenape City's evolving landscape. We've noted TPG's impressive portfolio and would appreciate the opportunity to discuss future projects.

Looking forward to your response,

Cassandra Maddox, CM Consulting

I hit send, a small thrill running through me. It's a long shot, but if they bite, it could open doors. Or trip alarms. Either way, it's information.

Closing my laptop, I grab my jacket. "Alright, Cassie," I mutter to myself, "time to hit the bank."

* * *

As I drive towards Lenape Savings and Loan, unease twists in my gut. Gregory's employment feels like a loose thread—one that could unravel everything if I tug too hard. How do I pull it without raising suspicions?

"Play it cool," I remind myself, gripping the steering wheel. "You're just a potential customer. Nothing more."

But as the sleek glass building comes into view, doubt nudges me. What if I'm walking into a hornet's nest? What if Gregory's secrets are beyond my reach?

I shake off the thoughts, parking and straightening my blazer. "No turning back now," I whisper, striding towards the entrance. Whatever lies ahead, I'm ready to face it. For Trudy. For justice. And perhaps, I admit, for the thrill of the chase.

The cool air of Lenape Savings and Loan washes over me as I enter, my heels clicking against the polished marble floor. I approach the reception desk, flashing a confident smile.

"Hi, I'm here to see Janette Dawson about small business funding options."

Moments later, I'm ushered into a plush office where a woman in her fifties rises to greet me. Janette Dawson exudes an air of professional warmth, her handshake firm.

"Ms. Maddox, welcome. How can I help you today?"

Opposite her, I take time to settle into a chair while considering my words. "I'm exploring funding options for my consulting business," I begin, leaning forward. "But I'm also curious about LSL's approach to employee development. I've heard great things about your programs."

Janette raises an eyebrow. "That's an interesting combination of inquiries. What would you like to know about our employee programs?"

Though her guard is up, I press on, keeping my tone light. "Well, I'm always looking to improve my own business practices. For instance, how do you handle employee transitions? I've had some... challenging departures."

Janette's lips thin out. "We pride ourselves on smooth transitions, Ms. Maddox. But I'm not sure how that relates to your funding needs."

I flash a disarming smile. "Oh, it's interconnected in my mind. Stable staffing, financial growth... you know." I pause, then add, "A week ago, one of your employees sold me on the idea of securing a small business loan through LSL. Gregory... Hunter, I think. But when I called, I heard he had suddenly left the company. That must have been difficult to manage."

Janette's face tightens, and I know I've struck a nerve. "Mr. Hunter's departure was... unexpected," she says. "But I'm afraid I can't discuss personnel matters."

My heart races. There's more to this story. "Of course, I understand," I say. "I just admire how LSL handles a situation like that with such discretion. It speaks volumes to the organization's integrity."

Janette relaxes, but I can see the wariness in her eyes. "Thank you. Can we discuss those funding options?"

As she launches into a rehearsed spiel about interest rates, my mind whirs. Her response neither confirmed nor denied the length of Gregory's abrupt departure from LSL. A week had been a guess, one drawn from the transaction history on his joint account with Trudy and the pressure put on him by Shayan Easton in the alleyway. As for the nature of Hunter's departure from the bank, Janette would remain tight-lipped. What was he involved in here? To what depth does this rabbit hole descend?

I nod along to Janette's words, but inside, I'm buzzing with anticipation. This lead feels hot, dangerous even. But that sure as hell won't stop me now.

* * *

Pushing through the revolving doors of Lenape Savings and Loan, I dial Rafi's number. Though we've only started digging into this case, I can't help but feel both grateful and guilty for not being able to meet him in person.

"Hey, sorry I couldn't make it today," I say as soon as he answers.

"You're always so busy," he sighs. "I've been sitting on this bombshell all day."

"I know, I know." I rush to explain. "The morning just got chaotic."

"Well, fasten your seatbelt, then." His voice crackles over the line with excitement and frustration. "There's more to that file. Shenandoah Partners is using multiple shell companies to launder money, and some of it leads right back to our city."

My feet freeze on the sidewalk, my grip tightening on the phone. "Who?"

"That's what I need to show you. It's too much to explain over the phone."

"I promise I'll be there as soon as I can."

"Please stop blowing this off, Cassie." His tone sharpens with urgency. "You have to see this now."

"I can't," I insist, trying to keep my voice level despite the panic bubbling in my chest.

"This isn't just about us anymore," he warns. "This is dangerous. If they catch wind that we're onto them—"

"I know," I cut him off. "I'll be careful, I promise. Back up the drive and print what you can."

"I already did that." His voice softens in concern. "Please be careful."

"I will. Thank you for everything." Dull heat creeps up my neck. Rafi is risking a lot for this investigation.

"There's something else I want to tell you, so come by when you're done with... whatever you're doing," he says before hanging up.

I stand in a whirlwind of speculation until I realize just how deeply Rafi and I care for each other. Yes, we're in this together. But it's not just our complementary skills and determination. There's something more to our relationship, something I want to protect. Though we might just be able to catch these criminals, a knot of unease settles in my stomach. This case carries with it monumental stakes. If we follow this path to its logical conclusion, will we be able to veer off before it's too late?

Another question looms in my mind. Old Town Plaza—a shining beacon of progress or a facade hiding darker truths? It's time to find out.

I pull out my phone, thumbs hovering over the screen before tapping out a message to Lila:

Hey, I'm headed over to Old Town Plaza if you're still free to check out the apartments. Be there in fifteen.

As I hit send, my stomach twists. I can't shake the feeling that Gregory's death is just the tip of a very large, very dangerous iceberg.

My phone buzzes with Lila's reply: *Sure thing! Coffee at that new place?*

I smile despite myself. Leave it to Lila to inject a cheer into... whatever this is. But as I type back a quick, *Sounds perfect*, my smile fades as I read her next text.

BTW. Last night was nuts! What happened?

How much should I tell her? Would telling Lila put her at risk? I craft a quick reply.

Turned out it was just my dad. LOL. My bad for the unnecessary alarm.

Leaning against a nearby wall, I close my eyes, trying to organize my thoughts. The bank records, the flash drive, Gregory's sudden "departure" from Lenape Savings and Loan, his death... it's like a jigsaw puzzle with half its pieces missing and the other half having irregularly shaped edges.

"Rafi's right," I mutter to myself, running a hand through my hair. "I've been blowing him off."

A passing couple gives me an odd look, and I straighten up, forcing a calm air. My insides are anything but calm. This case... it's not just white-collar crime anymore. It's something much darker.

* * *

I drive toward Old Town Plaza, each creeping mile feeling heavier than the last. The risks are mounting, but so is my determination. Dad often said concealed truths inevitably emerge.

"Well, Dad," I whisper, "I hope you're right. Because I've already started digging."

As I approach Old Town Plaza, my stomach tightens. The sleek glass facade of the new buildings looms before me, a stark contrast to the weathered brick warehouses nearby. In one of those warehouses, someone found Gregory Hunter's body. Thomas Pence's warning echoes in my mind: Stay away from Shenandoah Properties. But here I am, walking right into the lion's den.

I spot Lila's vibrant purple hair before she sees me. She's leaning against a newly planted tree, scrolling through her phone. I briefly envy her.

15

Suspicious Observations

I slam the car door shut, adjusting my sunglasses against the glare of the midday sun. Lila looks up from her phone, and a grin spreads across her face.

"Well, well, if it isn't the elusive Cassie Maddox," Lila calls out, her voice tinged with playful sarcasm. "I was thinking you'd stood me up."

I roll my eyes, but can't help smiling. "Please, as if I'd miss the chance to see this swanky new development. Besides, someone's got to keep you out of trouble."

Lila laughs, linking her arm through mine as we walk. "Speaking of trouble," she says, her tone shifting slightly, "what really happened last night? And don't give me that 'it was just my dad' line again. If we're going to be roomies, we need to trust each other."

I hesitate, weighing my words carefully. Part of me wants to spill everything—Dad's sudden and inconvenient arrival outside of Phantom Beats, Gregory Hunter's premature death, the gnawing fear of being followed that's been eating at me since. But another part, the cautious investigator in me, holds back.

"It's... complicated," I finally say, watching Lila's face for her reaction. "My dad and I, we've always had a rocky relationship. I've been on edge with this case and last night I overreacted big time. That was my dad in the car, not some..."

My voice trails off and Lila nudges closer. "Who'd you expect to be in the car, Cass?"

I come to a sudden halt. "I don't know, Lila. When I got into the car, my dad dropped a bomb on me—my client's husband was found dead."

Lila gives my arm a sympathetic squeeze. "You know I'm here for you, right? Whether it's just to vent or if you need any help." Her words offer comfort, but I can't help but feel conflicted and overwhelmed by the weight of this new information and my family issues.

"Thanks, Lila. That means a lot."

As we continue through the plaza, my eyes dart around, taking in the bustling construction site. The workers move with an urgency that seems out of place for a standard build.

"Is it just me," I muse aloud, "or does everyone look like they're in a rush to finish?"

Lila shrugs. "Deadlines, probably. You know how these big projects are."

I nod, but I'm not convinced. My gaze catches on a half-finished building to our left, its sleek glass facade jarringly modern next to the pseudo-historic brick structure beside it.

"That's... an interesting design choice," I comment, trying to keep my tone neutral.

Lila follows my gaze. "Oh yeah, I heard they're going for an 'eclectic' look. Personally, I think it's a bit much."

I hum in agreement as I take in the buildings. The inconsistent styles, the frantic pace—it all adds up to something, but what?

"So," I say, forcing a lightness into my voice that I don't quite feel, "tell me more about this Peterson Group you're working for. Sounds like things are really taking off for you there."

As Lila launches into an enthusiastic description of her new job, I listen with half an ear; my focus split between her words and the nagging sense that there's more to this development than meets the eye.

"Hey, speaking of The Peterson Group," I say, gently steering Lila towards a striking glass building at the corner of the plaza, "isn't that one of their designs? The amenities look amazing."

Lila frowns. "Maybe. I haven't had the chance to study every design, but it looks familiar. Want to check it out?"

As we approach, I scan the area, my senses on high alert. The building's lobby is all polished surfaces and modern art, but it's what's happening outside that catches my attention. A group of men in expensive suits huddled near the construction fence, their voices low but clearly agitated.

My heart skips a beat as I recognize one of them. Thomas Pence, the charismatic CEO of Shenandoah Partners, his silver hair catching the sunlight. What's he doing here?

"Earth to Cassie," Lila's voice breaks through my thoughts. "You okay? You kind of zoned out there."

I force a smile. "Sorry, just admiring the architecture. It's really something, isn't it?"

I try to catch snippets of the conversation between Pence and the others, but they're too far away.

"You know," I say casually to Lila, "Isn't that cafe around here? Do you want to grab a drink?"

"Ooh, coffee sounds perfect," Lila chirps, linking her arm through mine.

As we walk toward the bistro, I position us to pass closer to Pence's group. Whatever's going on here, I need to find out more. And I need to decide how much, if anything, I can tell Lila. The weight of secrets between us suddenly feels heavier than ever.

We approach the bistro, entering through its original stone façade, where tall, arched windows framed in black steel hint at the blend of history and modernity inside. As Lila talks animatedly about her favorite coffee blend, two people sitting at a nearby table catch my attention. I immediately recognize one member of the pair—Lisa Chenoweth, Thomas Pence's temporary assistant. Her sharp blazer and perfectly styled brown hair are unmistakable. The man she's talking to is unfamiliar to me—stout build, thinning hair, and a slightly disheveled appearance that contrasts with Lisa's polished appearance. Engrossed in conversation, Lisa does not notice me as I step in line to place my order.

From this vantage point, I sense Lisa's discomfort as she pinches her lips together and fidgets with her coffee cup. With my attention divided, I feign interest in Lila's work-related anecdote. Something about one of her coworkers getting locked in the bathroom.

I laugh. "Your department sounds like a fun bunch."

"They have their moments," Lila says. Her eyes sparkle. "You'll have to meet them sometime."

The barista calls out our orders—a venti latte, a tall black coffee, a blueberry muffin and a scone. Mine's the black coffee and I don't add any cream and sugar.

Lila crinkles her nose. "I still don't know how you drink it like that."

I shrug. "It's an acquired taste." I steer us toward an empty table and turn away from Lisa and her conversation partner as we pass by their table. "But I'd love to try one of your specialty drinks when we're roomies."

Lila's eyes light up. "Then you'll have to try my famous honey lavender latte."

We slip into our seats as Lila lists off the ingredients for the espresso drink and describes her perfected process. Meanwhile, I feign interest as I turn a listening ear toward the conversation happening at the nearby table. The man's voice is low and his tone urgent, tinged with barely concealed excitement.

"Lisa, see the potential here," he says intently, leaning forward. "Thomas and I have been working on this for months. This acquisition could completely change the course of Shenandoah Partners. We both agree that you're the right fit for this position."

Lisa furrows her brow, nervously tapping her fingers on her coffee cup. "Chuck, I appreciate you bringing this to my attention, but I'm not sure I feel comfortable—"

"Comfortable?" Chuck scoffs, his face turning red. "This isn't about comfort, Lisa. It's about seizing an opportunity. Do you have any idea how long I've been waiting for something like this?"

Lisa leans back in her chair, putting distance between herself and Chuck's intense enthusiasm. "I understand that, but I only started as Thomas' assistant a few weeks ago. I'm still learning the ropes, and this sounds... complicated."

Chuck's eyes dart around anxiously, reminiscent of a trapped animal. He lowers his voice, forcing Lisa to lean in despite her hesitation. "Look, it's very simple. Just think about it, okay?" Suddenly, he stands up and tries to smooth out the wrinkles on his suit.

My heart races with excitement. Whatever Shenandoah Partners is planning, it's bound to be significant.

Lila's voice interrupts my trance, bringing me back to reality. "What's so interesting over there, Cassie?"

I force a laugh, trying to sound nonchalant. "Just people-watching. You know how I am."

Lila rolls her eyes. "Only all too well."

Our conversation shifts toward our ideal apartment. Lila's preference leans toward modern luxury, while mine leans more toward comfort and functionality. Both of us agree on a central location, such as the many available in the heart of Lenape City.

As we finish our drinks, Chuck walks past us and I feel a shiver run down my spine. Did he just look at me?

"Ready to go?" I ask, attempting to keep my voice steady.

We stand up, and I quickly scan the area. Lisa Chenoweth is nowhere in sight, but my instincts tell me to follow Chuck. I guide Lila towards the main entrance of the plaza, my eyes constantly scanning reflective surfaces and dark corners.

"Hey, slow down," Lila chuckles. "What's the rush?"

I force myself to breathe. "No rush," I lie. "Just excited to see more."

But inside, my mind is racing. What have I stumbled into? And more importantly, who else knows I'm here?

* * *

We stroll through the plaza, Lila chattering excitedly about the amenities. I nod and smile, but my mind is a storm of conflicting thoughts. Should I tell her the real reason I wanted to check out Old Town Plaza? Can I trust her with this?

"Lila," I start, then hesitate. She looks at me, eyebrows raised. I can almost hear my father's voice: *Trust no one, Cassie. This business will eat you alive if you let it.* But this is Lila. My best friend. My rock.

"What's up, Cass? You look like you're about to spill state secrets," she jokes, nudging me with her elbow.

I force a laugh. "Just… thinking about how much has changed. This place, us…" I trail off, chickening out at the last second.

Lila's eyes soften. "Yeah, it's wild, isn't it? But hey, change can be good, right?"

As we round a corner, my breath catches. There, parked innocuously across the street, is the Lincoln Town Car. To anyone else, it might look like just another car. But I know better. From this angle and distance, I can't read the license plate. I need to get closer.

"Hey," I say, trying to keep my voice casual. "Check out that car over there. Doesn't it look like something out of a spy movie?"

Lila squints, then laughs. "Oh my god, it totally does! Maybe we're in the middle of a stakeout and don't even know it."

If only she knew how close to the truth she might be. I force a smile, linking my arm through hers. "Come on, let's check out that new boutique you were talking about."

As we walk, I can't help but wonder: Who's watching whom? And what have I gotten myself into?

My eyes dart between Lila and the Lincoln as we stroll through the plaza. Every few steps, I steal a glance over my shoulder, my heart quickening each time I spot the sedan.

"You okay?" Lila asks, her brow furrowing. "You seem… jumpy."

I plaster on a smile. "Just excited about all the new shops. Look, there's a new boutique we'll have to check out when we have more time!"

As we pass Everly Lane's storefront displaying women's casual wear, I notice the car's reflection in the windows. It's moving, slowly tailing us from a distance. From this vantage point, I can make out the entire plate *ADF-1058*.

A knot, sharper than the winter air, tightens in my stomach.

"Actually, can we sit for a sec?" I ask, gesturing to a nearby bench. "These new shoes are killing me."

Lila nods, and we settle onto the bench. I position myself to keep the sedan in my peripheral vision.

"So, about that apartment..." Lila starts, but her voice fades as I spot two men exiting the car.

My mind races. Are they here for me? Or is this all just a coincidence?

"Earth to Cassie," Lila waves her hand in front of my face. "Where'd you go?"

I blink, forcing myself to focus. "Sorry, just... thinking about work stuff. Hey, would you mind grabbing us some water? I'm parched."

* * *

As soon as Lila's out of earshot, I pull out my phone, my finger hovering over Officer Lutman's number. I hesitate, weighing my options. If I'm wrong, I'll look paranoid. If I'm right...

I hit dial before I can talk myself out of it.

"Lutman," his gruff voice answers.

"It's Cassie," I say, keeping my voice low. "I'm at Old Town Plaza, and there's this car that seems to be following me. Two men just got out. I can't be sure, but—"

"Slow down, Cassie," Lutman interrupts. "You said Old Town Plaza? What makes you think they're following you?"

I swallow hard. "Just... a hunch. Look, I know how this sounds crazy, but can you run a plate number for me?"

There's a long pause on the other end. "Go ahead with the number."

I read off the license plate *ADF-1058*

"Alright, I'll look into it. But Cassie, be careful about jumping to conclusions. You see ghosts everywhere and you might miss the real threat."

I nod, even though he can't see me. "I know. Thanks, Dan."

As I hang up, I spot Lila returning with our waters. The two men from the car are nowhere in sight, and I swear one of them was Stanton.

"Who was that?" Lila asks, handing me a bottle.

I take a long swig before answering. "Just a work thing. Nothing important."

The lie tastes bitter on my tongue, but as we stand to continue our tour, I can't shake the feeling that I'm being watched. Every shadow seems to hide a potential threat, every passerby a tail.

Welcome to the glamorous life of Cassie Maddox, I think grimly. Where paranoia is just another day at the office.

I pocket my phone, my mind racing. Did I overreact? Or is my gut telling me something crucial? Dad always said to trust my instincts, but right now, they're a jumbled mess.

"Earth to Cassie," Lila's voice cuts through my thoughts. She's grinning, but there's a hint of concern in her eyes. "You okay? You look like you've seen a ghost."

I force a laugh, hoping it doesn't sound as hollow as it feels. "Just thinking about work. You know how it is."

We continue our stroll through Old Town Plaza, Lila chattering excitedly about the various amenities. I nod and smile at the right moments, but I struggle to savor this moment with her. Every reflective surface becomes a tool to scan our surroundings. Every sudden movement in my peripheral vision sets my heart racing.

"Oh my god, Cass, look at that rooftop garden!" Lila exclaims, pointing to a nearby building. "Can you imagine having morning coffee up there?"

I follow her gaze, noting the lush greenery against the backdrop of Lenape City's skyline. It's beautiful, but all I can think about is how exposed I'd be up there. How vulnerable.

"Yeah, it's great," I manage, my eyes darting to a group of construction workers nearby. Are they moving too quickly? Their hardhats obscuring their faces a little too conveniently?

Lila nudges me playfully. "Okay, spill. What's really going on in that head of yours?"

I turn to her, torn between the urge to confide and the need to protect her.

"It's nothing, really. Just... a lot on my mind with this case."

She raises an eyebrow. "Cassandra Maddox, I've known you since we were stealing each other's crayons in kindergarten. You're a terrible liar."

I sigh, running a hand through my hair. "I promise, it's not a big deal. Let's just enjoy the tour, okay?"

As we continue walking, I can't help but wonder: how long can I keep up this facade? And more importantly, at what cost?

I bite my lip, considering my next move. The gleaming facades of Old Town Plaza suddenly feel oppressive, hiding secrets I'm not sure I'm ready to uncover. But I need an ally, and Lila's always been there for me.

"Hey, Lila," I say, trying to keep my voice casual. "The Peterson Group had a few residential developments, right? Any chance they have some less extravagant listings?"

Lila's eyes light up. "Oh my God, yes! I can't believe I didn't think of that. To be honest, I love the glamorous look of this place, but I'm not sure I can swing the rent."

I nod, relief flooding through me. "Tell me about it. So, what's it like working for Carl Peterson? You talked a lot about your new job and coworkers, but told me nothing about your boss."

"Carl? He's amazing!" Lila gushes, her pixie cut bouncing as she talks animatedly. "Most CEOs are these distant figures, you know? But Carl's different. He's always popping by our desks, asking about our projects, our families. He even remembered my cat's name!"

I raise an eyebrow, intrigued. "Sounds like a real people person."

"Totally. Hey, you know what? I could probably set up a meeting for you. He's always interested in helping friends of employees."

My heart races. This could be the in I need. "That would be great, Lila. How does Monday morning sound?"

"Sounds like a date," Lila says with a grin. "I'll text you the details."

Upon wrapping up our tour of Old Town Plaza, Lila and I part ways with a hug and a promise to shop apartments this weekend. As I drive, my mind whirls with the morning's events.

The hurried construction workers, Thomas Pence's heated discussion with his rumpled associate, the Lincoln possibly belonging to Stanton—it all points to something bigger. And how does Gregory Hunter fit into all this? I grip the steering wheel tighter, frustrated by the gaps in my knowledge.

I glance at Lila's car ahead of me, guilt gnawing at my insides. She's so excited to help, blissfully unaware of the potential danger. Should I tell her everything? Bring her into my confidence and have her as a true partner in this investigation?

Lila hangs a left on the next corner while I continue straight ahead toward the county. I glance through the rearview mirror and Old Town Plaza's eclectic blend of history and sleek architecture fades in the horizon.

Maybe I am just being selfish, wanting to share the burden at the cost of Lila's safety?

16

Shocking Information

The sleek high-rise of The Peterson Group's headquarters looms ahead, a monument to progress and ambition.

Upon pulling into The Peterson Group's parking lot, I cut the engine and peer at the building's modern arches and the sign above its glass entryway: *A Better Building, A Better Business.*

"Okay, Mr. Peterson," I say. "It's time to see what sets your business apart from the rest."

As if she'd been waiting with bated breath for my arrival, Lila exits the building and waves at me. I turn off the car and climb out, the cool damp air a contrast to the warmth of my car.

Lila pulls her soft, cropped sweater—a pale sage knit that sets off the streak of blue in her hair—tighter around her waist until I reach the building's entrance.

Lila opens her arms. "Cassandra. How was your weekend?"

I embrace her. "Long. I needed Sunday to feel human again. How was yours?"

She pulls back, a playful smile tugging at the corner of her mouth. "Saturday night, I met this guy. "Tall, nerdy-cute, sharp as hell, and total gentleman. He kind of reminded me of a certain someone who spends a lot of time on your tech support."

My cheeks warm. "Rafi is just—"

Lila holds up a hand. "I know, I know. 'Just Rafi.'" She gives me a playful nudge as she turns toward the building. "But you should've seen your face just now."

I roll my eyes. "So… this is The Peterson Group." I glance up at the glass and steel facade. "Swanky is an understatement."

Lila gives me a knowing look. "Wait until you see the view from upstairs." She links her arm into mine. "C'mon, let me show you around."

The Peterson Group's lobby hits me like a wall of luxury as Lila and I step through the revolving glass doors. Marble floors stretch out before us, reflecting the warm glow of avant-garde light fixtures that dangle from the impossibly high ceiling.

The opulence is almost overwhelming, but I can't let it distract me from why I'm really here. I need to stay focused on exploring those property options, no matter how dazzling this place is.

"Just wait until you see the rest," Lila says, leading me towards the elevators. "The view from the finance department is to die for."

As we take the elevator up to the third floor, I can't help but wonder what secrets this gleaming tower might hide behind its polished facade. The doors slide open, and Lila ushers me into a bustling open-plan office with cathedral ceilings and a lofted fourth floor.

"Everyone, I'd like you to meet my friend, Cassie," Lila announces, drawing the attention of her coworkers. "Cassie and I are looking at some apartments today. We're thinking of leasing one with one of our developments."

A chorus of enthusiastic greetings washes over me. I scan their faces, noting the genuine excitement in their eyes. It's not just politeness; these people seem genuinely thrilled to be here.

"I just leased a place at Avenue Heights," a young man in a crisp suit tells me. "Mr. Peterson has a real eye for design and a real vision for the city."

"Oh yeah," another chimes in. "Carl's always ten steps ahead of the competition. It's why working here is so exciting."

I raise an eyebrow at Lila, who just grins and shrugs. "What can I say? The man inspires loyalty."

As the conversation flows around me, I can't help but feel a twinge of skepticism. No company is this perfect, right? But the enthusiasm is infectious, and for a moment, I find myself caught up in it. I have to remind myself why I'm really here. Somewhere between the pretty surface of this perfect company lies a connection between Shenandoah and Peterson, a connection that likely points to corruption.

"So, Cass," Lila says, pulling me back to the present. "Ready to look at some places we have available?"

I nod, plastering on my best interested-investor smile. "Absolutely. Show me what you've got."

As Lila leads me to her desk, I can't shake the feeling that I'm walking a tightrope. One wrong step and this whole facade might come crashing down around me. But I've come too far to back out now. If The Peterson Group is hiding anything, my patience will cut through any red tape they might throw my way.

Lila's fingers fly across the keyboard as she pulls up property listings on her dual monitors. "Okay, so we determined Old Town Plaza is way out of budget, but let me show you something better," she says, her eyes sparkling with excitement.

I lean in, feigning interest as she clicks through a series of sleek, modern apartments. "This is Avenue Heights," Lila explains. "It's got all the swagger of Old Town, but at a fraction of the price. Carl's really outdone himself with this one."

My stomach tightens at the mention of Carl's name. "Speaking of Carl," I say, trying to keep my voice casual, "When will I get to meet the man behind all this?"

Lila's face lights up. "Oh, absolutely! He's looking forward to meeting you, but he's currently tied up in a meeting. As soon as he's done, he'll call us up."

I force a smile. "That's great. Any idea what he's meeting about?"

Lila turns and shrugs. "No idea. A man in a suit barged in here an hour ago demanding to see Carl."

Lila turns back to her screen. "Check this listing out."

I pull up a seat beside Lila as she gushes about a listing for a sleek eighth floor two-bedroom with a view of the city skyline. Meanwhile, curiosity pulls my attention to Peterson's seventh floor office.

"Li," I say, interrupting her spiel about the apartment's convenience to the city's nightlife. "Do you mind if I use the restroom quickly?"

Lila nods, gesturing vaguely. "Sure thing. It's just around the corner, past the elevators."

As I stand, one of Lila's coworkers catches her attention with a question. It's the perfect distraction. Instead of heading toward the restroom, I slip into the waiting elevator, my heart pounding as I press the button for the seventh floor.

As the doors slide shut, I square my shoulders. This is it, Cassie. No turning back now. I'm not just here to secure an apartment—I'm here for the truth. And if Carl Peterson knows anything about Gregory Hunter's death, I'm going to find out.

The elevator doors open with a soft ding, and I step out onto the seventh floor, my senses immediately on high alert. The plush carpet muffles my footsteps as I move cautiously down the hallway, guided by the sound of raised voices echoing from around the corner.

My pulse quickens as I approach. I press my back against the wall, inching closer to the source of the argument. The air feels thick with tension, and I can smell the faint scent of expensive cologne mingling with the sterile office air.

As I edge closer, the voices become clearer, and I can make out every word of their heated exchange. The first voice I recognize immediately—it's Chuck, his oily tone now sharp with anger. The other voice, unfamiliar but commanding, must belong to Carl Peterson himself.

"You can't back out now, Peterson," Chuck snarls, his words dripping with venom. "We're in too deep. If you pull the plug on this merger, I'll make sure everyone knows about your little side projects."

I hold my breath, pressing myself flat against the wall. Through the partially open door, I glimpse Carl's office—all sleek lines and modern art, with floor-to-ceiling windows offering a dizzying view of the city below.

Carl's response is cool, measured. "You're treading on dangerous ground. Remember who you're dealing with."

"Is that a threat?" Chuck challenges.

I'm so focused on their exchange that I nearly miss the sound of approaching footsteps from the opposite direction. Panic floods my system. I'm exposed, with nowhere to hide. My mind races, searching for an excuse for why I'm here, eavesdropping outside Carl Peterson's office.

As the footsteps draw nearer, I make a split-second decision. I straighten up, plastering what I hope is a convincing look of confusion on my face. Just a lost potential client, nothing to see here. But deep down, I know I've uncovered something big—something that could blow this whole case wide open.

A deafening crash shatters the tense silence, followed by a blood-curdling scream. My body reacts before my mind can catch up. "What the hell?" I gasp, throwing the door open.

The scene before me is chaos incarnate. Shards of glass litter the plush carpet, glinting in the afternoon sun that now streams unobstructed through a gaping hole in the window. Papers flutter in the sudden gust of wind, a mockery of normalcy in this moment of horror.

And there, at the shattered window, stands Chuck, his face pale with shock as he stares down at the street below.

"Oh God," he chokes out. "He... he just..."

I position myself close enough to the window so I can follow his gaze, and my stomach lurches. Far below, a crowd is already gathering around a crumpled form on the sidewalk. Carl Peterson's body lies broken on the concrete, a stark contrast to the power and authority he exuded just moments ago.

"I didn't... I swear I didn't push him," Chuck stammers, his eyes wild as they lock onto mine. "He just... he lunged at me, and then..."

Reeling, I struggle to process what I've just witnessed. This can't be happening. But the reality of the situation crashes over me like a tidal wave. I've just become a witness to... what? An accident? A suicide? Or something far more sinister?

My hand trembles as I reach for my phone. "I'm calling 911," I announce, my voice steadier than I feel. As I dial, a part of me wonders if I'm making a massive mistake. What have I gotten myself into? And how deep does this rabbit hole go?

"This is Cassie Maddox," I say when the operator answers. "I need to report an incident at The Peterson Group building. A man has... fallen from a window."

As I relay the details to the 911 operator, my eyes dart around the office, taking in every detail. That's when I spot a flash of red through the doorway. A figure with vibrant red hair moves swiftly down the hallway, away from the scene.

Then realization dawns on me. Could it be? The description matches Shayan Easton perfectly. But what would she be doing here? And why is she fleeing?

I end the call, my mind buzzing with questions. "Stay here," I tell Chuck, my investigative instincts kicking in. "The police will want to speak with you."

I step into the hallway, hoping to catch another glimpse of the red-haired woman, but she's vanished. The elevator dings at the far end of the corridor, and I curse under my breath. She's gone.

* * *

Returning to Peterson's office, I try to piece together what I just witnessed. If that was Shayan, what role does she play in all of this? Is she a witness, like me? Or something more?

The wail of sirens grows louder, and within minutes, the office swarms with police. Officer Dan Lutman spots me and approaches.

"Cassie," he says with a wry smile. "It seems we keep running into each other."

"Yeah," I say, and the tension in my chest eases. "But don't think this means we're going steady."

"Wouldn't dream of it," he says.

As he pulls out a notebook and flips the pages, he clenches his jaw. "Can you tell me what happened here?"

I open my mouth to speak, but hesitate. Do I mention the red-haired woman? My gut tells me to hold back, at least for now.

"I was visiting a friend," I begin, choosing my words carefully. "As I headed to the restroom, I heard raised voices, then a crash. When I came in, I saw..." I swallow hard, the image of Peterson's crumpled body vivid in my mind.

As I recount the events, I spot a familiar figure striding through the door. Detective Dylan Maddox—my father—surveys the scene with sharp eyes before they land on me. His brow furrows, a mix of concern and something else. Disappointment? Suspicion?

"Cassie," he says, his voice low as he approaches. "What are you doing here?"

I straighten my spine, pushing down the instinct to shrink under his gaze. "I was looking at properties with Lila, Dad. How would I know I'd end up in the middle of... this?"

His eyes narrow slightly. "You seem to have a knack for finding trouble, don't you?"

Biting back a retort, I remind myself that I'm a witness now. Not his daughter. "I'm just trying to help," I say, keeping my voice level. "I saw what happened. Let me give a statement."

As more officers file in, securing the scene and questioning the still-trembling Chuck by the window, I'm torn between my duty as a witness and my burning curiosity about the red-haired woman. My father's presence adds another layer of complexity. Can I trust him with what I know? Or am I already in too deep?

Officer Lutman flips a page of his notebook. "Cassie, walk us through what you saw."

Choosing my words carefully, I say, "I heard raised voices coming from this office. Two men, one over there by the window and the other... well, the other is now on the street. It sounded like a heated argument about their business endeavors."

"Did you see what happened just before the victim fell out of the window?"

"Like I said, I heard shouting followed a moment later by the crashing of what I assume to be the window. I wasn't in the room when it happened."

"Did you see anyone else in the room or fleeing from the scene?" Lutman presses.

My heart races. I think of the red-haired woman. Was that Shayan's footsteps I heard from the other end of the hallway? Was it she I heard just after Peterson's exit from the seventh story window? Whoever the woman was, she wasn't exactly fleeing from the scene. There'd have to be more than one door to the office for that to be possible.

"The office door was only open a crack," I say decidedly, my voice steady despite the internal conflict. "So, no."

Dad's eyes bore into me, and I know he senses I'm holding something back. But I can't shake the feeling that there's more to this than meets the eye.

As the questioning winds down, I feel my phone vibrate in my pocket. Excusing myself, I step into the hallway and pull it out. My breath catches as I read the message:

We need to talk. What you saw today is just the beginning. Meet me at Crossroads Cafe. 1 p.m. –S.E.

Roughly an hour from now, Shayan wants to meet. My mind races with possibilities. Do I follow this lead and potentially jeopardize the official investigation? Or do I stay put and risk missing crucial information?

I check the time, then glance back at the office. A deep conversation with other officers distracts my father for a moment. It's now or never, though the weight of the decision presses down on me, my investigator's instincts warring with the voice of caution. But it's clear that I have no choice. I can't ignore this lead, not when Shayan might be the key to unraveling the whole mess.

"Hey, Dad," I call out, poking my head back into the office. "I've got to run. Call me if you need anything else."

He nods, distracted by the crime scene. I feel a twinge of guilt as I hurry towards the elevator but push it aside. This is what I do—chase the truth wherever it leads.

* * *

Leaving my car in the parking lot, I step out onto the bustling street and hail a cab. "Crossroads Cafe, please," I tell the driver, my voice steadier than I feel.

The city blurs past the window, a mix of old and new that mirrors the conflict inside me. Am I making the right call? What if this is a trap?

"You okay back there?" the driver asks, catching my eye in the rearview mirror.

I force a smile. "Yeah, just... running late for a meeting."

As we near the cafe, my resolve strengthens. Whatever Shayan has to say, I need to hear it. This could be the breakthrough I've been waiting for, the chance to prove myself beyond my father's shadow.

The cab pulls up to the curb, and I step out, scanning the area for any signs of danger or surveillance. My heart pounds as I push open the cafe door, the smell of coffee and pastries a stark contrast to the tension coursing through me.

I spot a woman in a white scarf and hat in the corner booth, her eyes meeting mine with a mixture of relief and apprehension. This is it. No turning back now.

As I slide into the seat across from Shayan, I can't help but wonder: am I walking into the biggest case of my career, or the biggest mistake of my life?

17

Dangerous Confrontations

Shayan's hands tremble as she raises the coffee cup to her lips, the ceramic clinking softly against her teeth. I want to dive right in, ask her what the hell she was doing at The Peterson Group's building just over an hour ago. And Gregory Hunter—does she know what happened to him? What could be so urgent that she'd risk leaving her safe haven on that Amish farm?

Instead, I offer what I hope is a reassuring smile. "It's good to see you, Shayan."

Her eyes dart around the cafe, never settling on one spot for long. The white scarf around her head seems to emphasize the pallor of her skin.

"You too, Cassie," she murmurs, her voice barely audible over the hum of conversation around us.

I lean in, trying to catch her gaze. "Are you okay? You seem—"

"We don't have much time." Shayan cuts me off, her words hushed but intense. She leans forward, her coffee forgotten. "What I'm about to tell you... it's bigger than I thought. Shenandoah Partners, they're not just developing properties. They're laundering money, manipulating markets, and pulling others in with them."

My heart rate kicks up a notch. I've suspected something was off with Shenandoah for a while, but this? This is next level. "How do you know all this?"

When our gazes meet, I make a conscious effort to convey a sense of calm, even though her expression reflects fear. "I've seen the files, Cassie. The numbers don't lie. They're using their real estate projects as a front for all sorts of illegal activities. And it goes deep—city officials, maybe even higher."

I try to process this information, my investigative instincts kicking into overdrive. If what Shayan's saying is true, this could be the biggest story to hit Lenape City in decades. But it could also be incredibly dangerous.

"Shayan," I start, keeping my voice low, "I need to know—why were you at The Peterson Group today? And what about Gregory? Do you know what happened to him?"

She opens her mouth to respond, but something over my shoulder catches her attention. The blood drains from her face.

Shayan's eyes dart around the restaurant, her fingers fidgeting with the edge of her scarf. I can almost see the gears turning in her head, weighing what to say next. Her hesitation is palpable, hanging in the air between us like a thick fog.

Finally, she leans in close, her voice barely above a whisper. "Cassie, I swear to you, I had nothing to do with Carl Peterson's death. And that man claiming Peterson jumped? That's Chuck Albright, Shenandoah's VP of Property Acquisitions."

Albright. The name tugs at a memory of a teenage girl—Mel Albright. Three years younger than me, we grew close at lacrosse several years ago before I went off to the academy. I never met her family, but I wonder if there's any relationship between her and Chuck.

I study her face, looking for any sign of deception. But all I see is fear mixed with a steely determination. I nod slowly, encouraging her to continue.

"I was there for a meeting," she says, her words coming out in a rush now. "With Peterson. About... about our mutual acquaintance."

My eyebrows shoot up. "Gregory Hunter?"

For a split second, Shayan's eyes go wide with shock. It's only a moment, but it's enough to confirm my suspicion. She recovers quickly, her face smoothing into a mask of calm.

"Yes," she admits. "Gregory. I... I was able to retrieve what I came for."

Her hand disappears into her purse, and when it emerges, she's holding a small USB drive. My heart starts pounding as she slides it across the table.

"Be careful with this, Cassie," she warns, her voice low and urgent. "What's on here... it goes deeper than you can imagine. The corruption, it's everywhere. In places you'd never expect. And Carl Peterson is just another casualty who was unwilling to play the game."

I pocket the drive, feeling its weight like a stone. "Shayan, what exactly—"

But she cuts me off, already half-rising from her seat. "I can't say more. Not here. Just... be careful who you trust. And watch your back."

As she gathers up her scant belongings, I'm left with more questions than answers. And a sinking feeling that I've just stepped into something far bigger and far more dangerous than I ever could have imagined.

The sudden wail of a police siren pierces the air, and Shayan freezes mid-step. Her eyes, wide with panic, dart to the window. A police cruiser pulls up outside, its lights flashing an ominous blue against the cafe's windows.

"Oh God," Shayan gasps, her voice barely above a whisper. "They're here for me."

I open my mouth to reassure her, but before I can speak, she's in motion. Her arm sweeps across the table, knocking over her coffee. Dark liquid spreads across the white tablecloth like an inkblot.

"Shayan, wait—" I start, but she's already moving.

She bolts towards the back of the cafe, her white scarf trailing behind her like a surrender flag. The other patrons turn to stare, their forks paused midway to their mouths. I watch, stunned, as Shayan disappears through the kitchen doors.

My heart pounds so hard I can feel it in my throat. Did I just witness a fugitive fleeing the scene? Or is Shayan running from something—or someone—else entirely?

I glance down at my pocket, feeling the weight of the USB drive. Whatever's on this thing, it's big enough to make Shayan risk everything. Big enough to send her running at the first sign of law enforcement.

"Get it together, Cassie," I mutter to myself, trying to steady my breathing. I need to think clearly. I need to—

The bell above the cafe door chimes, and I snap my head up. A police officer steps inside, his eyes scanning the room. I force my face into what I hope is a neutral expression, willing my hands not to shake as I reach for my water glass.

As I take a sip, my mind races. What the hell have I gotten myself into?

* * *

Officer Lutman's gaze locks onto me, and I match his unwavering stare as I take a sip of water. He approaches my table with measured steps, his expression a mix of curiosity and suspicion. I set down my water glass, trying to keep my hand steady.

"Cassie," he says, nodding as he reaches my table. "You left in quite a hurry."

I force a smile. "And apparently, you did the same. Did you follow me on your own accord, or did my father have you track me down?"

He doesn't answer immediately, his eyes darting to the overturned coffee cup on the table across from me. I silently curse myself for not cleaning it up.

"A little bit of both," he says finally. "Mind if I sit?"

"Not at all," I reply, gesturing to the empty chair. As he settles in, I can feel the USB drive pressing against my thigh, a constant reminder of what's at stake.

Lutman leans forward, his voice low. "Listen, Cassie, I know you're working on something big. I've been around long enough to smell it." His eyes flick to the spilled coffee, then back to me. "That plate number you had me run? It came back restricted."

My pulse quickens. "Restricted?"

Lutman nods, his eyes narrowing slightly. "Restricted. As in, beyond my pay grade. The kind of plates you only see on vehicles belonging to high-level government officials or... other sensitive operations."

He pauses, letting the weight of his words sink in. The bustling cafe around us seems to fade away, the clinking of cutlery and murmur of conversations becoming a distant hum. I can feel the rough grain of the wooden table under my fingertips as I try to keep my expression neutral.

"You see, Cassie," Lutman continues, his voice barely above a whisper, "there's a whole world of information out there that most people don't even know exists. Plates that can't be traced, vehicles that don't officially exist, people whose names never show up in any database."

His eyes bore into mine, expectant. I can feel sweat beginning to form at the nape of my neck. The weight of the USB drive in my pocket suddenly feels like a ton of bricks.

"And now," Lutman says, his voice low and gravelly, "I need a favor from you, Cassie."

I swallow hard, trying to keep my face neutral. "What kind of favor?"

Lutman leans in closer, his cologne—a mix of sandalwood and something sharper—filling my nostrils. "We are looking for another person of interest who was seen fleeing the scene at The Peterson Group. Someone reported her meeting here with a 5' 6" brunette matching your description. Where is Shayan Easton?"

The name hangs in the air between us, heavy and loaded like a ticking time bomb. I can't give Shayan up, not after all she's done for me. But I can't lie to a cop either, especially one as perceptive as Lutman. In a split second decision, I opt for a half-truth, my heart pounding in my chest.

"You've got me, Dan. Shayan was just here." My voice is strained with adrenaline. "She ran the moment she heard sirens."

Lutman's piercing gaze locks onto mine; his eyebrow arched in suspicion. "Do you know where she is now?"

I swallow hard, knowing that any false move could ruin everything. "I don't," I admit through gritted teeth. "But she trusts me. I promise if you give me time, I will get her in to see my father."

His expression remains unreadable as he considers my words. "Speaking of your father..." He trails off and my heart drops to my stomach when he mentions my absence from the scene.

"He was more than a little peeved when you slipped away without being dismissed," Lutman says sternly.

"Without being dismissed?" I ask. "I let him know I needed to head out."

Lutman crosses his arms."Well, you're needed down at the station for further questioning."

"Of course," I force out, trying to maintain composure. "I was just about to check with my father, anyway. You know me, Dan. I always follow through."

I watch as he stands and his expression softens slightly, making it clear that he knows me better than anyone else on the force. "I do know you, Cassie," he says quietly. "That's why I'm trusting you on this one." His words hit me like a punch to the gut, making me question my every move. "Don't make me regret it."

As he turns to leave, a wave of guilt and doubt wash over me. Did I just make a huge mistake by covering for Shayan? But then I feel the weight of the USB drive in my pocket, a physical reminder of the secrets I'm protecting. Sometimes, doing the right thing and following the law are two completely different things. And I can only hope that my loyalty to Shayan won't come back to bite me in the ass.

I let out a long breath as Lutman's retreating figure disappears through the restaurant door. My hands are shaking slightly as I reach for my wallet, the adrenaline from our exchange slowly ebbing away.

"Can I get you anything else?" The waitress appears at my elbow, startling me.

I shake my head, forcing a smile. "Just the check, please."

As she calculates the bill, I can't help but notice her glancing at me curiously. "You okay, hon? That looked like a tense conversation."

"Oh, you know," I say, trying to sound nonchalant. "Just small town drama."

She nods knowingly, her eyes taking on a distant look. "Lenape City's got more than its fair share of that. Sometimes I think this place has more secrets than people."

I pause as I hand over my cash. "What do you mean by that?"

The waitress leans in, her voice dropping to a conspiratorial whisper. "Let's just say, in a town like this, even the walls have ears. And some of those ears belong to people you'd never suspect."

I scan the sparsely populated room as I process her words. Before I can press further, she's already moving away.

I gather my things and head for the exit, my mind whirling. I push open the door, the evening chill instantly clearing my head. But the reprieve is short-lived.

* * *

Across the street, the Lincoln Town Car sits idling, its tinted windows revealing nothing of its occupants. My heart rate picks up as I casually glance around.

"Screw it," I mutter to myself and march toward the car.

As I approach, my senses heighten. A gust of wind carries the scent of snow and something else—a hint of danger, perhaps.

I'm about ten feet away when the car's engine roars to life. The sound reverberates off the brick buildings, echoing down the narrow street. The headlights flare, momentarily blinding me. I raise a hand to shield my eyes, squinting to make out any details through the tinted windows.

For a split second, I swear I see a familiar face—is that Gregory Hunter? But before I can be sure, the car lurches forward. Its tires screech against the asphalt, leaving behind twin trails of burnt rubber. The acrid smell fills my nostrils.

I duck into an alley, my back pressed against the cool brick as I try to catch my breath and organize my thoughts. "Ghosts. I'm seeing ghosts," I whisper to myself, half-exhilarated, half-terrified.

The risks are undeniable. I've seen firsthand what happens to people who stick their noses where they don't belong in this town. But the truth... God, the truth is worth it, isn't it?

I close my eyes, picturing the web of connections I've uncovered so far. Shenandoah Partners, The Peterson Group, Gregory Hunter—all threads in a tapestry of corruption I'm only beginning to understand.

"I can't back down now," I say firmly, steeling my resolve. "Too many people are counting on me, even if they don't know it yet."

Just then, my phone buzzes. Unknown number. My heart leaps into my throat as I swipe to read the message:

Midnight. Old Clock Tower. Come alone if you want answers. -X

I stare at the screen, my mind racing. Is this a trap? Or the breakthrough I've been waiting for?

"Well," I mutter, a wry smile tugging at my lips, "looks like sleep isn't on tonight's agenda after all."

The cold air nips at my face as I step out of the alley, my mind a whirlwind of possibilities. Two USB drives, two bodies, and one hell of a mystery.

"What am I getting myself into?" I mutter, glancing around the street. I start walking, my steps purposeful despite the uncertainty churning in my gut. "Okay, Cassie, let's break this down," I whisper to myself. "Peterson's dead, but was it suicide or murder? And how does Hunter fit into all this?"

A group of joggers bundled in their running gear and knitted caps approach from behind. One of them yells, "On your right." I pause, letting them pass, and use the moment to collect myself.

"The USB drives," I continue my internal dialogue. "Both from Shayan. Both probably holding enough dirt on Peterson and Shenandoah to shut down their base of operations and bury half of Lenape City's elite."

I reach into my pocket, feeling the small device. The temptation to plug it in right now, to unravel its secrets, is almost overwhelming.

"No," I shake my head. "Not here. Not now. Too risky."

As I approach the corner, I catch my reflection in a storefront window. The determined set of my jaw reminds me so much of my father, it's almost unsettling. Would he approve of what I'm doing? Or would he tell me I'm in over my head?

"I'm sorry, Dad," I whisper. "But I have to see this through."

I signal a taxi.

"To The Peterson Group," I direct the driver. My final destination is Rafi's computer lab, a meeting that I have been postponing for far too long. As we drive away from the curb, I steel my determination. Tonight, at midnight, I am going to that clock tower. It may be a risky move, but it's one that I can't avoid any longer. Somewhere amidst all of these USB drives, dead bodies, and hushed accusations lies the truth.

18

Mysterious Package

The bell above R.A. Pharmacy's door chimes as I push it open, adrenaline still coursing through my veins from heisting my own car out of the parking lot of The Peterson Group. I had directed the taxi to drop me off a block from the offices. By the time I got there, the police activity had died down and only a handful of police milled about securing the crime scene. Still, I had to proceed with caution and managed to get the car started and out of the parking lot before anyone noticed me.

The weight of Dan Lutman's last words to me gives me pause. *I'm trusting you on this one... Don't make me regret it.* His comment rings with a double meaning—showing up at the police station to finalize my statement, yes. But he seemed too insistent that I report Shayan's whereabouts directly to him, and that troubles me. It troubles me in the same way Shayan's thumbdrive from The Peterson Group troubles me. What connects this real estate giant to Shenandoah Partners? Kickbacks? Shell companies? My detective instincts are on overdrive, piecing together a puzzle of high-rises and shady finances.

"Cassie? Hello?"

I blink, startled to find Ritvik, Rafi's father, standing before me with a quizzical smile. Crap. How long has he been trying to get my attention?

"I'm so sorry, Mr. Alvi. I was lost in thought."

He chuckles, waving off my apology. "No worries, Beta. Rafi and your friend Lila are already set up in the back. Go on through."

Lila? My stomach does a guilty flip. I'd completely forgotten about ditching her at The Peterson Group earlier. Some friend I am. Bracing myself for the inevitable verbal lashing, I follow Ritvik's gesture toward the storage area.

The moment I step through the door, my jaw drops. Rafi's "workshop" looks like mission control for a space launch. Banks of monitors line the walls, cables snaking everywhere, and the hum of powerful servers fills the air.

Rafi swivels in his chair, a mischievous grin spreading across his face. "Well, well, well. Look who finally decided to grace us with her presence. I was starting to think you'd gotten lost in one of those fancy Peterson Group elevators."

I roll my eyes, but can't help smiling. "Very funny, Raf. This place is... incredible. When did you upgrade to NASA-level tech?"

He shrugs, but I can see the pride in his eyes. "Oh, you know, just a little tinkering here and there. Welcome to my humble abode, Detective Maddox."

"It's... incredible," I manage, still taking it all in.

Rafi's expression sobers slightly. "Listen, Cass. Lila filled me in on the chaos at Peterson and I filled her on what we've—"

"Oh, there you are!" Lila's voice cuts through the room like a knife. I turn to see her emerge from behind a tower of equipment, her purple-streaked pixie cut somehow even more vibrant under the glow of the screens. Her eyes narrow. "Nice of you to finally show up after abandoning me at a crime scene!"

I wince. "Lila, I—"

But she's on a roll now. "Do you have any idea how terrifying that was? One minute I'm introducing you to my coworkers, the next there are cops everywhere and my new boss is splattered on the sidewalk! What the hell happened? Where did you go? And why didn't you answer any of my texts?!"

The questions come rapid-fire, each one a reminder of how spectacularly I've screwed up as a friend today. My jaw locks, each muscle screaming as I search for words that will heal the strain between me and Lila.

"I know, I know. I'm the worst," I begin, holding up my hands in surrender.

"Everything happened so fast, and I got swept up in the investigation. I should have checked in with you. I'm really, really sorry."

Lila's glare softens a fraction, but I can tell I'm not entirely forgiven. Fair enough. I've got some serious making up to do. I meet Lisa's expectant gaze. "I'm so sorry, Lila. It's been... intense. My dad's leading the investigation regarding Peterson's death, and I was needed for a statement." I run a hand through my hair, the weight of the day settling on my shoulders. "And then Shayan Easton messaged me to meet at Crossroads Cafe."

Lila's eyebrows shoot up. "Shayan Easton? The missing Shenandoah Partners assistant?"

I nod, fishing the USB drive from my pocket. "She gave me this. Says it's enough to connect The Peterson Group and Shenandoah Properties."

Rafi whistles low, already reaching for the drive. "Now that's interesting."

"Wait," Lila interrupts, her earlier annoyance replaced by excitement. "I've been digging into Shenandoah's financials from the other USB. There's something you need to see."

As I move to join her, Rafi grasps my hand. I turn.

"Are you okay with Lila helping us?" He asks, his eyes search mine with uncertainty. "I would've waited, but she stormed in a few hours before you, demanding to know everything."

I offer Rafi a smile and squeeze his hand. "It's okay. I was meaning to tell her, but I've been practically non-stop since this investigation began."

"I know. It's consuming you, but that's kind of your thing," he says, rolling the USB in his hand.

I sigh. "You're right, but there was something else. Dan Lutman. You know he's a police officer now, right?"

He nods. "I bumped into him at my interview with LCPD."

"Shit!" I say. "I forgot. How'd that go?"

"Promising," he says. "You'll be the first to know. What were you saying about Dan?"

"It could be nothing, but he showed up at Crossroads Cafe and pretty much gave me an ultimatum to track Shayan down and report back to him."

Rafi grunts. "Unusual, for sure."

"Cass!" Lila calls out.

"She's proving very helpful," Rafi says. He holds up the USB. "Better get to work on this."

As Rafi begins decrypting the new USB, Lila and I huddle over her laptop. My eyes scan rows of numbers, trying to make sense of the data. There's definitely something off, but...

"I don't know, Lila," I murmur, frowning. "It's suspicious, sure, but with your limited experience in accounting..."

She nods, frustration clear in her voice. "I know. It's like it's right there, but I can't quite pin it down."

We fall into a focused silence while Rafi rapidly clicks away at his keyboard. My mind races, piecing together fragments of the puzzle. Without The Peterson Group's USB decrypted, it would be impossible to cross-reference payments made to vendors or any ties employees may have to vendors. Whatever's on this little device, Shayan Easton promises could bring down a lot of people. The Peterson Group and Shenandoah Partners—two titans of urban development, their gleaming towers reshaping Lenape City's skyline. What dark foundation lies beneath all that glass and steel?

"Got it!" Rafi's triumphant voice breaks the silence, making me jump.

I leap to my feet, nearly knocking over my chair in my haste. Lila's right behind me as we crowd around Rafi's workstation. My eyes dart across multiple screens, trying to take in the wealth of information suddenly at our fingertips.

"Look here," Rafi points, his finger tracing a series of transactions. "These link The Peterson Group directly to Shenandoah Partners. And there's more—see this? A third company, LCH Withholdings."

My heart races as I process the implications. "This is huge. Lila, does this match up with what you found?"

Lila's already scrolling through her own data, her brow furrowed in concentration. "It does," she confirms, her voice tinged with excitement. "It's as if LCH Withholdings is an intermediary between Shenandoah and Peterson. Only, payments made to Peterson by LCH are several thousand dollars lower than payments made to LCH by Shenandoah."

Rafi does several quick calculations. "LCH appears to be taking anywhere between fifteen to twenty percent. Sometimes more."

Lila chimes in. "These transactions... they're like missing puzzle pieces. It all fits now."

I can't help but grin, the thrill of discovery coursing through me. "We've got them," I murmur, more to myself than anyone else. But my elation is short-lived as the weight of what we've uncovered settles on my shoulders.

"Okay, let's think this through," I say, grabbing a notepad. "What are we looking at here? A money laundering operation? Illegal property acquisitions?"

Rafi leans back in his chair, running a hand through his hair. "Could be both. The way these funds are moving... it's definitely not above board."

As I scribble down theories and questions, Lila paces behind us, her energy palpable. "This is way bigger than you thought, isn't it?" she asks, her usual jovial tone replaced by something more serious.

I nod, my pen flying across the paper. "Any idea who owns LCH?"

Rafi types away at his keyboard. "LCH is owned by Eschelon Nexus LLC, which is owned by Gregory Hunter, and–"

"Hunter?" I interrupt him. "That explains the large sums of cash deposits to his account at Lenape Savings and Loans. But who was he receiving those funds from?"

"That's what I was getting to," Rafi says. "Shayan Easton, along with another company, is named."

Lila chimes in. "Let me guess. That's a shell company as well."

Rafi nods. "This trail could be several layers deep."

"And following it could implicate half the city's elite," I add.

Silence settles over us as we ponder the implications. Until Rafi clears his throat, his expression is hesitant. "Cassie... I think it might be time to turn this over to the police. This is getting into dangerous territory."

I consider his words. He's right, of course. This is far beyond what we're equipped to handle. But a nagging doubt gnaws at me.

"You're probably right," I admit, chewing my lip. "But who do we trust with this? My dad's boss, Chief Burgess? Or that IRS agent, Stanton? He did offer to team up…"

The weight of the decision presses down on me. One wrong move could jeopardize the entire investigation. I look between Rafi and Lila, grateful for their support but acutely aware that the final call rests with me.

"What do you guys think?" I ask, my voice betraying my uncertainty. "Who do we bring this to?"

Just as Rafi opens his mouth to respond, my phone buzzes loudly, making us all jump. I fish it out of my pocket, frowning at the notification.

"Package delivery?" I mutter, confusion creasing my brow. "At my mother's house?"

Lila's eyebrows shoot up. "You weren't expecting anything?"

I shake my head, a knot of unease forming in my stomach. "No, and that's what worries me."

Rafi leans back in his chair, his dark eyes serious. "Be careful, Cassie. With everything that's going on—"

"I know," I cut him off, already gathering my things. "I'll be cautious. And I'll keep you both updated, I promise."

I pause at the door, turning back to my friends. "Thanks for everything today. Really."

Lila's smile is warm. "Anytime, boss lady. Just don't ditch me at any more crime scenes, okay?"

I manage a chuckle as I head out, but my mind is already racing ahead to the mysterious package. The drive to my mother's house—where I've set up my makeshift office—seems to take forever.

* * *

As I pull up, my eyes immediately lock onto the plain brown box sitting on the front porch. It's unremarkable, which somehow makes it even more ominous.

"Okay, Cassie," I mutter to myself, approaching it cautiously. "Don't let your imagination run wild."

But as I pick it up, noting its unexpected weight, my investigator's instincts kick into overdrive. Who could have sent this? Is it related to the case? Or is it something more sinister?

I carry it inside, my steps echoing in the empty house as I climb to my attic bedroom. Setting it down on my desk, I stare at it, uncertainty gnawing at me.

"To open or not to open," I say aloud, my voice sounding small in the quiet room. "That is the question."

My hands tremble slightly as I carefully open the package, half-expecting it to explode in my face. Instead, I stare at a cheap burner phone, a folded piece of paper, and a key. My hands tremble as I unfold the note: *Airport locker 217, 8 p.m.. Come alone.*

"What the hell?" I mutter, turning the paper over, searching for more clues. Nothing.

I pick up the burner phone, its weight unfamiliar in my hand.

"Who sent this? And why?"

My mind whirls with possibilities. Could it be connected to Carl Peterson's death? Or is it about the financial web I've been untangling?

I sink into my chair, the note clutched tightly in my fist. "Okay, Cassie, think this through," I say to myself. "This could be huge... or it could be nothing but trouble."

I close my eyes, taking a deep breath. When I open them, I start jotting down potential scenarios in my notebook.

"If it's legit," I muse aloud, "it could blow this whole case wide open. But if it's a trap..." I trail off, not wanting to finish that thought.

I lean back, rubbing my temples. "Dad would tell me to hand this over to the police immediately," I say with a wry smile. But I'm not my father, and this... this feels like it's meant for me.

"I can't ignore this," I decide, determination settling over me like armor. "But I need to be smart about it."

I outline a plan, considering every angle. "I'll need backup," I murmur, "but who can I trust with this?"

I can't stop feeling like whatever's in that airport locker will be trouble, but I still let my curiosity get the best of me. I reach for my phone, my fingers hovering over the screen for a moment before I tap out a quick message to Lila and Rafi:

Hey guys, need your input ASAP. Just got a mysterious package with a burner phone and a cryptic note about a locker at the airport. Feels like it could connect to our case. Thoughts?

I hit send and set the phone down, my stomach churning with a mix of anticipation and anxiety. While I wait for their responses, I pull out my notes, spreading them across my desk.

"Okay, let's go over this one more time," I mutter to myself, scanning through the financial records we uncovered earlier. My eyes flit from document to document, searching for any detail I might have missed.

As I pore over the data, my mind races. "The Peterson Group, Shenandoah Partners, and now the two shell companies Eschalon Nexus LLC and LCH Withholdings," I say under my breath. "Hunter's death, if he's truly dead, is clearly connected, and Shayan could be next. But what's the connection that ties it all together?"

I grab a marker and start drawing lines on a large whiteboard, connecting company names, transaction dates, and suspicious amounts. The web of information grows more complex with each addition, mirroring the intricate network of corruption we're trying to unravel.

"What am I not seeing?" I ask the empty room, frustration creeping into my voice. I take a step back, my eyes roving over the entire board. "At best, Hunter and Easton are middlemen for someone much more powerful who wants to remain nameless. But the trail of shell companies has to end with someone."

My phone buzzes, startling me out of my intense focus. I snatch it up, hoping for some insight from Lila or Rafi that might help me crack this case wide open.

I glance down at my phone, relief washing over me as I see Lila's name pop up on the screen. Her message reads:

OMG, Cass, a secret locker at the airport? Are you sure about this? Sounds risky AF. But you know we've got your back. What do you need? Stakeout snacks? A getaway car? Just say the word, partner in crime-solving!

I can't help but smile, picturing Lila's vibrant purple hair and the mischievous glint in her eye as she typed this. Her unwavering support warms my chest, easing some of the tension that's been building there.

Thanks, Li, I type back quickly. *Maybe hold off on the getaway car for now, but I might take you up on those snacks.*

As I hit send, I lean back in my chair, letting out a long breath. "At least I'm not in this alone," I murmur, grateful for Lila's mix of concern and enthusiasm.

My phone buzzes again, this time with Rafi's response:

Cassie, proceed with extreme caution. This could be a trap. If you decide to investigate, let me set you up with some covert tech. We can create a secure communication channel and maybe even get eyes inside that locker before you open it. Whatever you need, I'm here.

I nod to myself, appreciating Rafi's level-headed approach. His technical expertise could be a game-changer in navigating this potential minefield.

"Rafi's right," I say to myself, drumming my fingers on the desk. "I can't go in blind. But with their help, maybe I can turn this mystery package into a real breakthrough."

I type a response to Rafi and Lila: *Rafi, grab your gear. Both of you, be here in 15 minutes.*

A moment later, consecutive thumbs-up emojis light up my screen.

I feel a renewed surge of determination. Whatever's waiting for me at that airport, at least I know I've got a solid team behind me.

I turn to my laptop, fingers hovering over the keys as I stare at the blank document. "Time to put it all down," I mutter, typing up the day's events. The steady click-clack of keys fills the room as I recount the chaos at The Peterson Group, my meeting with Shayan, and the revelations from Rafi's decryption.

Halfway through, I pause, a knot forming in my stomach. "Chief Burgess is going to have a field day with this," I groan, rubbing my temples. The thought of handing over this report, potentially implicating some of Lenape City's most powerful figures, makes me queasy.

I force myself to keep writing, adding, "And don't forget Agent Stanton.

He'll want his piece of the pie too." The idea of the IRS getting involved makes me cringe even harder.

As I wrap up the report, my eyes drift to the burner phone and cryptic note. The airport locker beckons, a siren song of danger and potential breakthroughs.

"This could blow the whole case wide open," I whisper, excitement and apprehension battling in my chest. "Or it could be a trap that ends my investigation before it really begins."

I stare at the cryptic note: *Airport locker 217, 8 p.m.. Come alone.*

The note burns in my hand as I stare at it, my mind racing. Who sent this? What's waiting for me there?

I close my eyes. Focus, Cassie. This is what you do. Piece by piece, I dissect the message. The timing, the location, the secrecy—it all points to something big. Something dangerous.

19

Clues and Mission

Lila, Rafi, and I huddle around my kitchen table. I lay out everything—the note, my suspicions, the risks.

"This is crazy, Cass," Rafi says, running a hand through his hair. "We've barely sketched out a plan, and you have to be there in... what? A half hour?"

"Impossible," I admit. "But I need you two to be my eyes and ears. Can you do that?"

Lila reaches out, squeezing my hand. "Always. Let's review the plan one more time?"

"We'll track you through your phone," Rafi explains, his fingers flying over his laptop. "And I've got this." He holds up a tiny earbud. "Two-way communication. We'll be with you every step."

I nod, grateful for their support. "Remember, if anything goes wrong—"

"Call the cops and your dad," Lila finishes. "We've got your back, Cass."

"Alright, team," I say, standing up. "Let's do this."

As we head out, I catch my reflection in the mirror. The determined set of my jaw reminds me of my father, and I push away the complicated emotions that brings up. In less than an hour, I'm not Dylon Maddox's daughter. I'm Cassie Maddox, PI, and I'm about to crack this case wide open.

Or die trying.

* * *

I step into the bustling airport, my senses immediately on high alert. The cacophony of rolling suitcases, muffled announcements, and excited chatter washes over me as I scan the crowd, my eyes darting from face to face.

"Eyes open, guys," I mutter under my breath, knowing Lila and Rafi can hear me through the earbuds. "Anything look off to you?"

As I weave through the throng of travelers, Lila's voice crackles in my ear. "Woman in black by the restrooms, Cass. Been standing there a while, pretending to read a magazine."

I glance over, catching sight of the figure Lila mentioned. My heart rate picks up a notch. "Copy that," I whisper, adjusting my path to avoid her line of sight.

Rafi chimes in, his tone tense. "Heads up. Suit at your two o'clock, looking a bit too interested in you."

I resist the urge to turn and look directly. Instead, I casually pivot, pretending to check the departure board while getting a glimpse of the man Rafi spotted.

"Nice catch," I murmur. "I'm going to duck into Books-a-Million. Keep an eye out."

As I enter the store, the familiar scent of new books helps calm my nerves. I meander through the aisles, running my fingers along spines while keeping my peripheral vision sharp.

"Anyone follow me in?" I ask, picking up a paperback at random.

"Negative," Lila responds. "Coast looks clear for now."

I allow myself a small sigh of relief, flipping through the pages of the book in my hands. My mind races, wondering what I might find in that locker. Who sent the note? What am I walking into?

"You're good, Cass," Rafi's reassuring voice comes through. "No one's watching the store."

I nod, mostly to myself, and move to return the book to its shelf. As I do, the title catches my eye: "Airport: Code Red." A wry smile tugs at my lips.

"You've got to be kidding me," I mutter, shaking my head at the irony.

"What's that?" Lila asks, curiosity evident in her tone.

"Nothing," I reply, my resolve strengthening. "Just the universe having a laugh. I'm heading out now. You two ready?"

Their affirmative responses bolster my courage as I step back into the bustling terminal, ready to face whatever comes next. The weight of the situation settles on my shoulders, but I straighten my spine. I approach the airport lockers.

The cool metal of the key burns in my palm, a tangible link to the mystery I'm unraveling. I scan the locker numbers, my eyes darting from one to the next until—there.

"I'm at the locker," I whisper, more to steady myself than to inform Lila and Rafa.

I slide the key in and turn the lock. The locker door swings open with a soft click that seems to echo in my ears. Inside, a plain manila envelope sits innocuously, as if it doesn't potentially hold the answers to questions that have been keeping me up at night.

My hand trembles slightly as I reach for it. "Package secured," I mutter, tucking it quickly into my bag.

My mind races. Is this from Gregory Hunter, a message from beyond the grave? Or perhaps someone within The Peterson Group or Shenandoah Partners, unable to stay silent any longer? The possibilities are dizzying.

I catch myself shaking my head. "Get a grip, Cassie," I chide internally. "You're not some undercover agent in a James Patterson novel. Just a PI doing her job."

As I turn to leave, a familiar voice stops me cold.

* * *

"Ms. Maddox. Fancy meeting you here."

James Stanton stands before me, his tall frame blocking my path, his suit as impeccable as ever. My stomach drops, but I force a neutral expression.

"Agent Stanton. What a coincidence."

His eyes narrow slightly. "Is it? I'm curious about your interest in certain...

financial arrangements in our city."

My pulse quickens. How much does he know?

"I'm afraid I don't know what you mean," I reply, fighting to keep my voice steady.

"Come now, Ms. Maddox. Surely, a skilled investigator like yourself has noticed the interesting flow of capital between certain prominent entities lately?"

Alarm bells blare in my head. He's fishing, but he's dangerously close to the truth.

"Cassie, be careful," Rafi's voice warns in my ear.

"I investigate a lot of things, Agent Stanton," I say carefully. "You'll have to be more specific."

He takes a step closer, his voice lowering. "Shell companies. Intermediaries. Deceased partners with surprising connections. Ring any bells?"

I swallow hard. He knows about LCH Withholdings, maybe even about Echelon Nexus LLC. About Gregory Hunter and Shayan Easton. But how much?

"He's fishing, Cass," Lila whispers. "Don't give him anything."

I meet Stanton's gaze. "If you have specific concerns, Agent Stanton, I'd be happy to assist in any official capacity. But right now, I'm just a private citizen going about my day."

The tension between us is palpable, a silent battle of wills. I can't back down, can't show weakness. But beneath my calm exterior, my heart is racing, and I'm acutely aware of the weight of the envelope in my bag. Whatever this is, it's bigger than I imagined, and I'm in deep.

Stanton's eyes narrow, his tone shifting from probing to cautionary. "Ms. Maddox, I hope you understand the gravity of what you're potentially involving yourself in. This isn't some small-time operation you're poking around."

A trickle of sweat streams down my back, a nagging reminder of the danger lurking behind every corner. My instincts scream at me to turn back, but my burning curiosity fuels my resolve. "I appreciate your concern, Agent Stanton, but I've got the full force of Lenape City Police backing my investigation. I think I can handle myself."

"Can you?" he growls, leaning in closer with a dangerous glint in his eye. "Because make no mistake: there are powerful people who will stop at nothing to keep their secrets buried. They won't think twice about silencing anyone who dares to uncover the truth."

A cold tension coils in my gut, but I refuse to let him see my fear. With determination, I lift my chin and meet his intense gaze head on. "Is that a threat, Agent?"

"A warning," he corrects, his voice low. "From someone who's seen how ugly this can get."

For a moment, I waver. The weight of what I've uncovered presses down on me, and I consider coming clean, sharing what I know. But then I think of the cryptic messages, of the web of deceit I've only begun to unravel. I can't back down now.

"I appreciate the warning," I say, infusing my voice with a confidence I don't entirely feel. "But I've come too far to turn back. If I need help, Agent Stanton, I'll be sure to reach out."

As I turn to leave, his hand catches my arm. "Be careful, Cassie," he says, his tone softer now. "You're playing a dangerous game."

I nod once, then pull away. "Aren't we all?" I reply, striding towards the exit, my heart pounding but my resolve stronger than ever.

As I weave through the bustling airport, my phone vibrates. Lila's voice crackles through my earbud. "Cassie, Stanton's on the move. Two o'clock, about fifty feet behind you."

I resist the urge to look back. Instead, I duck into a nearby gift shop, pretending to browse postcards. "How many with him?" I murmur, keeping my voice low.

"Two suits," Rafi chimes in. "One's hanging back near the information desk. The other's tailing Stanton."

My heart races, but I force myself to stay calm. "Options?"

"There's a service corridor coming up on your left," Lila says.

"Staff only," Rafi adds. "But the lock's basic. I can guide you through bypassing it."

I weigh the risks. Getting caught in a restricted area could be trouble, but so could letting Stanton corner me again. "Let's do it," I decide.

As I make my way towards the corridor, I can't help but marvel at the absurdity of the situation. Here I am, playing cat-and-mouse in an airport like I'm in some kind of spy thriller. But this isn't fiction—the danger is very real.

"Cassie," Rafi's voice is urgent. "Stanton's picked up his pace. You need to move, now."

I quicken my steps, my hand brushing against the package in my bag. Whatever's inside, it's clear Stanton wants it. And that makes me all the more determined to keep it out of his reach.

I reach the service door, my fingers trembling slightly as I follow Rafi's instructions to bypass the lock. "Come on, come on," I mutter.

"You've got this, Cass," Lila encourages.

The lock clicks open, and I slip inside, closing the door quietly behind me. The narrow corridor stretches out before me, dimly lit and eerily quiet compared to the bustling terminal.

"Which way?" I ask, my voice barely above a whisper.

"Take a right," Rafi instructs. "There should be a stairwell at the end. It'll lead you down to the baggage claim area."

I start moving, my footsteps echoing in the empty hallway. "Any sign of Stanton?"

"He's arguing with security near the service door," Lila reports, a hint of satisfaction in her voice. "Looks like he doesn't have the clearance to follow you."

A small smile tugs at my lips. "Small victories, right?"

"Don't celebrate yet," Rafi warns. "His associates are still out there. And Stanton's not the type to give up easily."

He's right, of course. This is far from over. I push open the door to the stairwell. "Okay, guys. Let's get me out of here."

I burst through the stairwell door into the baggage claim area, my heart pounding against my ribs. The carousel nearest me creaks to life, spitting out a stream of suitcases. Perfect cover.

"Blend in, Cassie," Rafi's voice crackles through my earbud. "Act like you're waiting for luggage."

I nod, though he can't see me, and sidle up to the carousel. My eyes dart around, scanning faces in the crowd. "Any sign of Stanton's goons?"

"Not yet," Lila replies. "But stay alert."

I pretend to check my phone, using the reflection to keep an eye on my surroundings. A businessman in a crisp suit catches my attention, his gaze a little too focused. "Guys, three o'clock. Suit. Could be one of them."

"I see him," Rafi confirms. "Don't react. Just keep moving towards the exit."

I grab a random suitcase off the carousel, pulling it behind me as I weave through the crowd. My pulse quickens as I near the exit, freedom so close I can taste it.

"Cassie, duck left!" Lila's urgent whisper makes me freeze. "Woman in a red blazer, coming your way."

I veer sharply, nearly colliding with a family of tourists. "Sorry," I mutter, my eyes locked on the automatic doors ahead.

The cold night air hits my face as I step outside, and I allow myself a shaky exhale. "I think I'm clear."

"Not quite," Rafi warns. "Black SUV, approaching from your right. Could be Stanton."

I don't hesitate, abandoning the suitcase and breaking into a run. My feet pound the pavement as I sprint towards the parking garage, ducking between cars.

"You're doing great, Cass," Lila encourages. "Almost there."

I reach my beat-up Cadillac, fumbling with the keys. As I slide into the driver's seat, I glimpse a black sedan cruising past.

As I catch my breath, a sudden vibration jolts me back to high alert. It's not my phone—the buzz is coming from my bag. The package.

* * *

My hands tremble as I reach for the phone, a mix of anticipation and dread coursing through my veins. The manila envelope feels heavier now, almost alive with potential. I tear it open, my fingers fumbling in my haste.

Inside, nestled among crumpled paper, is a sleek burner phone. Its screen flashes to life, an unknown number lighting up the display. My heart leaps into my throat.

"Guys," I whisper to Lila and Rafi, "the package—it's a phone. And it's ringing."

"Answer it," Rafi urges, his voice tight with tension.

"Hello?" I answer cautiously.

No response, just a series of beeps and clicks. Then, silence.

"What the hell?" I mutter.

The phone buzzes again—a text message this time. The sender's name is simply "X."

I pull over, my hands shaking slightly as I open the message. It's a jumble of numbers and letters, clearly encrypted. But as I stare at it, patterns begin to emerge. My investigator's mind kicks into high gear, decoding on instinct.

"Oh my god," I breathe as the message takes shape. Shenandoah Partners, The Peterson Group, LCH Holdings, Echelon Nexus LLC—they're all there, along with names of shareholders we've only just begun to track.

But there's more. Hints of shell companies I've never heard of, offshore accounts, and political connections that make my stomach churn. This goes deeper than I ever imagined.

I recall the final chilling line of the decrypted message: *Nice work, Ms. Maddox. But the rabbit hole goes much further than you think. See you tonight. –* *X*

I lean back in my seat, my mind reeling. Who is X? How do they know what I've uncovered? And more importantly, what am I supposed to do with this information?

One thing's for certain – I'm in way over my head now. But as fear and excitement battle within me, I realize I've never felt more alive. Whatever comes next, I'm ready for it.

I grip the steering wheel, my knuckles turning white as I weigh my options. The logical part of me screams to hand this over to Stanton or the police. But something doesn't sit right.

"Damn it," I mutter, hitting the dashboard. "Why can't this be simple?"

I close my eyes, picturing Stanton's probing questions at the airport. His words echo in my mind, laden with hidden meaning. No, I can't trust him. Not yet.

Then there's Chief Burgess. Known him since I was knee-high to a grasshopper, as Dad would say. But even he feels like a wild card in this high-stakes game.

"Hey, super sleuth," Lila's cheerful voice fills the car. "What'd you find?"

I sigh. "Listen, guys. I need a favor. Are you two free in two hours?"

"Of course," their voices respond in unison.

"Thanks," I say, drumming my fingers on the steering wheel. "I've got a meeting. Midnight at the Old Clock Tower. It's... sensitive. I need to go alone, but I'd feel better knowing you two were nearby."

"Cassie," Rafi's voice cuts in, concern evident. "That sounds more risky than your encounter with Stanton in the airport. Are you sure about this?"

"No," I admit. "But my gut says this is big. Way bigger than we are equipped to handle. I have to see it through."

There's a pause, then Lila speaks. "We've got your back. Always."

Relief washes over me. "Thanks, guys. I owe you."

As I end the call, a weight lifts from my shoulders. Whatever lies ahead, I'm not facing it alone. With renewed determination, I start the car and head home to prepare for my midnight rendezvous.

20

The Old Clock Tower

The Old Clock Tower looms before me, its weathered bricks absorbing the feeble glow of nearby streetlamps. My footsteps echo off cobblestones as I approach, each click-clack amplified in the still night air. I scan the shadows, my senses on high alert.

"You've got this, Cassie," Lila's voice crackles through my earpiece. "Rafi and I are watching from two blocks away. We've got your back."

I take a deep breath, willing my racing heart to slow. "Thanks, guys. I'm going in."

The tower's arched entryway yawns before me, pitch black within. I hesitate for a heartbeat, then step inside. The musty scent of age and disuse fills my nostrils as my eyes adjust to the gloom.

"Hello?" I call softly, my voice barely above a whisper. "I'm here."

A figure detaches itself from the darkness, moving with cautious grace. I tense, my hand instinctively reaching for the concealed weapon at my hip.

"Ms. Maddox," a low voice intones. "Thank you for coming."

The speaker–X, I assume–stays mostly in shadow, but I catch glimpses of a tall frame and glinting eyes. Male, probably, though I can't be certain.

"You said you had information," I reply, keeping my tone even. "About the development deals in Lenape City."

X nods, glancing furtively over his shoulder before speaking. "It goes deeper than you know. There's a man—powerful, connected. He's the puppet master behind it all."

My mind whirs, piecing together fragments of the investigation. "Who?" I press. "Give me a name."

"Someone you know," X says, his voice barely above a whisper. "Someone who's embedded himself at the highest levels of the city's power structure."

I frown. Who could he mean? A face flashes in my mind—but no, it can't be. Can it?

"This man," X continues, "he's got his fingers in every major development deal for the past decade. Bribes, blackmail, shell companies—he's built an empire on corruption."

I lean forward, hungry for more details. "How do you know all this?"

X shifts uneasily. "I've... worked for him. Seen things. But I can't be part of it anymore. That's why I reached out to you."

I nod, understanding dawning. "You're taking a huge risk."

"We both are," X replies grimly. "But someone has to stop him before he destroys everything that makes Lenape City special."

I think of the city I love—its blend of history and progress, its vibrant neighborhoods. The thought of all that being corrupted makes my blood boil.

"I need proof," I say firmly. "Concrete evidence I can take to the authorities."

X hesitates, then reaches into his jacket. "The burner phone from the locker. That's only the tip of the iceberg. I have files. Documents. But you need to be careful. He has eyes everywhere."

As he speaks, a flicker of movement catches my eye. Someone else is here, lurking just beyond the edge of my vision. My heart pounds as I struggle to maintain my composure.

"Cassie," Lila's voice hisses in my ear. "We've got movement outside. Be ready."

I lock eyes with X, seeing my tension mirrored there. Whatever happens next, I know this night is far from over.

X's voice drops even lower, barely above a whisper. "The reach of this conspiracy extends further than you can imagine, Cassie. It's not just about real estate. It's about—"

A sudden movement to my right cuts him off. My head snaps around, adrenaline surging through my veins. There, emerging from the shadows is a flash of red hair and a familiar face I didn't expect to see tonight.

Shayan Easton.

She's breathing hard, eyes wide with a mix of fear and determination. She takes a step towards me, hands slightly raised, as if to show she means no harm.

"Cassie," she calls out, voice trembling. "I need to speak with you. It's urgent."

X tenses beside me, his masked face turning towards the newcomer. He shifts his stance, positioning himself between Shayan and me. I can feel the tension radiating off him in waves.

My mind races. What's Shayan doing here? How did she know about this meeting? I try to keep my voice steady as I address her. "Shayan, this isn't a good time. How did you—"

"Please," she interrupts, desperation clear in her tone. "You don't understand. There's something you need to know about—"

X cuts her off, his voice sharp. "That's enough. I told you I'd handle things from here."

I'm caught in the middle, my instincts screaming at me to be cautious. Shayan has always seemed trustworthy, but in this world of shadows and secrets, can I really be sure of anyone's motives?

"Cassie," Lila's voice crackles in my ear again. "Something's not right. Be ready to move."

"Okay," I say, addressing both X and Shayan. "Let's all just take a step back. We need to—"

But before I can finish, the wail of distant sirens cuts through the night air. X's head snaps up, his body language screaming alarm.

"We're out of time," he hisses.

Shayan takes a step forward, her white scarf fluttering in the cool night breeze. "Cassie, please," she pleads, her eyes darting around nervously. "Listen to me. The corruption goes deeper than you know. And this man—"

"Stay back!" X's voice cuts through the darkness, sharp and urgent. "You've meddled enough."

I raise my hands, trying to defuse the situation. "Both of you, calm down. Shayan, what's so urgent?"

Shayan's voice trembles as she speaks. "It's about this man. He's just—"

"Enough!" X interrupts, moving closer to me. His masked face turns towards Shayan. "You've done enough. Leave now, before you're captured."

I feel torn, my investigative instincts warring with caution. Shayan's always been a reliable source, but X's warnings echo in my mind. Can I trust either of them?

As the tension builds, I notice X's hand moving subtly. In a blink, he presses something small and cold into my palm—a USB drive.

"Keep this safe," he whispers urgently. "It's everything you need."

I nod, discreetly slipping the drive into my pocket. My heart races as I try to process the chaos unfolding around me. What secrets does this tiny device hold? And why is Shayan so desperate to talk to me?

"Cassie," Shayan tries again, her voice filled with desperation. "You don't understand the danger you're in. I have to tell you about—"

The piercing wail of police sirens slices through the night air, shattering the tense standoff. My heart leaps into my throat as I whip my head around, scanning the darkened streets.

"Shit," I mutter, adrenaline surging through my veins. "This is about to get real messy."

X's head snaps up, his body tensing like a coiled spring. "They're coming, Cassie. Trust no one."

I turn back to face him, questions burning on my tongue. "Wait, what about—"

But he's already melting into the shadows, his dark form blending seamlessly with the night. In the blink of an eye, he's gone, leaving me alone with Shayan and a whirlwind of unanswered questions.

"Dammit!" I hiss, frustration bubbling up inside me. The USB drive feels heavy in my pocket, a tangible reminder of how close I'd been to unraveling this mess.

The sirens grow louder, red and blue lights painting the walls of the Old Clock Tower. I glance at Shayan, her face a mask of fear and indecision.

"Cassie, please," she starts, but I cut her off with a sharp gesture.

"Not now," I say, my mind racing. "We need to figure out how to handle this."

As the sound of screeching tires reaches my ears, I can't help but wonder: How did it all go sideways so fast? And more importantly, what am I going to do now?

Shayan's eyes dart frantically between me and the approaching lights. In a blur of motion, she rushes forward, pressing something small and hard into my palm.

"Take this," she whispers urgently, her breath warm against my ear. "Don't let them see it. And remember, trust no—"

Officer Dan Lutman and another officer materialize from the darkness, their hands already reaching for their cuffs. Dan's eyes gleam with victory, and he moves with flaunting deliberation as he briefly makes eye contact with me. By his side, the second officer is practically invisible as he follows protocol, professional and without any fanfare. Shayan's shoulders slump in resignation as they take her into custody, but her eyes lock onto mine one last time, blazing with a mix of fear and determination.

I clench my fist around the object—a burner phone; I realize, and slip it discreetly into my jacket pocket. My heart pounds a frantic rhythm against my ribs as I watch Shayan being led away, questions flooding my mind. What was she about to say? Who can't I trust?

"Cassie."

The familiar voice cuts through my spiraling thoughts like a knife. I turn slowly, readying myself for the confrontation I've been dreading. There he is—Detective Dylan Maddox, my father, striding towards me with that perfect blend of paternal concern and professional authority that I've come to both admire and resent.

"Dad," I manage, trying to keep my voice steady.

His eyes narrow, scanning my face. "What are you mixed up in this time, Cass?"

I cross my arms, adopting a defensive posture I know he'll recognize. "Just following a lead. You know, doing my job."

"Your job," he repeats, a hint of exasperation creeping into his tone. "Right. First, you're a witness to a suicide, maybe a murder. Now this. Your duties as a hired PI are getting dangerously close to interfering with an ongoing police investigation. This meeting, whatever it was, better have resulted in gathering reliable evidence for Chief Burgess."

I bite back a sharp retort, reminding myself of the stakes. The USB drive and the burner phone feel like they're burning holes in my pockets. I can't let him know about them—not yet, not until I understand what's really going on.

"Look, Dad," I say, softening my tone. "I'm following every lead. Shayan was ready to spill everything she knows until you guys showed up. I can handle this."

His expression flickers, concern momentarily overtaking the stern detective facade. "That's what worries me, Cassie. You don't know what you're getting into here."

For a split second, I consider turning over X's USB drive and Shayan's burner phone. But Shayan's unfinished warning echoes in my mind: Trust no one. Even those closest to you?

I swallow hard, forcing a smile. "I appreciate the concern, Dad. Really. But I've got this under control. Let me do the job Chief Burgess hired me to do."

We stand there, locked in this familiar dance of protection and rebellion, as the sirens fade into the distance. The night feels charged with unseen dangers and unspoken truths.

What have I gotten myself into? And more importantly, how deep does this conspiracy really go?

Agent James Stanton strides forward, his presence commanding attention even in the chaos of flashing police lights. His eyes lock onto mine, cold and determined.

"Ms. Maddox," he says, his voice clipped and authoritative. "I need you to turn over all materials related to your investigation. Immediately."

My heart races, but I keep my expression neutral. "I'm not sure what you're referring to, Agent Stanton. This is a private matter—"

"This is now a federal investigation," he cuts me off. "When we ran into each other at the airport, it was out of courtesy that I let you go. To be clear, your cooperation isn't optional."

I glance at my father, hoping for support, but his face is unreadable. Stanton's words hang in the air, heavy with implied threat. I weigh my options, acutely aware of the USB drive and burner phone burning holes in my pockets.

"Fine," I say finally, my voice steadier than I feel. "I'll get you what I have at my office tomorrow morning."

Stanton's eyes narrow. "Now, Ms. Maddox."

As I reluctantly nod, my gaze sweeps the scene. Blue and red lights pulse over dark pavement while a uniformed officer murmurs into his radio. Beside me, Dad nudges me while I catalog the faces I recognize from LCPD and strain to get a glimpse of the road. How many patrol cars arrived on scene? Something's off. I take a moment to place it—Officer Lutman has gone, and along with him, Shayan Easton. A cold dread pulls me out of the moment.

"Is there a problem, Ms. Maddox?" Stanton's voice snaps me back to the present.

I force a smile. "No problem at all, Agent Stanton. Just making sure I understand exactly what you need."

As the words leave my lips, a wave of understanding washes over me. This USB drive and whatever secrets Shayan was trying to reveal hold more weight than I ever imagined. My thoughts race, trying to piece together exactly how Stanton fits into the puzzle, but fear and uncertainty cloud my mind.

My father's voice breaks through my frantic thoughts as he turns to Stanton. "I assure you, Ms. Maddox will provide everything required, Agent Stanton."

Stanton's cold gaze pierces into me, his words dripping with malice. "You may have escaped me once, Ms. Maddox, but you won't get away again."

My heart pounds in my chest as Stanton orders his team to search the premises. Meanwhile, my father reminds me of my duty to the police force. "Tomorrow, Cassie. Hand over all evidence to Chief Burgess."

"I will," I promise, though neither my father nor Stanton know the full extent of what I've uncovered.

* * *

Leaving the Old Clock Tower, each step feels like a heavy burden as I try to process all that has transpired. The USB drive and burner phone weigh heavily in my pockets, pulling me down into murky depths. My mind races with confusion and fear, unsure of what secrets I've stumbled upon.

Suddenly, Lila's voice breaks through the silence in my earpiece, jolting me back to reality. "Cassie, are you alright?" Her concern only adds to the weight pressing down on me as I realize the danger I am now facing.

"Yeah, I'm fine. Just... processing."

"Want us to meet you?" Rafi chimes in, concern evident in his tone.

"No," I reply, perhaps too quickly. "I need some time to think. I'll catch up with you both tomorrow."

As I start my car and round the corner onto Main Street, the familiar sights of Lenape City's nightlife blur into a haze of neon and shadows. The Old Town Plaza looms ahead, its modern glass façade a stark contrast to the historic buildings surrounding it. It's a physical reminder of the changes sweeping through our city.

My phone buzzes. Not my regular phone—the burner Shayan slipped me. I pull over and my heart races as I pull it out, glancing around to ensure I'm alone before reading the message.

Trust no one. Not even those closest to you.

The words send ice through my veins, especially since Shayan is in Officer Lutman's custody. Shayan and X could both be working for someone else who either wants to point me in the right direction or throw me off the trail. It's no coincidence they both showed up ready to hand over information. But what about Lutman?

The weight of suspicion settles over me like a shroud. Is it possible that Dan Lutman is involved? That would explain his persistence in nabbing Shayan. The thought makes me sick, but I can't ignore it.

I pull onto the road and hit the gas, faster now, eager to get home where I

143

can examine the USB drive's contents. As I pass the sleek high-rise housing Shenandoah Partners, I can't help but wonder how deep this conspiracy runs.

"One step at a time, Cassie," I tell myself, shifting in the driver's seat. "You wanted a big case. Well, congratulations—you've got one. Now solve it."

I pause at the intersection, the streetlights casting long shadows across the empty sidewalks. My mother's house is only a few blocks away, but it feels like miles. Every passing car makes me tense, causing me to wonder if I'm being followed.

"Okay, think," I mutter. "What do I know for sure?"

Not much, if I'm honest. A conspiracy involving Lenape City's development sector. A powerful figure, who I evidently know, pulling strings. And now, a warning not to trust anyone—even those closest to me.

I fish the USB drive out of my pocket, turning it over in my hand. "You better have some answers," I whisper.

As I park the car on the street, I spot a familiar figure seated on the front porch of my mom's house. I turn the car off and get out.

"Hey," Rafi calls out, standing up. "You okay"

I hesitate, Shayan's warning echoing in my mind. Can I trust Rafi? I've known him all my life, but...

"Yeah, I'm fine," I say, careful to keep my voice neutral. "Just a long night."

Rafi's brow furrows. "Did you get anything useful from X?"

"Maybe," I shrug. "If that truly was X. I need to go through some things. Why don't we reconnect in the morning?"

"Sure," he nods, but I catch a flicker of... something in his eyes. Concern? Suspicion? "Stay safe, Cassie."

As I watch him walk away, I can't shake the feeling that I'm standing on the edge of a precipice. One wrong move and I could lose everything—my career, my relationships, maybe even my life.

But I didn't become an investigator to play it safe.

I unlock my apartment door, my mind already racing with the next steps. The USB drive. Shayan's burner phone. The web of connections between Shenandoah Partners, The Peterson Group, and every player still on the board—Pence, Easton, Stanton, X, my father, Chief Burgess.

"Time to pull threads," I mutter, booting up my laptop. "Let's see where this leads."

21

Those Closest to Us

The fluorescent lights of Rafi's tech shop flicker to life as I push open the door, my heart still pounding from last night's chaos. The familiar scent of electronics and coffee hits me, a slight comfort in the storm of uncertainty swirling around me.

Rafi hunches over his computer, surrounded by a sea of blinking gadgets and glowing screens.

"Rafi," I call out, my voice shakier than I'd like. He swivels in his chair, his warm brown eyes widening as he takes in my disheveled appearance.

"Cass? You look like you've seen a ghost," he says, concern etching his features.

Pulling up a chair, I sit and look Rafi in the eye. "I'm sorry about last night. I was short with you, and you didn't deserve that."

Rafi's expression softens. "Hey, no worries. What's going on?"

My hand trembles slightly as I pull out the burner phone and USB drive. "I need your help, Rafi. And I need to know I can trust you completely."

He leans forward, his gaze intense. "Always, Cass. You know that."

I nod, swallowing hard. "This USB... X gave it to me last night... or, more like this morning. He said it contains everything I need. But Rafi, it could implicate someone close to me in all this corruption with Shenandoah and Peterson."

146

Rafi's eyebrows shoot up as he takes the drive. "Did he say who this could implicate?"

I shake my head, my mind racing. Should I tell him about X's and Shayan's warning? I decide to keep it simple for now. "Stanton wants the files, and my father wants me to hand everything over to Chief Burgess. I should be able to trust my father and the police chief, but they both seem to have their own angle. And Stanton? I didn't trust him when I met him. Can I even trust anyone right now?"

He turns the drive over carefully. "You can trust me, right?"

I manage a small smile. "Yes. You and Lila, of course."

As Rafi inserts the drive into his computer, I can't help but think about how much is riding on what we might find. The familiar skyline of Lenape City looms outside the shop window, a reminder of all that's at stake. How many of those gleaming towers hide secrets of corruption and greed?

"Cass," Rafi's voice pulls me back. "Whatever's on here, we'll figure it out together. Okay?"

I nod, grateful for his steady presence. "Okay. Let's see what X thought was so important."

As the files load, I hold my breath, hoping for answers but dreading what they might reveal about the city I love—and the people I thought I knew.

The sound of my feet echoes around the tiny space of Rafi's makeshift office, tucked away in the pharmacy's storage area among the walls of screens and equipment. My mind's a tornado, whirling with fragments of information—shell companies, shady real estate deals, whispered threats in dark alleys. How deep does this corruption go?

"You're gonna wear a hole in my floor, Cass," Rafi quips, his eyes never leaving the screen.

I pause, running a hand through my hair. "Sorry. It's just... everything's connected, Rafi. The Old Town Plaza project, Shenandoah Partners, The Peterson Group—it's like a giant spider web, and I'm caught right in the middle of it."

Rafi's fingers dance across the keyboard, lines of code reflecting in his glasses. "I get it. But we'll untangle this mess, I promise. Look here—"

I pause and lean in, squinting at the screen. Rafi points to a complex diagram of transactions.

"See these shell companies? They're funneling money through a series of offshore accounts. Classic laundering scheme, but on a massive scale."

My heart races. "Can you trace where it's all coming from?"

Rafi's brow furrows. "It's not that simple. Whoever set this up knew what they were doing. But…" He taps a few more keys. "I can follow the money trail backward. It might lead us to the source."

I nod, a mix of determination and dread settling in my gut. "Do it. We need to know who's pulling the strings."

As Rafi works his technological wizardry, a thought crosses my mind: Am I prepared for the reality that awaits me? What if it exposes someone I hold dear? My father's face appears in my mind, followed by my mother and Lila. Even Uncle Alfred comes to mind. But I push those concerns aside, determined to see this through to the end.

"Cass," Rafi's voice cuts through my thoughts. "You okay?"

I realize I've been gripping the edge of his desk, knuckles white. "Yeah, I'm fine. Just… a lot on my mind."

"Holy shit," Rafi mutters, his eyes widening as he scrolls through the newly unlocked data. "Cassie, you need to see this."

My heart races as I take in the complex web of financial transactions linking Shenandoah Partners and The Peterson Group to a dizzying array of shell companies. It's a tangled mess of numbers and names, but one that's hauntingly familiar.

"Most of this… we already knew," I say, my voice tight. "But there's something else here, isn't there?"

Rafi nods, opening another spreadsheet. "Yeah, look at this. It's not just companies. It's individuals, their holdings…"

As we dig through the fresh data, my investigative senses heighten. The names stand out to me—city officials, affluent investors, individuals I've spotted on social media and at fundraising events. People I've served food and drinks to when I worked at The Genesee Country Club. These are the last people who should be involved in this mess.

"Rafi," I say, my mouth suddenly dry. "Can you search for my last name?"

He glances at me, concern etched on his face, but doesn't argue. A few keystrokes later, and there it is. Maddox. Buried deep, but undeniably there.

"Cass..." Rafi starts, his voice heavy with suspicion. "You don't seem surprised."

I meet his gaze, weighing how much to reveal. "I recognized some names. I... I needed to be sure."

"Sure of what?" he presses.

Before I can answer, my phone buzzes. It's Lila, her voice tight with anxiety. "Cassie, you need to get to The Peterson Group's office. Now. Something's happening, and it doesn't look good."

As I end the call, my mind reels.

"I've got to go," I say, already moving towards the door. "Lila needs me at The Peterson Group."

Rafi stands, concern in his eyes. "Cassie, wait. What's going on? What aren't you telling me?"

I pause, one hand on the doorknob. "I don't know. Lila might be in danger. I need to help her, but..." I trail off, the words sticking in my throat.

Rafi's eyes soften. He steps closer, his voice low and steady. "But you're worried about what you might walk into."

I nod, grateful for his understanding. "Exactly. We have a scattering of pieces, but not the complete picture. And now Lila's right in the middle of it."

"I've got your back, Cassie," Rafi says, his hand on my shoulder. "I'll keep working on this data. Whatever you need."

His loyalty warms me, a small beacon in the growing darkness. "Thanks, Rafi. There is one more thing." I hesitate, then push forward. "Can you share all my case files with my dad? For his eyes only."

Rafi's eyebrows rise, but he doesn't question it. "Consider it done."

As I reach for the door again, my phone vibrates. A text from an unknown number flashes on the screen:

DANGER IMMINENT. WATCH YOUR STEP.

I show Rafi the message, my hand shaking slightly.

"Jesus," he mutters. "Cassie, maybe you shouldn't—"

"I have to," I cut him off, my resolve hardening. "Lila needs me. Just... keep digging, okay? And be careful."

The cold air slaps me in the face as I step out of Rafi's shop, sharpening my senses and steeling my resolve. Lenape City's bustling streets stretch before me, a maze of possibilities and dangers. My heart pounds, but I force myself to breathe steadily, focusing on the task ahead.

"One step at a time, Cassie," I mutter to myself, weaving through the morning crowd. "Find Lila, uncover the truth, protect the innocent. Simple, right?"

A bitter laugh escapes me. Simple. As if anything about this case has been simple.

I turn the corner, my mind racing with potential scenarios involving armed thugs at The Peterson Group office, when I slam to a halt. My blood runs cold.

* * *

There, not ten feet away, stands my Uncle Alfred Maddox.

His steel-gray eyes lock onto mine, a predator sizing up its prey. Every instinct screams at me to run, but I force myself to stay rooted to the spot. Uncle Alfred's lips curl into a smile that doesn't reach his eyes.

"Cassandra," he says smoothly, taking a step towards me. "What a pleasant surprise. I was just thinking about you."

I swallow hard, desperately trying to keep my face neutral. "Uncle Alfred," I reply, my voice steadier than I feel. "I didn't expect to see you in this part of town."

He chuckles while I offer a lighthearted laugh. "Oh, you know me. Always keeping an eye on the city's... development. Speaking of which, I hear you've taken quite an interest in some of our local projects lately."

My mind races. How much does he know? Is this a threat? A warning? I force a casual shrug. "Just doing my job, Uncle. Following leads where they take me."

"Of course, of course," he nods, his gaze never wavering. "Your father must be proud. Though I worry, sometimes, about the dangers a young woman might face in such... delicate investigations."

I notice the barely veiled threat. I clench my fists, fighting the urge to confront him outright. Not here, not now. I need more proof than a name buried deep within a spreadsheet.

"I appreciate your concern," I say, injecting as much sincerity as I can muster into my voice. "But I can handle myself."

Uncle Alfred's smile widens, cold and calculating. "I'm sure you can, my dear. I'm sure you can."

I stand my ground, meeting Alfred's calculating gaze with a steady one of my own. The bustling sounds of the city fade into the background as we face off on the sidewalk, two players in a dangerous game of chess.

"You know," Alfred says, smoothing his already impeccable suit, "I've always admired your tenacity, Cassie. It reminds me of your father in his younger days."

I force a smile, my mind working overtime to decipher his angle. "Thank you. I learned from the best."

Alfred takes a step closer, his cologne—expensive and overbearing—filling my nostrils. "Indeed. Which is why I'm surprised you haven't come to me with any of your... concerns about our city's development projects. I could be a valuable resource, you know."

My heart pounds. Is this an invitation or a trap? I choose my words carefully. "I appreciate that, Uncle Alfred. But you know how it is—I like to gather all the facts before involving anyone else."

He laughs, the sound as polished as his appearance. "Ah, the impetuousness of youth. Sometimes, Cassie, it's not about what you know, but who you know. And in this city, well..." He trails off, leaving the implication hanging in the air between us.

I fight the urge to back away, to run. Instead, I stand taller, channeling all my determination into my voice. "I'll keep that in mind. Now, if you'll excuse me, I have an appointment to keep."

Alfred's eyes narrow slightly. A flicker of something—approval? Amusement?—passing through them. "Of course, of course. Don't let me keep you. But Cassie?" He pauses, his tone shifting to something almost paternal. "Do be careful out there. The truth can be a dangerous thing in the wrong hands."

I try to steady my breathing as I process Alfred's words. Every syllable feels like a loaded gun, and I'm tiptoeing through a minefield of hidden meanings. My eyes dart around, taking in the bustling street, searching for any sign that we're being watched or followed.

"You seem distracted, Cassie," Alfred says, his voice cutting through my thoughts. "Is something troubling you?"

I force a smile, meeting his gaze. "Just a busy day ahead. You know how it is in this city—always something happening."

He nods, a knowing smile playing on his lips. "Indeed. Speaking of which, I hear there was quite a commotion at the old clock tower last night. Anything you'd care to share about that?"

My pulse quickens. How does he know? Dan Lutman's face flashes in my mind. Could he be the leak? But whose payroll is he on? I keep my voice steady as I reply, "I'm afraid I know nothing about that. Police business, you understand."

Alfred's eyes bore into mine, searching. "Of course. It's just that these things have a way of... affecting our community. I'd hate to see anything disrupt the progress we've been making."

As I formulate a response, a sleek black limousine glides to a stop behind Alfred. He turns, a satisfied smile on his face. "Ah, perfect timing. Our ride awaits," he says, gesturing toward the car. "After you, Cassie."

Caught off guard, I freeze. "I... I'm not sure I—"

"Nonsense," Alfred interrupts, his tone brooking no argument. "I insist. We have much to discuss, and I believe you'll find our conversation most illuminating."

As he opens the door, I realize I'm trapped between curiosity and caution. Every instinct screams danger, but this could be my chance to uncover the truth. But then again, he's always looked out for number one. I step forward, wary of my uncle's intentions.

22

Veiled Warnings

The sleek black leather of the limousine's rear seat creaks softly as I shift my weight, my eyes locked on Uncle Alfred's face. He lounges across from me, the picture of ease in his tailored suit, a slight smile playing at the corners of his mouth. The air between us feels thick, charged with unspoken questions and barely concealed suspicion.

"So, Uncle Alfred," I begin, keeping my tone light despite the rapid beating of my heart, "I've been hearing a lot about Shenandoah Partners and The Peterson Group lately. Any exciting projects they're working on?"

I note the way his eyebrows lift slightly at my question. Is it surprise or just polite interest? It's hard to tell with Uncle Alfred; he's always been a master of masks.

"Ah, Cassie, always the inquisitive one," he chuckles, leaning forward slightly. "I'm glad you asked. Those two have quite a few irons in the fire, as they say. Revitalizing the old warehouse district, for one. Quite an ambitious undertaking."

I nod, trying to keep my face neutral even as my mind races. The warehouse district? They found Gregory Hunter's body there. Is it just a coincidence, or is there more to it?

"Sounds interesting," I say, aiming for casual curiosity. "I've heard The Peterson Group has been making waves in urban development. Any truth to that?"

Uncle Alfred's smile widens, and I can't shake the feeling that he's enjoying this exchange far too much. "Oh, absolutely. Carl Peterson—God rest his soul—had quite the vision for Lenape City. The Peterson Group has been at the forefront of transforming our skyline."

I file away the mention of Carl Peterson's death, noting the lack of genuine emotion in Uncle Alfred's voice. My fingers itch to jot down notes, but I resist the urge. This isn't an official interview; it's a dangerous dance of half-truths and veiled implications.

"And Shenandoah Partners?" I press, leaning forward slightly. "I've heard they're involved in some pretty innovative projects."

Uncle Alfred's eyes gleam with what might be pride—or something darker. "Thomas Pence is a visionary, no doubt about it. Shenandoah's work in sustainable urban living is truly remarkable. You should see their plans for the riverside development."

I nod, trying to piece together the connections in my head. Shenandoah, The Peterson Group, the warehouse district, the riverside... It's like a complex web, and I can't shake the feeling that Uncle Alfred is at the center of it all.

"Sounds like exciting times for Lenape City," I say, forcing a smile. "You must be proud to be associated with such forward-thinking companies."

Uncle Alfred leans back, his expression unreadable. "Oh, I'm just a humble country club owner, Cassie. But I do like to keep an eye on progress in our fair city."

I bite back a snort. Humble is the last word I'd use to describe Uncle Alfred. As the limousine glides through the city streets, I can't help but wonder just how deep his involvement goes—and what secrets lie buried beneath the shiny facade of Lenape City's urban renewal.

A disarming smile playing across his lips. His perfectly tailored suit doesn't crease as he relaxes into the plush leather seat.

"You know, Cassie," he says, his voice smooth as aged whiskey, "if you're looking for an interesting lead, you might consider Hathaway Realty."

My eyebrows shoot up involuntarily. "Hathaway Realty?" I echo, trying to keep my voice neutral. My uncle is not the first to suggest looking into

Hathaway.

Uncle Alfred nods, his eyes twinkling. "Indeed. I heard the police paid their offices a visit recently. And Rhonda Hathaway, their CEO? She's quite the elusive figure."

I study his face, searching for any hint of deception. How does he know about the police activity, or about my failed attempts to meet with Ms. Hathaway? And why is he, along with Pence, so eager to point me in that direction?

"That's... certainly interesting," I say carefully. My mind races, trying to connect the dots. "I wasn't aware Hathaway Realty was involved in all this."

Uncle Alfred shrugs, the picture of nonchalance. "Oh, I'm sure it's nothing. Just thought it might pique your investigative curiosity."

I can feel him trying to steer me away from something, but what? I decide to change tack.

"Actually, Uncle Alfred," I say, leaning forward slightly, "I've been curious about two other companies—Echelon Nexus LLC and LCH. Have you heard of them?"

I watch his face intently, looking for any flicker of recognition or alarm. My heart pounds, but I keep my expression neutral.

Uncle Alfred's brow furrows slightly. "Echelon Nexus? LCH? Can't say either of them rings a bell. What sort of business are they in?"

I hesitate, torn between pushing harder and playing it cool. "I'm not entirely sure," I admit. "They seem to operate in the shadows. I was hoping you might have some insight, given your... connections."

He chuckles, but there's an edge to it. "My dear, I'm afraid you give me too much credit. I'm just a simple businessman, not some kind of corporate mastermind."

I don't believe that for a second, but I nod as if considering his words. I weigh the risks of revealing what I know about Gregory Hunter and Shayan Easton. No, I decide. It's too soon to show my hand.

"Of course," I say with a smile that doesn't quite reach my eyes. "I just thought, with all the people you rub shoulders with at The Genesee, you might have heard something."

The air in the limo feels thick with unspoken truths and carefully constructed lies. As we continue to circle each other with words, I can't shake the feeling that I'm playing a dangerous game—and Uncle Alfred might hold all the cards.

Alfred leans back, his fingers tapping lightly on the leather armrest. "If I had to guess," he says with a casual shrug, "Echelon Nexus is probably just another shell company. You know how it is these days–every corporation has a dozen of them for tax purposes."

His dismissive tone doesn't match the calculated look in his eyes.

"Tax purposes," I repeat, trying to keep the skepticism out of my voice, knowing full well what shell companies hide. "That's certainly possible."

Uncle Alfred's nonchalance only fuels my suspicion. I've known my uncle long enough to know when he's deflecting. But why? What is he trying to hide?

"Speaking of corporations," I say, deciding to change tactics, "I've been meaning to ask you about Gregory Hunter's death." I watch him closely, searching for any flicker of emotion. "Given his connections to some of these companies and the people he associates with at The Genesee, I can't help but wonder if there might be a link."

For a split second, I see something—a tightening around his eyes, perhaps, or a slight pause in his breathing. But it's gone so quickly, I almost doubt I saw it at all.

"Gregory Hunter?" Alfred repeats, his voice tinged with what sounds like genuine sadness. "Such a tragedy. He was a brilliant man, taken far too soon."

I lean forward slightly, my gaze locked on his face. "Did you know him well?"

Uncle Alfred sighs, running a hand through his silver hair. "We've interacted a few times at the country club and crossed paths occasionally in business circles. But Cassie, dear, you shouldn't go looking for conspiracies where there aren't any. Sometimes, terrible things just happen."

His words are reasonable, even kind. But there's an undercurrent of... something. Warning? Threat? I can't quite put my finger on it, but it makes the hair on the back of my neck stand up.

"I'm not looking for conspiracies," I say carefully. "I'm looking for the truth."

Our eyes meet, and for a moment, the facade slips. I see a flicker of something cold and calculating in Uncle Alfred's gaze. Then it's gone, replaced by his usual charming smile.

"Of course you are," he says warmly. "It's what makes you such an excellent investigator. Just... be careful where that search leads you, Cassie. Not everyone appreciates having their secrets exposed."

I feel my jaw tighten as I process Uncle Alfred's veiled warning. My mind races, connecting dots and seeking patterns. I won't be deterred, not when I'm this close.

"What about Shayan Easton?" I press, leaning forward in my seat. "Why was she arrested? It can't be a coincidence that her name keeps coming up alongside Gregory's and these companies."

Alfred's eyebrows lift slightly. "Shayan Easton? I'm afraid I'm not familiar with—"

"Don't," I cut him off, surprising myself with the sharpness in my voice. "Please don't pretend you don't know. Shayan, Gregory, Echelon Nexus, Shenandoah Partners, The Peterson Group—they're all connected. I need to understand how."

I watch as Alfred's expression shifts, his practiced smile faltering for just a moment. His gaze shifts, and I can almost see him recalibrating his approach.

"Cassie," he says, his tone gentle but firm, "I understand your drive. It's admirable. But you're treading into dangerous waters. These are powerful people and organizations you're investigating."

I feel a flicker of frustration. "I'm aware of the risks, Uncle Alfred. But if there's corruption happening in Lenape City, someone needs to expose it."

He reaches out, as if to pat my hand, but I subtly shift away. His eyes narrow slightly at the movement.

"You're so much like your father," he muses, a note of something I can't quite identify in his voice. "Always chasing after the next big case, oblivious to the personal cost."

The comparison stings, but I push the feeling aside. "This isn't about personal glory. It's about justice."

Alfred leans back, studying me. "And what if pursuing that justice puts you in harm's way? What then?"

I meet his gaze steadily. "Then that's a risk I'm willing to take."

Alfred's hand lands on mine, his grip firm but not forceful. His voice drops to a low, measured tone while my shoulders tense.

"Cassie, my dear," he says, "I admire your tenacity, but you need to focus on building your career, not chasing potentially dangerous leads. Corporate CEOs don't take kindly to outsiders meddling in their affairs or exposing their... let's call them 'trade secrets.'"

I feel the weight of his words, the subtle threat beneath them. I think of Gregory Hunter's untimely death, and I wonder if Alfred's warning is more than just a hypothetical concern.

"You know," he continues, his eyes never leaving mine, "what happened to Gregory Hunter is a tragic example of what can occur when one pokes their nose where it doesn't belong."

My breath catches. Is he really implying what I think he is?

"As for Ms. Easton," Alfred adds smoothly, "I believe you already know the reason for her arrest. Your client, Thomas Pence, filled you in on all the details, didn't he?"

I blink. How does he know about my connection to Pence? The realization that Alfred might be more involved than I thought sends a wave of unease through me.

Before I can respond, the limousine slows to a stop. I glance out the window, surprised to see the imposing structure of The Peterson Group looming before us.

"What are we doing here?" I ask, unable to keep the confusion from my voice.

Alfred's smile is enigmatic. "Ah, perfect timing."

As I turn back to him, movement outside catches my eye. A tall, silver-haired man in an impeccably tailored suit approaches the limo. My heart races as I recognize Thomas Pence.

"Uncle Alfred," I begin, my voice tight, "what's going on?"

He chuckles softly. "Thomas and I are old associates, Cassie. Nothing to worry about."

The tension in the car is palpable as the driver opens the door opposite me. Thomas Pence slides in, his piercing gaze immediately finding mine. He doesn't seem surprised to see me here, and that unsettles me even more.

* * *

I lock eyes with my uncle, searching for any hint of explanation. But all I see is that maddeningly calm smile as he says, "Shall we get down to business, then?"

My mind races, trying to piece together the puzzle before me. Lila's frantic call echoes in my ears, urging me to get to The Peterson Group. And now, here I am, sandwiched between my enigmatic uncle and Thomas Pence, the very client who hired me to track down Shayan Easton.

Alfred clears his throat, breaking the tense silence. "Cassie, you should know that Thomas and I share a mutual interest in salvaging The Peterson Group." His eyes flicker to Pence before returning to me. "Especially now that Carl Peterson is no longer with us."

My breath catches. Uncle Alfred's precision in mentioning Carl Peterson's death swirls in my mind. Before I can voice questions, Thomas Pence turns to me with a disarming smile.

"Ms. Maddox," he says, his tone warm yet formal. "I must commend you on your excellent work in locating Ms. Easton. Your reputation is well-deserved."

I swallow hard, unsure how to respond. "Thank you, Mr. Pence. I—"

He cuts me off smoothly, reaching into his suit jacket. "Now that she's in police custody, I believe our contract has been fulfilled." He produces a check, holding it out to me. "Shenandoah Partners appreciates your diligence in this matter."

My hand moves almost involuntarily, taking the check. As I glance down at the amount, my eyes widen. It's double what we agreed upon.

"I... this is..." I stammer, completely thrown off balance.

Pence's smile never wavers. "Consider it a bonus for your discretion and efficiency."

I clutch the check, my mind reeling. What am I missing here? Why does this feel like a bribe? And what the hell is going on at The Peterson Group?

Uncle Alfred's hand lands on my knee, startling me from my thoughts. His eyes gleam with pride, but there's something calculated behind his smile that makes my skin crawl.

"Well done, Cassie," he says, his voice dripping with approval. "I always knew you had it in you. Handling a case for the CEO of Shenandoah Partners. That's no small feat."

I force a smile, my throat tight. "Thanks, Uncle Alfred. I just did my job."

Pence leans toward me, his expensive cologne filling the space between us. "And a thorough job it was, Ms. Maddox. I trust you'll forward all your findings to my office by tomorrow?"

My mind races. What findings? I've barely scratched the surface of this case. But I hear myself saying, "Of course, Mr. Pence. First thing."

Uncle Alfred pats my arm, his touch feeling more like a warning than affection. "That's my girl. Now, I hate to cut this short, but Mr. Pence and I have some urgent matters to discuss." He gestures to the door. "You understand, don't you, Cassie?"

I nod mechanically, my hand on the door handle. "Sure, of course."

As I step out onto the sidewalk, the cool air hits me like a slap. The limousine purrs away, leaving me standing alone in front of The Peterson Group's towering headquarters. My head spins, and I feel nauseous.

I glance down at the check in my hand; the numbers blur before my eyes. Double my fee. A sick feeling settles in my stomach. Pence and my uncle bought me off, and I didn't even see it coming.

Lila's frantic call echoes in my mind as I stare up at the gleaming building before me. Something's going down inside, she'd said. And here I am, right where Uncle Alfred and Pence wanted me to be. This is no coincidence.

Whatever game they're playing, I refuse to be just another pawn. It's time to find out what's really going on in there.

23

Dramatic Turn

The heavy glass doors of The Peterson Group headquarters glide open, and a wave of warm, artificial air immediately engulfs me. The faint smell of lemon cleaner fills my nostrils as I step into the bustling lobby, my heart racing with anticipation. My eyes scan searching for any sign of Lila.

I take a deep breath and smile as I approach the reception desk. A familiar face greets me, and my stomach does a little flip. It's Lisa Chenoweth, Thomas Pence's interim assistant. What's she doing here?

"Cassie Maddox," Lisa says, her voice warm but professional. "It's good to see you again."

I force a smile, trying to mask my surprise. "Lisa, hi. I wasn't expecting to see you here."

She leans in slightly, lowering her voice. "I've taken on a new role. I'm handling the merger between The Peterson Group and Shenandoah Partners."

My eyebrows shoot up before I can stop them. A merger? This is news to me, and it sets off alarm bells in my head. I struggle to keep my voice casual as I reply, "Wow, that's quite a step up from interim assistant. Congratulations."

Lisa offers a smile, thin and practiced. "Thank you. It's been... an interesting transition." She pauses, then adds, "You know, I was just thinking about our first meeting just over a few weeks ago. When Thomas hired you to find Shayan Easton."

I nod, my mind racing. Why is she bringing this up now? "Right, of course. That feels like ages ago."

"Time flies in this business," Lisa says with a small laugh that sounds a bit forced. "Anyway, I hope your investigation is going well."

I'm torn between wanting to press for more information and maintaining my cover. Surely she knows the police have taken Shayan into custody. I settle for a noncommittal, "It's... progressing." My eyes scan the lobby again, hoping to glimpse Lila. Where is she?

Lisa seems to sense my distraction. "Were you here to see someone specific?" she asks, her tone just a touch too casual.

I hesitate, weighing my options. What does Lisa know? I certainly can't trust her. Between encountering her once during our initial meeting and overhearing her conversation with Chuck Albright, I realize I know next to nothing about this woman who's suddenly at the center of a major corporate merger.

"I was hoping to catch up with Lila, actually," I finally admit, deciding that honesty might be the best policy here. "Is she around?"

A flicker of... something... passes across Lisa's face. Concern? Worry? It's gone before I can be sure. "Lila's in a meeting right now, I'm afraid," she says. "But perhaps I can help you with whatever you need?"

I force another smile, my instincts waging a battle. Though I know something isn't right here, my curiosity is more than a little piqued. "I'd be happy to have your help. At least until Lila is free."

A smile reaches Lisa's eyes. "Follow me."

Lisa leads me down a sleek corridor, her heels clicking against the polished marble floor. The air feels heavy, charged with an undercurrent of anxiety that sets my nerves on edge.

"The merger has been a challenge," Lisa says softly, her eyes darting to a framed photo of Carl Peterson on the wall. "Especially with Carl's unexpected passing yesterday."

I nod, studying the faces we pass. Furrowed brows, hushed conversations that halt as we approach. "I can imagine," I reply, my mind racing. "Big shoes to fill."

As we round a corner, I catch sight of a familiar purple-streaked pixie cut. Lila. My heart leaps, but the feeling is short-lived. Our eyes lock for a moment, and the look she gives me sets me on high alert. It's subtle—a slight widening of her eyes, a barely perceptible shake of her head—but the message is clear: Danger.

I stumble slightly, my breath catching. *What's going on?*

"Are you alright?" Lisa asks, touching my arm.

I plaster on a smile. "Fine, just clumsy today. This place is quite the maze."

Lisa chuckles. "You get used to it. The meeting room is just ahead."

As we walk, my mind races. Lila's warning, the merger, Carl's death—how does it all fit together? And more importantly, what am I walking into?

Whatever's waiting behind that door, I need to be ready. My father's voice echoes in my head: "Trust your gut, Cassie. It'll never lead you wrong."

Right now, my gut is screaming that I'm in way over my head.

Lisa opens the door to a sleek conference room, and I'm immediately hit by the scent of expensive cologne. A stocky man with thinning hair rises from his seat, a wide smile plastered on his face.

"Cassie Maddox, I presume?" His voice is smooth, almost oily. "Chuck Albright, VP of property acquisitions. It's a pleasure to see you again."

As we shake hands, one question comes to my mind. How is he not in police custody?

"Chuck is Thomas Pence's right-hand man," Lisa explains, taking a seat.

I nod, my investigator instincts kicking into high gear. "Nice to meet you, Mr. Albright."

"Please, call me Chuck," he insists, gesturing for me to sit. "We're all friends here."

I seriously doubt that. I think about yesterday morning's scene and keep my expression neutral as I settle into a chair. *If this guy is related to Mel Albright, I'm not seeing it. I decide not to bring it up.*

Chuck leans forward, his eyes gleaming. "Now, I'm sure you're curious about this merger. It's quite exciting, isn't it?"

I nod, choosing my words with caution. "It certainly seems that way. I can only imagine the immense pain and struggle everyone must be going through after losing Mr. Peterson."

A dark cloud, barely noticeable, crosses over Chuck's face. He leans back in his chair, his fingers forming a steeple beneath his chin.

"Mr. Peterson's passing has been more than just difficult," he says, his voice low and filled with an underlying sense of dread. "As you already know, I was there when he jumped from the building."

"As you might recall," I say, keeping my tone steady. "I was in the hallway. I heard the shouting. The crash. The scream."

Chuck blinks rapidly and his lips part, ready for a response. Lisa's eyes dart to her presumptive boss. Chuck clears his throat. "Perspective, Ms. Maddox. As you noted, you weren't in the room when it all happened."

I concede with a nod and observe the folding of Chuck's hands. Then I ask. "Do you think *it* had anything to do with the merger? Or was something else going on?"

A tense silence hangs in the air between us, Chuck and Lisa both avoiding eye contact as if we are all daring each other to break first.

Finally, Lisa speaks up, her voice laced with hesitation as she forces a smile. "Here at Peterson, we're all grieving in our own way. But that's not why you came here today, is it Ms. Maddox?"

Chuck's piercing gaze locks onto mine.

"Of course not," I say, trying to infuse cheer into my tone. "I've heard Shenandoah Partners is dedicated to preserving Carl Peterson's legacy."

Lisa nods solemnly. "The Peterson Group and Shenandoah Partners share many common goals. This merger will allow us to accomplish great things for Lenape City."

I listen closely, searching for any cracks in their perfectly polished facade. "That sounds promising," I say neutrally. "I'm curious, though. How long has this merger been in the works?"

Chuck and Lisa exchange a quick glance that sets off alarm bells in my head. Have I revealed too much of my hand?

"Well, these things take time," Chuck says smoothly. "But we've been in talks for a few months now. Carl was very excited about the possibilities."

I nod, filing away the non-answer. "I can imagine. It must be a lot of pressure, trying to carry on his legacy while mourning his recent passing. Honestly, I'm surprised to see the offices open."

Chuck's smile falters for just a moment. "The late Carl Peterson believed in momentum," he says, voice tightening. "We share that belief and intend to honor his legacy by finishing what he started. The future of Lenape City depends on it."

As the conversation continues, I can't shake the feeling that if I ask just the right question, I can get Chuck Albright to open up. But what don't I know?

Chuck leans forward, his eyes gleaming with what I can only describe as predatory interest. "Speaking of the future, Ms. Maddox, we have an exciting proposition for you."

My guard immediately goes up. "Oh?"

"Indeed," he continues, his voice smooth as oil. "Lila Baker spoke highly of your investigative services. And, of course, I know firsthand about what you did for Mr. Pence. That being said, we believe your business would be a perfect fit for our new luxury mixed-use space in the Old Town Plaza development."

I blink, genuinely taken aback. "That's... very generous. I'm flattered."

But even as the words leave my mouth, my mind races. Thomas Pence just paid me twice the amount for my investigative services. Why would they—or Albright—offer me prime real estate? What's the catch?

Lisa chimes in, her tone warm but measured. "We believe in supporting local businesses, especially those with such a sterling reputation."

I force a smile, buying time as I process this unexpected turn. "That's certainly an intriguing offer. I'd need to look over the details, of course."

"Of course," Chuck agrees readily. "We'll have the paperwork sent over to you."

As the discussion progresses, I find myself hyper-aware of every gesture, every fleeting expression. Chuck's hands move animatedly as he speaks, but there's a tension in his shoulders that belies his easy charm. Lisa remains still, her posture perfect, hands folded neatly on the table. Only the occasional tightening around her eyes hints at emotion.

"So, Ms. Maddox," Chuck says, leaning back in his chair, "what do you think about the revitalization efforts in the East Side? I'm sure you've seen the changes firsthand."

I choose my words carefully. "It's certainly bringing a lot of fresh energy to the area. Though I wonder about the impact on long-time residents."

Lisa's eyebrow twitches slightly, and she quickly reassures me that their company prioritizes responsible development and the needs of the community. But I can't help but notice Chuck's eyes darting to the side, a hint of annoyance or impatience crossing his expression.

As I ponder the situation, I wonder what is really happening here. The last time I saw Chuck and Lisa together, she had many reservations about taking this position. So why the sudden change of heart? Is Thomas Pence using Lisa as a puppet for The Peterson Group?

One thing is certain: this offer goes beyond just my business. They want something from me, and I'm determined to figure out what it is before agreeing to their proposal for office space or before cashing the check Pence gave me for my services.

* * *

The door opens, and my heart skips a beat as a polished middle-aged man escorts Lila into the office. Her vibrant pixie cut, a purple streak catching the light, stands out against the room's muted tones. But there's a tightness around her eyes that I've rarely seen before.

"Ah, Lila," Chuck says, his voice dripping with false warmth. "Perfect timing. We were just discussing the exciting opportunities ahead."

Lila's gaze meets mine, and in that split second, I see a storm of emotions— fear, uncertainty, and a silent plea for help. My protective instincts surge. Whatever's going on here, they've pulled Lila into it as well.

"Hi, Cassie," Lila says, her usual bubbly tone subdued. "What do you think of their proposal?"

I nod, trying to convey reassurance with my eyes. "It's certainly a surprise.

I was just about to ask about the timeline for the Shenandoah merger."

Lila's eyebrows lift slightly—a tiny tell that speaks volumes. She doesn't know about this. My suspicions deepen.

"Oh, it's all moving quickly," Lisa interjects smoothly. "We're excited to combine our strengths and expand our reach."

I lean forward, keeping my tone casual. "Lila, you must be thrilled. This kind of growth is exactly what you were hoping for when you joined The Peterson Group, right?"

Lila smiles, forcing the corners of her mouth upward. "It's certainly... unexpected. There's a lot to process."

My mind races. How can I get Lila alone? How can I warn her without tipping off Chuck and Lisa? I need to know what she knows, what she's seen inside these offices.

"Speaking of processing," I say, "Lila, would you mind showing me where the restroom is? I could use a quick break before we dive into more details."

Chuck waves a hand. "Of course, of course. Take your time."

As Lila and I step out of the office, I can feel the weight of Chuck and Lisa's gazes on our backs. The corridor feels charged with unspoken tension.

"Lila," I whisper urgently as soon as we're out of earshot. "What's going on? Are you okay?"

Her eyes dart nervously down the hall. "Cassie, I can't—" She swallows hard. "It's not what it seems. Be careful."

Before I can press further, footsteps echo from around the corner. Lila's face shutters, and just like that, the moment is gone. Behind us, the same polished individual follows as Lila leads me to the restroom.

Lila looks back. "We've got it from here."

He nods. "Just following procedure, ma'am."

Lila and I exchange a glance and enter the restroom. As soon as the restroom door swings shut behind us, Lila's demeanor shifts dramatically. Her voice takes on an almost exaggerated cheeriness, loud enough to be heard through the door.

"Oh my gosh, Cassie! We absolutely have to get drinks tonight. It's been way too long since we've had a proper girls' night out!"

I blink, momentarily thrown by the abrupt change, but quickly catch on. Lila's eyes are wide, meaningful, as she continues to chatter away.

"There's this adorable new speakeasy-style bar that just opened up in Old Town. It's called The Blind Tiger—how cute is that? They have these incredible craft cocktails. I had this lavender gin fizz last week that was to die for."

As she speaks, Lila's hands move in quick, subtle gestures. She points to her ear. I get the hint.

"Oh my gosh, The Blind Tiger? I've been dying to check that place out!" I exclaim, matching Lila's enthusiasm while my mind races. "Didn't their mixologist used to work at that fancy place in New York—you know, the one with the gold-leaf cocktails?"

I turn on the faucet, letting the water run as I continue, "And the decor is supposed to be absolutely stunning. Didn't they restore an old bank vault or something?"

Lila nods vigorously, her eyes conveying a silent message of danger even as she chatters away. "Yes! It's gorgeous. All dark wood and brass fixtures. They have these vintage-style Edison bulbs that cast the most amazing warm glow. It makes everyone look like a movie star!"

I flush the toilet, adding to the ambient noise. "That sounds incredible. I could use a night out to unwind."

"So it's settled, then," Lila says as she turns on a faucet. "Tonight, 7 p.m."

"Ooh, and you have to try their signature cocktail," Lila gushes as we exit the restroom. "It's called the Bootlegger's Bliss. They smoke the glass with cedar chips and garnish it with a candied orange peel. It's like drinking liquid velvet!"

I laugh, playing along. "That sounds dangerously delicious. I might need to stick to just one of those."

We pause as we encounter the security guard, his polished appearance doing little to soften his imposing presence. I decide to take a risk, letting a flirtatious smile play across my lips.

"Well hello there," I say, my voice taking on a playful lilt. "I don't think we've been properly introduced. I'm Cassie."

The guard blinks, clearly thrown off by my sudden shift in demeanor. "Uh, Michael."

"Michael, huh?" I say, letting my eyes linger on him. "You know, I've always had a thing for men in uniform. I bet you keep this place safe and sound, don't you?"

Michael shifts his weight, a faint blush creeping up his neck. "Just doing my job, ma'am."

I lean in slightly, lowering my voice to a conspiratorial whisper. "And you do it so well. Say, what do you think about giving me your number? I'd love to hear more about what it's like keeping The Peterson Group's secrets."

Michael's face turns a deeper shade of red, and he clears his throat awkwardly. "I, uh... that wouldn't be very professional of me, Ms. Maddox. I'm on duty, you see."

I let out a dramatic sigh, waving my hand dismissively. "What a shame."

I turn to Lila, who's grinning from ear to ear, barely containing her laughter. "Well, it was worth a shot," I say with an exaggerated wink. "Come on, let's head back before they send out a search party."

As we walk down the corridor, the walls seem to close in around us. The sleek, modern design that had impressed me earlier now feels cold and oppressive. Every reflective surface seems to hide watchful eyes, and the muffled sounds of hushed conversations leak from behind closed doors.

Michael follows a few paces behind, his footsteps echoing in the hallway. I can feel his gaze boring into my back; no doubt still flustered from my flirtatious advance. Good. Let him be off-balance. It might make him less observant.

As we near the meeting room, I glimpse our reflections in the polished chrome of a nearby water cooler. Lila's purple-streaked hair seems muted, her usual vibrancy dimmed by the weight of whatever secret she's carrying. My face looks drawn, eyes sharp with barely concealed tension. We're both actors on a stage, playing parts in a drama we don't fully understand.

Lila and I exchange a meaningful glance as we pause at the conference room door. The weight of unspoken words hangs heavy between us, a silent promise to unravel the mysteries that have ensnared us both.

"Well," I say, my voice deliberately light, "I guess this is where we part ways for now. But I'll see you tonight at The Blind Tiger, right?"

Lila nods, her purple-streaked hair catching the light. "Absolutely. Seven o'clock sharp. Don't be late, or I might start without you!"

We laugh, the sound echoing off the polished surfaces around us. It's a brittle sound, tinged with an edge of desperation that I hope only we can hear.

I turn to Michael, who's still hovering nearby, his posture rigid but his eyes betraying a hint of curiosity. "You sure you don't want to join us for a signature cocktail?"

Michael nods, clearly embarrassed. "I'm sure."

With a smile and a wave, I say, "Farewell, my friends."

As I step into the conference room, I take my previous spot and settle back into my chair. I'm struck by the stark contrast between Chuck and Lisa. Chuck's eyes gleam with barely contained excitement, like a child on Christmas morning, while Lisa's face is a mask of cool professionalism.

* * *

The late afternoon sun slants through the floor-to-ceiling windows, casting long shadows across the polished conference table and highlighting the fine sheen of sweat on Chuck's forehead.

"Welcome back, Ms. Maddox," Chuck says, his voice smooth as aged whiskey. "I trust the facilities more than suited your expectations."

I nod, forcing a smile. "Absolutely. You run a tight ship here."

Lisa leans forward, her manicured nails tapping a gentle rhythm on the glossy tabletop. "Now, before we conclude our meeting, I'd like to revisit our offer regarding the office space at Old Town Plaza."

Chuck's face lights up, his eyes gleaming with an almost manic enthusiasm. "Ah yes, the Old Town Plaza development. Cassie, you're going to love what we have in store." He reaches into a sleek leather briefcase and pulls out a glossy brochure, sliding it across the table to me.

As I flip through the pages, I'm bombarded with images of a glittering urban oasis. Towering glass structures reflect the sky, their facades adorned with cascading greenery. Wide, tree-lined boulevards teem with happy pedestrians, and charming cafes spill out onto sun-dappled sidewalks.

"It's not just office space we're offering," Chuck continues, his voice taking on a dreamy quality. "Our goal is to establish a lifestyle and community for our clients. Just picture walking out of your modern office and into a limitless world—"

I quickly cut him off, saying, "Thank you, Mr. Albright." My voice sounds steady, but inside, I'm a whirlwind of suspicion and fear. "This is all very wonderful, but let's stick to one thing at a time for now. I'd love to see your proposal for the office space."

Chuck Albright's eyes glitter with something I can't quite place. Amusement? Threat? "The pleasure's all ours, Ms. Maddox. We look forward to a fruitful partnership."

I shake their hands, hyper-aware of every gesture, every fleeting expression. Lisa Chenoweth's grip is firm, professional, but there's a flicker of... something in her eyes. Uncertainty? Guilt?

As Michael escorts me to the front door, we pass the finance department, where I catch one last glimpse of Lila. She offers me a wave and a smile, but I know her well enough to see the tension in her shoulders.

* * *

The cold and damp midday air sends a chill down my spine. As I pull my coat around me, my mind races. What have I gotten myself into? The doors behind me slide shut, and I let out a shaky breath.

"Okay, Cassie," I mutter to myself. "Think. What do you know, and what don't you know?"

I hail a cab, directing the driver back to RA Pharmacy. As we merge into the midafternoon traffic, I watch as the city slides past—businessmen walking too quickly, a shuttered café that should be open, and a woman arguing with no one on a street corner. The pulse of Lenape City feels off, like it's holding its breath. Something about this case isn't lining up, and I'm no closer to figuring out what piece I'm missing.

I attempt to fit together the pieces of the puzzle—the merger, Carl Peterson's untimely death, Lila's warning look, Chuck Albright's slick charisma. But none of it seems to make sense. Like carrion birds, Albright and Chenoweth swooped into the Peterson building before the deceased CEO's seat had time to cool. There's no way Pence could've moved in so quickly without the help of very influential people capable of scattering evidence like ash into the wind.

A sports car zips past the cab, forcing my driver to veer sharply to the left, reminding me I need to be careful. One wrong turn, and I could jeopardize everything—the investigation, Lila's safety, maybe even my own. But as I walk towards my car, determination settles in my chest.

"Whatever's going on here," I think, clenching my fists, "I'm going to figure it out. For Lila, for justice, and for myself."

My phone buzzes in my pocket, jarring me from my thoughts. I fish it out, expecting a text from my mom or maybe Lila, but the number on the screen is unfamiliar. My heart rate quickens as I open the message.

Getting warmer, Cassie. The fire's about to start. Central Park fountain, midnight. Come alone.

I clench my jaw and look out the window, those words pulsing behind my eyes like a warning flair. Across the street, the afternoon sun glints off the hood of my old Cadillac, waiting at the curb like a loyal hound—warn, quiet, and ready.

After the incident at the Old Clock Tower, I thought X, my elusive informant, would disappear into the shadows forever. But this message feels like a spark tossed into dry kindling.

Urgency coils in my gut as the cab slows, then rolls to a stop with a squeal of brakes. I pay the driver, tipping him generously. "Thanks for the ride," I say, already reaching for the door. He barely mumbles a your-welcome and a thank-you before I step onto the sidewalk and close the door behind me.

I slip into the safety of the Cadillac and shut the door. "Damn it," I whisper, gripping the wheel. Even here, I feel exposed, and every passerby is a potential threat.

I key the ignition and pull out of the parking spot. A car behind me blares its horn. Some asshole in a pickup truck roars by me at a neck breaking speed that reminds me of how fast this investigation has moved. Yet, despite the speed, I still find myself on the edge of something big, I know that. But this message from X... it feels like a tipping point.

I have to be at the Old Clocktower, I decide. Whatever X knows, it could blow this whole thing wide open.

But doubt creeps in. Can I trust X?

The road noise offers no answers. I press my foot against the gas and urge Dad's old car forward.

"Bring it on, X," I think, a grim smile tugging at my lips. "Let's see what you've got."

The first flakes of snow drift lazily past my windshield as I navigate the familiar streets back to Mom's house. Lenape City transforms around me, its edges softening under winter's gentle touch as the cityscape merges with the suburbs of Greater Lenape City. My knuckles are white on the steering wheel, my mind racing faster than my car.

"God, what a mess," I mutter, flicking on the wipers. "The Peterson Group, Shenandoah Partners, Lila caught in the middle... and now X wants to meet again."

A red light forces me to stop, and I take the moment to breathe. Snow falls harder now. It reminds me of nights spent with Dad, poring over case files while a storm raged outside.

"What am I missing, Dad?" I whisper, a familiar ache in my chest. "What would you see?"

The light changes, and I press on. As I drive, I piece things together out loud, a habit I picked up from him.

"Okay, so we've got Chuck Albright, slippery as an eel. Lisa Chenoweth, suddenly more than just an interim assistant. And that offer for office space and an apartment way below market value... way too good to be true."

I turn onto Mom's street, the old Victorian houses looming like sentinels in the growing dusk.

"It all connected somehow," I continue, pulling into the driveway. "The merger, the deaths of Gregory Hunter and Carl Peterson's death, the arrest of Shayan Easton... But how?"

Killing the engine, I sit for a moment, watching the snow accumulate on the windshield. The house looks warm and inviting, a stark contrast to the chill settling in my bones.

"One thing's for sure," I say, grabbing my bag. "I need to dig deeper before meeting X. No more walking into situations blind."

I trudge through the growing snowdrift to the front door, already plotting my next moves. The attic office awaits, a sanctuary where I can unravel this tangle of lies and corruption.

As I fumble for my keys, a neighbor across the street catches my eye. They wave, calling out, "Storm's coming in fast, Cassie! You picked a good time to be home!"

I force a smile and wave back, thinking, "If only you knew. The real storm's just beginning, and it's got nothing to do with the weather."

24

Uncertain Allegiances

The snow falls in thick, lazy flakes as I step out of my house, pulling my coat tighter around me. I fish my phone out of my pocket, my gloved fingers clumsy as I type a quick text to Lila:

Headed to Rusty's on the edge of town. See you at 7.

I'm barely in my car when my phone buzzes with Lila's reply. I ignore it, knowing it's confirmation that she'll be there. As I navigate the slippery streets, I can only hope Lila's bathroom ruse about meeting at The Blind Tiger would throw off anyone intent on intercepting us.

But what isn't she telling me? And why?

I grip the steering wheel tighter, my mind racing. If Albright and Pence have pulled Lila into something dangerous, I need to know. I know she wouldn't betray me, at least not willingly... I swallow hard, pushing the idea away. She's learned something at The Peterson Group she needs me to know.

The rest of the drive passes in a blur of swirling snow and uneasy thoughts. Before I know it, I'm pulling into the gravel lot outside Rusty's Bar. The neon sign flickers weakly in the gathering darkness.

Inside, the bar is dim and cozy, smelling of wood smoke and whiskey. I spot Lila immediately; her purple-streaked pixie cut standing out even in the low light. She waves me over, a familiar grin on her face that doesn't quite reach her eyes.

"Hey, stranger," she says as I slide into the booth across from her. "Shame we couldn't hit up The Blind Tiger. I've been dying to try their new winter cocktail menu."

I force a smile. "Rain check? We can go after... all this is over." I wave my hand vaguely, encompassing the whole mess we've found ourselves in.

Lila's eyes dart around the bar. "Yeah, for sure. Though I bet Michael would've enjoyed tailing us there more than to this dump."

I lean in, lowering my voice. "You think he followed us here?"

Lila shrugs, but her casual tone feels forced. "Wouldn't put it past them. The Peterson Group seems pretty invested in keeping tabs on us since, you know."

My heart races. Us? Or just me? I study Lila's face, searching for any hint of deception. But all I see is my oldest friend, looking tired and scared.

"Lila," I start, not sure how to ask what I need to know without shattering the fragile normalcy of the moment. "What's really going on?"

A waitress approaches, momentarily halting our conversation. I order a whiskey neat, while Lila opts for a vodka tonic. As the waitress leaves, I notice Lila's eyes following her, scanning the nearby tables.

"Lila," I press gently, "talk to me. What happened?"

Averting her eyes, she fidgets with a cocktail napkin. "Cass, I... I'm way over my head." Her voice drops to barely above a whisper. "Chuck Albright, he's not just some corporate suit. He's dangerous."

My stomach tightens. "How so?"

Lila leans in closer, her eyes wide with genuine fear. "He's got his hooks in everything at The Peterson Group. Lisa Chenoweth? She's just a reluctant figurehead. Albright's the one pulling all the strings."

I process this, thinking back to my interactions with both of them. It fits in a sickening way. "How do you know all this?"

"Because," Lila swallows hard, "ever since I got on board, they've had me doing their dirty work. Falsifying documents, moving money around. If I don't play along..." She trails off, glancing nervously over her shoulder.

The waitress returns with our drinks. We fall silent until she's out of earshot.

"Jesus, Lila," I breathe, my mind reeling. "Why didn't you come to me sooner?"

"I didn't know I needed to," she says, her voice cracking. She takes a prolonged sip, downing half her drink. "It was only just the other day I saw what you and Rafi had. Then, this morning, seeing the receipts, I realized what they'd assigned me to do. When I brought it to the attention of my immediate supervisor, she brought me before Albright and Chenoweth. They made it clear what would happen if I talked. To me, to you, to anyone I care about. Then they forced me to reach out to you. They know what you... we... have uncovered."

I reach across the table, squeezing her hand. "We'll figure this out, I promise."

But even as I say the words, I'm acutely aware of how deep this conspiracy might go, and how dangerous unraveling it could be for both of us.

I lean back in my chair, my mind racing. Part of me wants to dive headfirst into this investigation, to uncover every dirty secret Pence and Albright are hiding via The Peterson Group. But another part, the part that values Lila's friendship, screams caution.

"Lila," I say, my voice low and steady, "I need you to be careful. We both do."

She nods, her purple-streaked hair catching the dim light. "I know. But what about you, Cassie? You're not backing down, are you?"

I sigh, running a hand through my hair. "I can't. Not now. But something doesn't add up." I lean in closer, lowering my voice. "If Chenoweth is just Albright's puppet, why go through the charade? Why not just run things openly?"

Lila's brow furrows. "Maybe it's about appearances? Or... plausible deniability?"

"Maybe," I mutter, my mind drifting back to that meeting with Chenoweth and Albright. The way Lisa had deferred to Chuck, her carefully measured responses, and the practiced delivery of their intentions to shape Lenape City. Their attempts to buy me off with office space make sense now. Though I wonder how long they've suspected we were getting close to uncovering their scheme.

In the uncomfortable silence between us, Lila and I raise our glasses. A salute to the foreboding immediate future. Lila downs the rest of her drink, and I down half of mine.

But something else is on my mind now. "You know, Albright should be in police custody."

Lila's expression shows surprise. "Spill it! What did I miss?"

I lean in closer. "Yesterday morning, I overheard a heated exchange between Albright and Carl Peterson. Shenandoah had some dirt on him, possibly the records we recently acquired. From what I heard, it sounds like Albright resorted to physical force."

Lila scoots closer to me and speaks in hushed tones. "But if that's true, who do Albright and Pence have connections with? Who's protecting them?"

The realization hits me like a punch to the gut. "Chief Burgess."

Lila's eyes widen. "The police chief? You think he's involved?"

"I can't be certain," I say. "But it would explain a lot. The convenient capture of Shayan Easton, his insistence on discretion when he hired me as a private investigator instead of putting someone like my father on the case."

My hand unconsciously moves to my pocket, where Pence's check still sits. The overpayment. Was it really just hush money? Did they know I'd eventually stumble onto their scheme?

"Cassie?" Lila's voice pulls me back to the present. "What are we going to do?"

The weight of everything we've uncovered presses down on me. "We keep digging," I say, meeting her worried gaze. "But carefully. Very careful."

My phone buzzes, startling me. I glance down, my heart rate quickening as I see Rafi's name on the screen. The message preview is a string of nonsensical characters, encrypted.

"I need to take this," I tell Lila, my fingers already working to decrypt the message. The anticipation is almost unbearable as I wait for the contents to reveal themselves.

"What is it?" Lila leans in, her voice hushed.

"It's from Rafi," I murmur, my eyes scanning the now-decrypted text.

"Oh, my God."

My hands start to shake as I read through Rafi's findings. The familiar thrill of a big break washes over me, mingled with a growing sense of dread.

"Cassie?" Lila prompts, concern etched across her face.

My throat tightens. "Rafi's dug deep into Shenandoah Partners' finances. It's... it's worse than we thought."

I turn the phone so Lila can see, pointing out key details as I explain. "Look here. Fake invoices, shell companies. It's all a smokescreen."

Lila's eyes widen. "But what does it mean?"

"It means," I say, my voice barely above a whisper, "that Shenandoah Partners is just the tip of the iceberg. The Peterson Group, LCH Withholdings, Echelon Nexus LLC–they're all connected. And at the center of it all?"

I pause, the weight of the revelation settling over me. "Thomas Pence."

Lila gasps. "Thomas Pence? But he's—"

"A pillar of the community? Yeah, that's what they want us to think." I run a hand through my hair, my mind racing. "But there's more. My uncle, Alfred Maddox? His name's all over this too."

The implications hit me like a tidal wave. Family, corruption, danger—it's pulling me, and possibly my father, deep into its tangles.

"What are you going to do?" Lila asks, her voice trembling slightly.

I stare at my phone, at the damning evidence laid out in black and white. "I don't know," I admit. "But I can't ignore this. It's too big, too important."

As I look up at Lila, I see my fear and determination reflected in her eyes. We're in deep now, and there's no turning back.

My phone buzzes again, and I feel a jolt of adrenaline. It's Rafi.

Cassie, we've got a problem, his message reads. *I think someone's keeping tabs on your activity. You need to move.*

My heart races as I read his words aloud to Lila. "Shit," I mutter, glancing around the dimly lit bar. Suddenly, every patron looks suspicious.

"What does that mean?" Lila asks, her voice hushed.

I run my fingers through my hair, my mind whirling. "It means we've attracted attention. The wrong kind."

Dread invades my mind. "The burner phone Shayan gave me... what if it's being tracked? That would explain how my uncle knew exactly where to find me outside RA Pharmacy."

Lila's eyes widen. "You don't think Shayan—"

"I don't know what to think anymore," I interrupt, frustration edging my voice. My phone buzzes again with another message from Rafi: *Get rid of the burner ASAP. It's not safe.*

I nod, more to myself than to Lila. "I need to ditch it. Tonight."

Forcing myself to focus, I turn back to the financial data on my screen. "But first, I need to make sense of this. There's something here; I can feel it."

As I scroll through the numbers, patterns emerge. "Look at these transactions," I say, tilting the screen towards Lila. "They're all routed through shell companies, but they all lead back to one place."

Lila leans in, squinting at the screen. "The mayor's office? But that's—"

"A kickback scheme," I finish, the pieces falling into place. "The Peterson Group has been funneling money through these fake companies, straight into City Hall's pockets."

I feel a surge of excitement mixed with dread. "This is big, Lila. It's not just corporate corruption; it goes all the way to the top of Lenape City's government."

Lila sits back, her face pale. "What are you going to do?"

"I'm going to follow this trail wherever it leads. Someone needs to expose the truth, despite the danger."

As I say the words, I realize how true they are. Despite the risks, despite the fear churning in my gut, I know I can't walk away from this. Not now. Not when I'm so close to figuring out who's pulling the strings in this real estate scheme in Lenape City.

I stare at my phone, the weight of Rafi's message pressing down on me. The dimly lit bar seems to close in, the soft chatter of patrons fading into white noise. My fingers hover over the screen, itching to dial a familiar number.

"Damn it," I mutter, setting the phone face-down on the sticky table.

Lila leans in, concern etching her features. "What's wrong, Cassie?"

I shake my head, struggling to articulate a storm of thoughts. "We can't do this alone anymore."

"The police?" Lila asks, her voice barely above a whisper.

I nod, then pause. "Maybe. Or... my dad."

The words hang between us, heavy with implication. I've spent years trying to carve out a path of my own, to prove I'm more than just Detective Maddox's daughter. But now, faced with the sprawling web of corruption we've uncovered, I feel like I'm drowning.

"If I bring the cops in, it could blow this whole thing wide open," I say, more to myself than to Lila. "But if I'm wrong, if I've misinterpreted anything..."

"You could put your dad in danger," Lila finishes, understanding dawning in her eyes.

I nod, a lump forming in my throat. "Exactly. And not just him. Every honest cop on the force could be at risk if this thing goes sideways."

Replaying every conversation, every clue that led me here, I think back to the kickback scheme, the mayor's office, and my uncle's involvement. It's all tied up in Lenape City's power structure.

"But your dad's a good detective," Lila offers. "Wouldn't he want to know?"

I laugh, but there's no humor in it. "That's the problem. Rafi's already sent him my case files. I thought that was enough until this. If I tell him about this, he won't be able to let it go. And I can't... I can't put him in the crosshairs."

I pick up my phone again, turning it over in my hands. My father's number is right there, a few taps away. I can almost hear his voice, steady and reassuring, telling me we'll figure it out together.

But then I remember the look in his eyes when I told him I was becoming a PI. The disappointment, the worry. The unspoken fear that I was throwing away my potential on a pipe dream.

"I need to do this without his help for now," I say finally, meeting Lila's gaze. "I need to prove that I can handle this, that I'm not just playing at being an investigator."

Lila nods slowly. "I get it. But Cassie, be careful. This isn't about proving yourself."

"I know," I reply with resolve. "But that's exactly why I have to see it through. If I can crack this case, maybe then…"

I trail off, leaving the thought unfinished. Maybe then my dad will see me as an equal. Maybe then I'll finally step out of his shadow.

I slip my phone back into my pocket, decision made. The weight of it feels both terrifying and exhilarating.

"So," Lila says, breaking the tension. "What's our next move?"

I lean in, lowering my voice. "We follow the money. Every dirty deal leaves a trail, and I intend to tie the evidence we gathered right around its source."

I gather my coat, a nervous energy thrumming through my veins. "I've got a lead to follow up on," I tell Lila, trying to keep my voice steady. "Someone who might have more information."

Lila's brow furrows with concern. "At this hour? Cassie, are you sure that's safe?"

I force a smile, hoping it looks more confident than I feel. "Don't worry. I'll be careful. Will you be okay?"

The waitress hands Lila another drink, and she wraps her fingers around the glass, eyes fixed on bubbling tonic. "I'll be fine."

I remain for a moment longer. "If anything feels off, call me. Promise?"

She raises her eyes, glistening in the dim light of the bar. "You too."

Neither of us moves. I consider pressing, but I let the moment slip by and turn to go. "Lila can take care of herself," I tell myself.

The heavy wooden door of the bar creaks as I push it open, and a gust of frosty night air blows in, bringing with it heavy snowflakes. A blanket of snow covers the streets of Lenape City, creating an eerie silence. My footsteps crunch through the freshly fallen snow as I head towards my car.

I glance at my watch, noting the time: 11:30 p.m.. There is just enough time to reach Central Park Fountain. I pull the burner phone apart and toss the pieces into the gutter. Then, I open the trunk and lift the floor paneling, revealing a gun safe. I rarely carry, but tonight is different… more dangerous. After strapping on my 9 mm and tucking it beneath my coat, I slide into the driver's seat and ease out of the parking lot.

As streaks of snow and light rush past, my thoughts swirl. Who is X? Can I rely on him? What if this is all a setup?

But beneath the fear, there's an undercurrent of excitement. This is what I've been working towards—a chance to prove myself, to unravel a conspiracy that goes deeper than I ever imagined.

I park a block away from the fountain, my heart pounding. As I walk the final stretch, I can't shake the feeling of being watched. Every shadow seems to hide a potential threat.

The fountain comes into view, and I scan the area, looking for X in the wintery shadows.

"This is it," I whisper to myself, clenching my fists to stop my hands from shaking.

25

Dangerous Situation

The crunch of snow beneath my boots echoes in the stillness of Central Park. Each step sends a jolt of anticipation through my body as I make my way toward the fountain, my breath visible in the frigid night air. My eyes dart from shadow to shadow, searching for any sign of movement or threat.

The park is eerily quiet, save for the whisper of snowflakes falling around me. Danger seems to lurk just beyond the reach of the dim lamplight. My hand instinctively moves to my hip, where my 9mm rests, safely concealed in its holster. The familiar weight is comforting, even as I hope I won't need to use it.

As I approach the fountain, the wind picks up, sending snow swirling in graceful eddies. I pause, my senses on high alert. The hairs on the back of my neck stand up as I scan the area, searching for any sign of X or potential threats.

"Get it together, Cassie," I mutter to myself, trying to calm my racing thoughts. "You've handled tougher situations than this."

But have I? This feels different, bigger than anything I've tackled before. The corruption I've uncovered in Lenape City runs deep, touching powerful people who won't hesitate to protect their interests. For a moment, I consider turning back, returning to the relative safety and warmth of my attic bedroom in my mother's house.

No. I've come too far to back down now. Whatever X has to tell me could be the key to blowing this whole thing wide open.

* * *

"Show yourself," I call out, my voice steady despite the tremor in my hands. "I'm here, just like you asked."

The wind carries my words away, and for a long moment, there's nothing but silence. Then, a twig snaps somewhere to my left, and I whirl toward the sound, my heart leaping into my throat.

A figure emerges from the shadows, and my breath catches in my throat. It's Gregory Hunter, the man I'd spotted in that Lincoln with the restricted plates. The man who's supposed to be dead.

"Ms. Maddox," he says, his voice low and measured. "Thank you for coming."

I take an involuntary step back, my mind reeling. "How... what..." I struggle to form coherent thoughts, let alone sentences. Finally, I blurt out, "You're alive?"

Gregory nods slowly, his eyes darting around as if checking for eavesdroppers. "I am. And I know you have questions. I'm here to provide answers."

My investigator instincts kick in, overriding my shock. "What's your endgame here, Hunter? Who are you working for? Does Trudy know you're alive?" The questions tumble out rapid-fire.

He holds up a hand, a pained expression crossing his face. "Please, let me explain. It's... complicated."

I cross my arms, fixing him with a hard stare. "I'm listening."

Hunter paces, etching a pathway in the snow, as he speaks. "My endgame is survival, Ms. Maddox. And bringing down the real criminals—Pence and Albright. They used me as a pawn in their schemes at The Peterson Group."

"How does Shayan Easton fit into their schemes? Who's she working for?"

Hunter clears off a section of a bench and sits. From where I'm standing, he's framed in shadows. "Shayan's a complicated one. Early on, I figured she was my counterpart at Shenandoah. But as time passed, I realized she was working for Stanton, until she went completely rogue."

"Can we trust her?" I ask, though I suspect the answer before Hunter speaks.

"No," Hunter says. "Not with the company she keeps."

"You mean she's playing for the highest bidder?" I ask, my skepticism warring with curiosity.

Hunter sighs. "She had me fooled until Pence brought you in to track her down."

"A lot of good I did," I say, as frustration rises in my gut.

Hunter brushes snow off the space next to him. A nervous tick or an invitation to sit? "They used you, Ms. Maddox, just like they used me. That's why I had to get out."

"Go on," I say, approaching the bench.

"Faking my death was the only way out of their web," he continues. "I'm not working for anyone now. When I tried to get out, they threatened my life. I had to disappear to gather evidence without their interference."

I process this, my mind racing. "And Trudy?"

Gregory's face crumples. "She doesn't know. It kills me, but keeping her in the dark is the only way to keep her safe. If they knew I was alive, they'd use her against me in a heartbeat."

"The body…" I start, remembering what my father had told me about the police finding Hunter's corpse.

"Not mine," Gregory interjects. "Your father—Detective Maddox — he helped arrange for a coroner to misidentify a transient with similar features. It sold the illusion, at least for now."

My head spins. My father involved in this deception? I push that revelation aside for the moment, focusing on Hunter. "Why reveal yourself to me now?"

"Because you were getting too close to the truth," he says, urgency creeping into his voice. "Without my intervention, they might have silenced you, just like they nearly did to me. The files I shared with you and Rafi? That's only the beginning."

I narrow my eyes. "Why me?"

A ghost of a smile flickers across Gregory's face. "Your persistence, Ms. Maddox."

As Gregory speaks, I feel my initial disbelief slowly giving way to a grudging understanding. With the pieces now fitting together, I see the dangerous game I've been pulled into. Anxiety and relief flood through me simultaneously. Anxiety at teetering on a precipice. Relief that my father had my back this whole time, protecting me within the shadows.

"As you may have already concluded, this has ties to the mayor's office and your uncle," Gregory says, his voice barely above a whisper. "We're running out of time, and proving your uncle's involvement may be more difficult."

"How long has my father been involved?" I ask, my voice sharper than I intended.

Gregory's eyes dart around the park. "Detective Maddox understood the stakes. We needed someone on the inside, someone with the authority to make this believable."

"How does Chief Burgess play into all this?" I ask.

Gregory rises and carves a path in the snow as he paces. "That's what we still need to find out. It was a wise choice to have Rafi send the files directly to your father."

A lump forms in the pit of my stomach. "Are you saying the chief is on the take?"

Gregory freezes in his tracks and casts me a stony stare. "Feed him enough to satiate his appetite and fulfill your contract. Your father will handle the rest."

I laugh bitterly. "And here I thought I was finally carving my own path."

"You are," Gregory insists, reaching into his coat. "That's why we need you now more than ever."

He pulls out a thick manila folder, holding it out to me like an offering. I take it, feeling the weight of secrets within.

"Lisa Chenoweth and Chuck Albright," Gregory explains, his voice low and urgent. "They're the key to unraveling this whole mess. Everything you need to expose their roles is in there."

I flip open the folder, catching glimpses of financial statements, emails, and grainy surveillance photos. My investigator's instincts kick in, already piecing together connections.

"Why them?" I ask, looking up from the documents.

Gregory's mustache twitches. "Chenoweth's the perfect fall guy—competent enough to be believable, but ultimately expendable. And Albright? He's the weasel who knows where all the bodies are buried. Metaphorically speaking, of course."

I close the folder, my mind churning. "And what exactly am I supposed to do with all this?"

"Use those skills of yours," Gregory says. "Connect the dots, follow the money. Your father will be in touch about the next phase."

I bristle at the mention of my father again. "And I'm just supposed to play along? After all the lies?"

Gregory's expression softens slightly. "I know it's a lot to ask, Cassie. But we're talking about exposing corruption that goes to the very heart of Lenape City. Sometimes the ends have to justify the means."

I stare at the folder in my hands, feeling the weight of responsibility settling on my shoulders. Part of me wants to throw it back at Gregory, to wash my hands of this whole mess. But I can't deny the thrill of the chase, the chance to prove myself on a case bigger than anything I've tackled before.

"I'll think about it," I say finally, tucking the folder into my coat.

Gregory nods, relief visible in his eyes. "Sleep on it. That's all we ask, but we're going to need to move on this quickly. Be careful, Cassie. Trust only your inner circle."

As he melts back into the shadows, I'm left alone with my thoughts, the wind whipping snow around me. I've always prided myself on my independence in building Maddox Investigative Services from the ground up. Now, I discover that I've been circulating in my father's orbit this whole time. The irony isn't lost on me.

I purse my lips as I test the weight of the folder in my hands. Upon flipping it open, I scan each page. Financial statements, email transcripts, photographs—it's a treasure trove of evidence against Lisa Chenoweth and Chuck Albright. My keen eye picks up on subtle patterns, connecting dots that others might miss.

"Jesus," I mutter, tracing a series of transactions that scream money laundering. The Old Town Plaza project suddenly looks a lot less like urban renewal and more like a massive front for illegal activities.

My heart races as I absorb the implications. This goes beyond simple corruption—it's a cancer eating away at the heart of Lenape City. I can feel my investigative instincts kicking into high gear, the familiar rush of adrenaline coursing through my veins.

"This is huge," I whisper to myself, my breath visible in the frigid air.

For a moment, I allow myself to imagine breaking this case wide open. The prestige, the vindication—it would put Maddox Investigative Services on the map in a way I've only dreamed of. But then reality comes crashing back.

I pause, looking up at the city skyline looming beyond the park. The risks are enormous. If I'm caught digging into city corruption without the protection of LCPD, I could lose my business, my reputation, maybe even my freedom.

"Is it worth it?" I ask myself, closing the folder and hugging it to my chest.

The answer comes almost immediately, surprising me with its certainty. Yes, it is. Beyond the personal glory, beyond proving myself to my father or anyone else, there's a deeper drive—a pursuit of truth and a fight for justice in a city I love.

"Okay, Cassie," I mutter. "You wanted to play in the big leagues. Time to step up to the plate."

With renewed determination, I tuck the folder securely inside my coat and hasten towards the park exit. The game has changed, and I'm all in.

My father has a lot of explaining to do if he expects me to go along with whatever he's got planned.

It's a strange moment—leaving a clandestine meeting in a snowy park with a man who I was initially hired to catch in spousal infidelity. In a way, Trudy's hunches were right. Hunter was cheating in a game with stakes much greater than one's marriage.

I exit the park, my footsteps crunching in the freshly fallen snow. The city that never sleeps looms ahead, a glittering backdrop to the corruption I'm now determined to expose.

I'm already piecing together a plan to nail Albright and Pence, but where do I start? My comfortable, warm bed beckons, but my mother's house is unsafe since someone tracked me. I need a safe place to review more closely the contents of this folder, somewhere off the grid. Close to here is an old diner, an old stop for truckers needing rest and rejuvenation en route to their next destination. It's a risk, but so is this whole endeavor.

* * *

As I reach my trusty old Cadillac at the park's edge, I pause, scanning the area one last time. The shadows seem to stretch and shift, and I can't shake the feeling of being watched.

"You wanted to prove yourself, didn't you?" I whisper, a wry smile tugging at my lips. "Well, here's your chance."

Once nestled in the safety of Dad's old car, I navigate the slushy streets of Lenape City. At this hour and in this weather, traffic is light. As I drive, I can't help but wonder about the other players in this game. Who else might be involved? How deep does this conspiracy go?

Beneath a flickering street lamp, I park my car outside of Route 1 Diner - an unassuming name for those seeking warmth and sustenance on frigid nights. I reach for the folder Hunter handed me earlier and tuck it into my coat before stepping out of the car and entering the 24-hour diner.

As the doorbell chimes, I quickly glance around the restaurant. The only other patron is an elderly man sipping coffee at the counter where a tired waitress refilling ketchup bottles. I opt for a booth in the back corner and slide onto the vinyl bench, causing it to squeak under my weight. Sitting with my back against the wall, I have a clear view of both the parking lot and the front entrance.

"Just coffee, please," I tell the waitress when she approaches. As she walks away, I pull out my phone, my fingers hovering over the keypad.

Should I call Dad? The thought makes my stomach churn. Our relationship is complicated enough without adding this layer of deception and danger.

"Here you go, hon," the waitress says, setting down a steaming mug.

"Thanks." I wrap my hands around the warm ceramic, letting out a long breath. "Actually, could I get some pie too? Any kind."

As she heads back to the kitchen, I notice a man in a dark coat enter the diner. He takes a seat at the counter, his back to me. Something about the way he moves sets my nerves on edge.

I try to focus on the folder Gregory gave me, but my mind keeps drifting. What if I'm in over my head? What if—

The bell above the door chimes again. Two men in suits walk in, their eyes sweeping the room. My heart rate spikes.

"Everything okay, sweetie?" the waitress asks, setting a slice of apple pie in front of me.

I force a smile. "Just fine, thanks."

But I've already made my decision. I pick up my phone and text my father.

I'm in. Meet me at Route 1 Diner.

Be there in 15 minutes.

Settling back in my seat, I take a sip of the steaming coffee. The hot liquid does nothing to calm the nerves. Instead, I'm on edge as I watch the diner. One of the men in a suit sits at the counter; the other fills a booth a few tables away, directly across from mine. He watches me, facing my direction. I look away, turning to the road outside.

I wait for my father to arrive while the untouched apple pie remains on the table in front of me, its cheerful appearance contrasting with my anxious state.

26

Ties that Bind

The fluorescent lights of Route 1 Diner cast a harsh glow over the worn vinyl booths, making the two men in suits stand out like sore thumbs. I can't shake the feeling they don't belong here, especially at this hour. The one at the counter keeps fidgeting with his cufflinks, while the burly one a few tables away hasn't stopped glaring in my direction since he sat down.

I check my watch again. 2:17 a.m.. Dad's seventeen minutes late. So much for his promise to be here in fifteen.

"Come on, Dad," I mutter under my breath, tapping my fingers on the sticky tabletop. "Where are you?"

As if on cue, the bell above the door chimes. A gust of frigid air sweeps in, carrying with it the unmistakable figure of my father, Detective Dylan Maddox. But he's not alone.

Rafi Alvi trails behind him, looking oddly at ease for someone who just stepped into this powder keg of tension. My stomach does a little flip as they approach. Relief wars with a new anxiety blooming in my chest.

"Sorry we're late, kiddo," Dad says, sliding into the booth across from me. Rafi hesitates for a moment before joining him.

I force a smile. "We? I wasn't expecting company."

Dad at least has the decency to look sheepish. "Rafi's been helping with some aspects of the case. I thought it might be useful to have him here."

My eyes narrow as I look between them. "How long have you two been working together?" I ask, unable to keep the edge from my voice. "Just since I asked Rafi to send you those files, or longer?"

Rafi shifts uncomfortably, but Dad meets my gaze head-on. "Cassie, I know you have questions—"

"You're damn right I do," I interrupt, leaning forward. "Starting with why you've been keeping me in the dark about Gregory Hunter. I thought I was supposed to run a discreet investigation in tandem with Lenape City Police."

Dad sighs, running a hand through his salt-and-pepper hair. "It's complicated, sweetheart. There are protocols, risks—"

"I'm already neck-deep in this, Dad. I can handle the risks."

"Can you?" His voice is quiet but sharp. "Because from where I'm sitting, you're getting awfully close to a very dangerous situation."

I open my mouth to argue, but Rafi clears his throat. "Maybe we should order some coffee before diving into all this?" he suggests, glancing meaningfully at the men in suits who still linger nearby.

I nod reluctantly, my mind racing. As the waitress approaches our table, I can't help but wonder just how deep this conspiracy goes—and whether I can truly trust anyone sitting at this table, even my closest friend.

As the waitress retreats with our coffee orders, I notice the two men in suits suddenly rise, tossing a few bills on the table. They shuffle out, the burlier one casting a final glance our way before the door chimes their exit.

"Friends of yours?" I ask Dad, arching an eyebrow.

He frowns, shaking his head. "Never seen them before."

I lean in, lowering my voice. "Really? Because they seemed awfully interested in our little reunion."

Dad's eyes flick to the lone man still perched at the counter, then back to me. "Cassie, not everything is part of some grand conspiracy. Sometimes people just want to grab a late-night meal."

I bite my lip, frustration bubbling up inside me. "Like Gregory Hunter? Was he just grabbing a late-night meal when he faked his own death?"

Dad's jaw tightens. "That's different. Hunter is—"

"A key player in this whole mess," I interrupt. "A mess you've been keeping me in the dark about. Why, Dad? Don't you trust me?"

His eyes soften, but there's still a wariness there. "Of course I trust you, sweetheart. There are dangerous people involved, people who wouldn't hesitate to—"

"To what? Hurt me? News flash, Dad: I'm already involved. I've been careful, I've been smart, but I can't do my job if I don't know what I'm walking into."

I watch the conflict play across his face, torn between protecting me and respecting my abilities. Part of me aches for the simplicity of childhood, when I thought my dad could shield me from anything. But I'm not that little girl anymore, and Lenape City's underbelly of corruption won't wait for me to grow up.

"Just tell me what you know," I plead, softening my tone. "Let me help."

Dad exchanges a look with Rafi, and I feel a pang of jealousy at their unspoken communication. How long have they really been working together? And where does that leave me?

Dad leans in, his voice dropping to a murmur. "Cassie, the people we're dealing with... they're not just white-collar criminals. We're talking about individuals who've orchestrated murders, who have their fingers in every corrupt pie in this city. They won't hesitate to eliminate anyone who threatens their operation."

My body stiffens with unease, but I hold firm. "I understand the risks, Dad. But I'm already knee-deep in this. Keeping me out isn't protecting me; it's leaving me vulnerable."

His brow furrows and I can see the internal struggle play out behind his eyes. "You don't know what you're asking, Cass. The protocols exist for a reason. I can't just—"

"Can't what? Treat me like a professional?" I counter, trying to keep the hurt out of my voice. "I'm not asking to be deputized. My job is to operate outside the lines you have to color in."

Dad's shoulders slump slightly. "It's not that simple. Sharing details of an ongoing investigation, even with family... it violates department protocol. I could lose my badge."

I lean forward, my voice urgent but quiet. "Dad, listen. My position gives me flexibility you don't have. I can follow leads, talk to people who'd clam up the second they see a badge. We should work together, not at cross purposes."

As I speak, I notice Rafi watching us with an unreadable expression. Is he evaluating the emotional stability of those involved in this case, or is he fantasizing about being a part of our family drama? I push the thought aside, focusing on my father's conflicted face.

"I know you want to protect me," I continue, softening my tone. "But keeping me in the dark isn't the way. Let me help, Dad. Let me do what I do best."

Dad's eyes meet mine, and I see a flicker of something—pride, maybe, or resignation. He sighs, running a hand through his graying hair.

"Cassie, I... I was worried," he admits, his voice low. "Your connection to this case, your drive to prove yourself—I feared it might cloud your judgment. Make you take risks you shouldn't."

I feel a twinge of annoyance, but I force myself to consider his words. "You're right," I concede, surprising myself. "My emotions are involved. How could they not be? But Dad, I'm not some rookie blundering around. I know the stakes. I'm committed to following the evidence, whether you like it or not."

The diner's fluorescent lights flicker, casting strange shadows across our faces. For a moment, I'm struck by how much my father has aged in the past few years. The weight of his responsibilities, the secrets he carries, seem to press down on his shoulders.

"I kept you out of the loop to protect you," he confesses, his voice barely above a whisper. "To prevent you from taking impulsive actions that might derail everything we've been working towards."

I lean back, crossing my arms. "And how's that working out for you?" I ask, unable to keep a hint of sarcasm from my voice. "Dad, my insights, my unconventional methods—they could complement your approach, not hinder it. We're stronger together."

I glance at Rafi, who's been silent throughout this exchange. His eyes dart between us, and I wonder what he's thinking. Is he seeing a family drama unfold, or evaluating potential assets and liabilities in an investigation?

Turning back to my father, I continue, "I'm already in this. Let me help. Let me do what I do best."

Dad's expression softens, but I can see the conflict in his eyes. He leans forward, his coffee mug cradled between his hands. "Cassie, it's not just about your methods. It's about Hunter. I don't fully trust his motives or his information. He's a wild card, and I'm worried he might manipulate you."

The words sting, but I push past the hurt. "I get it, Dad. Hunter's not exactly a Boy Scout. But his revelations align with what I've found independently. We can't just dismiss them."

I tap my fingers on the table. "Look, I know Hunter's flawed. But so is this whole situation. His information deserves further scrutiny, at the very least."

Out of the corner of my eye, I catch Rafi trying to suppress a smirk. His amusement at our family drama suddenly irks me.

"Something funny, Rafi?" I snap, my frustration boiling over. "How long have you been working with my father, anyway? Were you in on keeping me in the dark, too?"

Rafi's eyes widen, his smirk vanishing. Dad quickly jumps in, "Cassie, no. Rafi's only been briefed recently. He's not part of some conspiracy against you."

My eyes, wide with dread, fix on the melting snow, its chilling grey mirroring the weariness of the last few days. I force a weak smile towards Rafi. "I'm sorry, Rafi. That wasn't fair."

As I look between my father and Rafi, I can't help but wonder how much I still don't know. Trust is a fragile thing in our line of work, and right now, it feels as delicate as spun glass.

Dad leans forward, his eyes intense. "Cassie, tell me about your meeting with Gregory Hunter. What exactly happened at Central Park Fountain?"

I take a sip of my now-cold coffee, buying time to organize my thoughts. The memory of that encounter floods back, sharp and vivid.

"It was surreal," I begin, my voice low. "There he was, a man everyone thought was dead, sitting on a bench like it was the most normal thing in the world."

I describe Gregory's strength and determination. "He looked... calm, despite living in the shadows and being on the run from men like Pence. Like a man ready to face whatever challenges lay ahead. He told me you helped stage his death."

Dad's eyebrows shoot up. "He wasn't supposed to— "

"Supposed to, or not, he said it was the only way to gather evidence against Thomas Pence and Chuck Albright without them suspecting."

Rafi leans in, his earlier amusement replaced by intense focus. "What kind of evidence?"

I pull out the manila folder and slide it over, intentionally placing it between Rafi and my father. Neither of them makes a move to open the files. I shake my head, frustrated. "That's everything we need on Lisa Chenoweth and Chuck Albright, provided we can trust Hunter."

The weight of the situation settles over our table like the heavy blanket of snow falling outside. In the diner's quiet, with the faint clink of dishes in the background, I realize we're standing on the edge of something monumental. And there's no turning back now.

"We need to move on this," I say, my voice firm. "I know working with Gregory is risky, but he's our best shot at uncovering the truth."

Dad opens his mouth, likely to voice his concerns, but I cut him off. "I'm not being naive, Dad. I know Gregory has his own agenda. But right now, our goals align. We can use that."

I look between Dad and Rafi, my resolve solidifying. "I'm going to see this through. With or without your help. But I'd rather have you both on my side."

The diner's fluorescent lights flicker, casting shadows across our faces. In this moment, I feel the weight of my decision, the path ahead fraught with danger and uncertainty. But there's no turning back now. We're going to bring down this corrupt operation.

Dad leans back in the booth, his weathered face a canvas of conflicting emotions. His eyes, so much like my own, hold a mixture of pride and fear that makes my chest tighten.

"Cassie," he says, his voice rough with concern, "this isn't just about exposing corruption. We're dealing with people who've already proven they're willing to kill to keep their secrets."

I nod, acknowledging the gravity of his words. Carl Peterson's murder still hangs heavy in the air.

"I know, Dad. But that's exactly why we can't back down now."

Rafi clears his throat, drawing our attention. "She's right, Detective. We've got a real shot at bringing these guys down. But we need to move fast."

Dad's jaw clenches, but I can see the wheels turning in his mind. After what feels like an eternity, he nods sharply.

"Alright," he says, turning to Rafi. "Brief her on the plan."

Rafi leans forward, his eyes bright with excitement. "We're going to wire you up, Cassie. Get you in a room with Pence and record everything he says."

My heart races at the prospect. It's dangerous, but it's also our best chance at nailing Pence.

"How are we going to get me close enough?" I ask, already running through scenarios in my head.

Rafi grins. "That's where it gets interesting. We're going to use Pence's ego against him..."

As Rafi outlines the details, I can't help but feel a mix of exhilaration and fear. This is it! Our chance to bring down the corrupt operation that's been plaguing Lenape City.

As Rafi wraps up the plan, a nagging thought rises to the surface. I bite my lip, hesitating for a moment before speaking.

"Dad," I begin, my voice low, "what about Uncle Alfred? And Chief Burgess? How deep does this corruption go?"

The diner suddenly feels too small, too exposed. Dad scans the room before settling on me, his expression guarded.

"Cassie," he says, his tone cautious, "we're monitoring your uncle closely. There's no concrete evidence yet, but we're not ruling anything out."

I lean in, lowering my voice further. "And Chief Burgess?"

Dad's hesitation speaks volumes. "That's... more complicated. We can't be certain of his involvement or loyalties at this point."

The uncertainty in his voice bears the weight of dread. If we can't trust the Chief of Police, who can we trust?

Rafi clears his throat softly. "We're operating on a need-to-know basis right now. The fewer people involved, the better our chances of success."

I nod, understanding the gravity of the situation. The web of corruption seems to stretch farther than I'd imagined, and for a moment, the task ahead feels overwhelming.

Dad reaches across the table, his hand covering mine. "I know it's a lot, Cassie. But we're in this together now. Are you sure you're ready for this?"

I meet his gaze, seeing a mix of concern and pride in his eyes. Despite our differences, despite the secrets and the tension, I realize we're on the same side. For once, we're truly working together.

"I'm ready," I say, my voice steady. "We need to do this."

Rafi grins, his enthusiasm infectious. "That's the spirit. We make a pretty good team, don't we?"

As we stand to leave, I feel a strange mix of emotions—determination, fear, and cautious optimism. Whatever comes next, at least I'm not facing it alone.

* * *

The bell above the door chimes as we step out into the frigid night air. I glance back at the counter, noticing for the first time that the lone man in the suit is gone. A strange prickle runs down my spine.

"Dad," I start, "did you see when that guy at the counter left?"

Dad follows my gaze, his brow furrowing slightly. "Hm? Oh, must've slipped out while we were talking. Nothing to worry about, Cass."

I'm not so sure, but before I can press the issue, Dad turns to Rafi. "Why don't you ride with Cassie? Make sure she gets home safe."

Irritation immediately rises within me. "I'm not a child, Dad. I can drive myself home."

"It's just a precaution, honey. With everything going on—"

"No," I cut him off, my voice sharper than intended. "You two have been conspiring together. You can leave together too.”

Rafi raises his hands in mock surrender, a small smile playing at his lips. “Hey, no conspiracy here. Just trying to help.”

I soften slightly at his easy-going tone, but stand my ground. “I appreciate it, but I’ll be fine. I’ll see you both tomorrow.”

Dad looks like he wants to argue but eventually nods. “Alright. Drive safe, Cassie. We’ll be right behind you.”

As I slide into the familiar leather seat of Dad’s old Cadillac, I can’t help but feel a twinge of nostalgia. How many times had I ridden in this car as a kid, dreaming of the day I’d be solving cases just like my father?

I start the engine, watching in the rearview mirror as Dad and Rafi climb into Dad’s unmarked police car. As I pull out onto the empty street, I see their headlights flicker on a few car lengths behind me.

Flakes of snow fall as I drive, creating a hypnotic dance in my headlights. It matches my swirling thoughts perfectly—a mix of hope and uncertainty, just like the delicate balance between rain and snow.

I think about the fragile alliance we’ve formed tonight. Dad and I have been at odds for so long, both of us too stubborn to truly hear each other. But now, with Rafi in the mix, it feels like something has shifted. His easy-going nature seems to soften the edges of our relationship, providing a buffer between our strong personalities.

As I navigate the familiar streets of Lenape City, now ghostly quiet in the early morning hours, I wonder if Rafi might be the key to bridging the gap between Dad and me. His presence seems to bring out a different side of Dad—less rigid, more willing to listen.

The snow falls harder now, creating a soft blanket over the city. It feels like a clean slate, full of possibilities. I’m scared. There’s no denying that. The corruption we’re facing runs deep, and the stakes are higher than I’ve ever dealt with before. But there’s also a spark of excitement, a readiness to face whatever comes next.

As I turn onto my street, I catch sight of Dad’s car in my mirror, still faithfully following at a distance. Despite everything, knowing he’s there brings a small comfort. We may not always see eye to eye, but when it really matters, we have each other's backs.

I pull into my driveway, the Cadillac's engine rumbling to a stop. For a moment, I sit there, watching the snow fall and listening to the tick of the cooling engine. When daylight comes, we dive headfirst into dangerous waters. But tonight, in these wee quiet hours, I allow myself to feel cautious optimism.

Whatever comes next, we'll face it together. And maybe, just maybe, we'll come out stronger on the other side.

27

The Unmasking

I step out of my car, the crisp winter air biting at my cheeks. The sun's warmth fights the lingering cold, melting Wednesday night's snow from the sidewalk. The gleaming glass facade of Shenandoah Partners, with its sleek lines a stark contrast to the historic buildings around it, catches my eye.

I smooth my blazer and adjust my bag. "You've got this, Cassie," I mutter under my breath, trying to quell the nervous energy coursing through me.

I can't help but glance across the street, spotting the innocuous-looking pastry van where Dad, Ravi, and the team are holed up. My stomach clenches, knowing they're listening to my every word, monitoring my every move. It's reassuring and terrifying all at once.

As I approach the building's entrance, my mind races through the evidence we've painstakingly gathered over the past two weeks. The financial irregularities, the questionable permits, the whispered rumors of blackmail—it all points to Thomas Pence and his web of corruption. But proof is one thing; getting him to incriminate himself is another entirely.

"Just get him talking," Dad's voice echoes in my head. "Stay calm, stay focused."

The lobby doors whoosh open, and I'm hit with a wave of warm air and the faint scent of lemon-scented cleaner. My eyes dart around, taking in every detail—the security guard at his desk, the click of heels on marble floors, the hushed conversations of employees hurrying to and fro.

I approach the elevator bank, my heart pounding so loudly I swear others must hear it. As I wait for the car to arrive, I discreetly adjust the hidden microphone nestled beneath my collar.

"Testing, testing," I whisper, hoping the tech is picking up my voice clearly. "Dad, Ravi—if you can hear me, everything's set."

The elevator dings and I step inside, my reflection in the polished doors staring back at me. For a moment, I see the scared little girl who used to play detective in the backyard, desperate to impress her father. But as the doors close, I know that little girl is gone. In her place stands a woman determined to uncover the truth.

"Alright, Pence," I whisper as the elevator begins its ascent. "Let's see what skeletons are hiding in that corner office of yours."

The elevator glides upward, and I catch a bird's eye view of the lobby below. At the center of which is the impressive miniature model of Shenandoah's planned projects. The lobby serves as a marbled throne encasing Shenandoah's crowned jewel.

"It's a shame," I mutter, noting the skyscraper as even this disappears from my line of sight. "All this vision, all this potential… crumbling because of one man's greed."

My father's voice echoes in my head: "Remember, Cassie, the city is bigger than any one person or company." I can almost see his stern yet caring expression, the same look he'd give me when I'd come home frustrated after a tough day at the academy.

"You're right, Dad," I whisper, straightening my shoulders. "Lenape City will survive this. Someone else will step up, build something even better."

The elevator chimes, signaling my arrival at the executive floor. As the doors slide open, I push aside thoughts of my father and our complicated relationship. Now isn't the time for introspection. I have a job to do.

A young woman sits at the desk outside Pence's office, her perfectly coiffed hair and crisp blazer a stark contrast to Lisa Chenoweth's more approachable style. She looks up as I approach, her smile practiced and impersonal.

"Can I help you?" she asks, her tone clipped and efficient.

I flash my most disarming smile. "Cassie Maddox to see Mr. Pence. I believe he's expecting me."

She nods curtly, tapping away at her keyboard. "Of course, Ms. Maddox. Please, go right in."

As I push open the heavy oak door to Pence's office, I can't help but feel a twinge of sympathy for this nameless assistant. Does she know she's just a placeholder, a convenient face to put between Pence and the outside world now that Albright is pulling Lisa's strings at The Peterson Group?

The thought vanishes as I step into Pence's domain. The opulence hits me like a physical force—plush carpets that swallow my footsteps, floor-to-ceiling windows offering a breathtaking view of Lenape City, and artwork that probably costs more than I'll make in a lifetime adorning the walls.

"Impressive," I murmur, my eyes drawn to a striking abstract piece. "But at what cost, Thomas?"

I settle into one of the leather chairs facing his massive desk, my senses on high alert. Any minute now, I'll come face to face with the man behind it all. The thrill of the hunt, mixed with a healthy dose of fear, courses through my veins.

"Game on," I whisper, welcoming the confrontation to come.

* * *

Thomas Pence sweeps into the room, his presence immediately filling the space. He exudes confidence, every inch the successful businessman in his tailored suit and perfectly coiffed silver hair.

"Cassie, always a pleasure," he greets me warmly, his handshake firm. "What brings you to my humble abode today?"

I flash him a bright smile, leaning into the persona of an eager young professional. "Mr. Pence, I hope I'm not interrupting. I just had to come by and congratulate you on the Old Town Plaza project. It's absolutely stunning."

His eyes light up at the compliment, and I can practically see his ego expanding. "You're too kind. We're quite proud of how it's shaping up. Have you had a chance to visit the site?"

"I have," I nod enthusiastically. "The way you've blended modern design with the historical elements is remarkable. It's really breathing new life into that whole area."

As I speak, I'm carefully gauging his reactions. He's clearly basking in the praise, but there's a slight tightness around his eyes. Is he wondering why I'm really here?

"You know," I continue, leaning forward slightly, "it got me thinking about the scale of what Shenandoah Partners is accomplishing. Carl Peterson must've felt the pressure to keep up."

I watch closely as Pence's demeanor shifts ever so slightly at the mention of Carl Peterson. His smile doesn't falter, but there's a flicker of something—unease? Annoyance?—in his eyes.

"Competition keeps us all on our toes," he says smoothly. "Some just don't have what it takes. But I assure you, Shenandoah Partners is more than capable of holding its own."

I nod, my mind racing. That wasn't quite the reaction I was expecting. Is he truly that confident, or is there more to the story?

"Of course," I agree. "Though I have to admit, I was surprised to see Lisa Chenoweth and Chuck Albright at the helm of The Peterson Group. Heard the merger between Shenandoah and The Peterson Group has been finalized. It seems like convenient timing, don't you think?"

This time, the change in Pence's demeanor is unmistakable. His jaw tightens, and for a split second, I see a flash of something dangerous in his eyes before his mask of affability slides back into place.

"Speculations can be such troublesome things, can't they?" he says, his tone light but with an underlying edge. "I wouldn't follow that thread much further than you already have, Cassie."

My heart is pounding, but I keep my expression neutral. I've struck a nerve; that much is clear. But how far can I push before he realizes this isn't just a casual visit?

"Of course," I say with a small laugh. "Though in this business, sometimes where there's smoke, there's fire. I just find the whole idea fascinating from a development perspective."

As Pence launches into a carefully worded response about Shenandoah's commitment to independent growth, I'm hyper-aware of every micro-expression, every subtle shift in his body language. There's definitely more to this merger story, and I'm determined to push Pence further to the edge.

I lean forward slightly, my eyes never leaving Pence's face. "Speaking of fascinating developments, I couldn't help but notice some… irregularities in the financial reports for the Old Town Plaza project. Particularly where Gregory Hunter's position was concerned."

Pence's smile falters for a moment, a barely perceptible twitch at the corner of his mouth. "Irregularities?" he scoffs. "Our books are impeccable. Evidence to the contrary would have been gained and doctored through illicit means."

I can feel the tension in the room ratcheting up, but I press on. "I don't think so, Mr. Pence. In fact, I've uncovered verifiable evidence that suggests a rather concerning misuse of Mr. Hunter's position."

Pence's facade is crumbling now, his eyes hardening as he leans back in his chair. "That's a very serious accusation, Ms. Maddox. I hope you have substantial proof to back it up."

My insides reel, but I give nothing away in my voice. "Oh, I do. And it goes beyond just Hunter. There seems to be some interesting connections to the mayor's office, not to mention certain elements within law enforcement."

The gleam in Pence's eye transforms into something dark and angry. He chuckles dryly. "You know, Ms. Maddox, loyalty has a price. So does silence. And that substantial proof of yours… let's just say the leak stopped after a quiet conversation between one officer and one redhead who needed a little perspective."

I swallow a lump that's formed in my throat. He knew Shayan was in police custody, and now I know why. I take a gamble, choosing my next words carefully.

"You mean Shayan Easton," I say, my tone measured. "Funny—she was supposed to be delivered to the downtown precinct. But someone made sure she didn't show up, didn't they?"

In an instant, Pence's demeanor shifts completely. He surges to his feet, his face contorted with rage as he rounds the desk towards me. "You little bitch," he snarls, looming over me. "You just can't take a hint, can you?"

I stand my ground, even as my pulse thunders in my ears. Pence continues, his words dripping with venom. "Wasn't the additional pay in your check enough? But you keep poking, don't you? Chuck Albright warned me against hiring the daughter of a prominent detective. I should've listened, and you should've taken the payout as it was handed to you."

As Pence towers over me, his words confirming my worst suspicions, I realize I've pushed him to the breaking point. But there's no going back now. I've come too far to back down, even as the danger of my situation becomes terrifyingly clear.

Pence's words hang in the air, heavy with menace. I swallow hard, my mind racing to find the right angle. "And what about Carl Peterson?" I ask, my voice steadier than I feel. "Did he take the payout you offered?"

Pence's eyes narrow, a flicker of surprise crossing his face before he can mask it. "Peterson was a stubborn fool," he spits out. "Wouldn't budge on the merger, despite our exorbitant offer. But he's out of the way now, isn't he?"

My heart leaps. This is it—the confession I've been waiting for. I open my mouth to respond, but before I can, the office door bursts open with a thunderous crash.

"LCPD! Thomas Pence, you're under arrest!"

My father's voice booms through the room as he and his team flood in, guns drawn. The chaos is immediate and overwhelming. Pence's face drains of color, his earlier bravado evaporating in an instant.

"What the hell is this?" he shouts, stumbling backward. "You can't—I have rights!"

As the officers move to restrain Pence, I catch my father's eye. There's a mixture of pride and concern in his gaze that makes my chest tighten. I did it. We did it. But why does this victory feel so hollow?

Pence struggles against the officers, his perfectly tailored suit now rumpled and disheveled. "You don't know what you're dealing with," he hisses at me. "This goes deeper than you can imagine, Cassie. You're in over your head!"

I watch as they cuff him, my mind whirling. What did he mean by that? How deep does this corruption really go? And why do I have the sinking feeling that this is just the beginning of something much bigger and more dangerous than I ever anticipated?

Suddenly, Pence's body tenses like a coiled spring. In a burst of desperate energy, he shoves past the officers, knocking one to the ground. He's out the door before anyone can react.

"Stop him!" my father shouts.

I'm already moving, my legs carrying me after Pence before I can even think. My heart pounds in my ears as I race down the hallway, catching glimpses of his retreating figure. He's heading for the stairwell—the roof.

"Cassie, wait!" I hear my father call, but I can't stop now. I've come too far to let Pence slip away.

* * *

I burst through the stairwell door, taking the steps two at a time. My breath comes in ragged gasps, but adrenaline pushes me forward. I can hear Pence's footsteps echoing above me, growing fainter with each passing second.

God, what am I doing? I'm not a cop. I'm not trained for this. But I need answers, and Pence is the key to everything.

I reach the roof access door, slamming it open. The bright sunlight momentarily blinds me as I step out onto the gravel-strewn surface. Wind whips at my hair, and the city sprawls out below us in a dizzying panorama.

Pence stands at the edge of the roof, his back to me, chest heaving. He turns slowly, and I'm struck by the wild look in his eyes.

"It's over, Pence," I call out, trying to keep my voice steady. "There's nowhere left to run."

He laughs, a harsh, bitter sound. "You think you've won, don't you? Little Cassie Maddox, playing at being a real investigator."

I take a cautious step forward. "I know about Carl Peterson. I know about the blackmail, the merger. It's all going to come out now."

Pence's lips curl into a sneer. "You know nothing. This goes so much deeper than you can imagine. I have friends in high places, Cassie. Powerful allies who won't let this stand."

A chill runs down my spine despite the warmth of the sun. "What are you talking about? Who are these allies?"

He shakes his head, a strange, almost pitying look crossing his face. "Oh, you poor, naive girl. You don't know what you've stumbled into, do you? This city, this entire system, is built on secrets you can't even comprehend."

My voice catches before it can leave—behind me, the door bursts open. My father and his team pour out onto the roof, guns drawn.

"It's over, Pence," my father calls out. "Step away from the edge and lay face down on the ground."

Pence looks at me one last time, his eyes boring into mine. "Remember what I said, Cassie. This is just the beginning."

As the officers move in, aiming a taser in Pence's direction, I can't shake the feeling that Pence is right. This isn't the end of something—it's the start of a much darker, more dangerous chapter.

Pence's drops to his knees as the officers close in. His gaze locks onto mine, filled with a mixture of spite and something else—a knowing glint that sends a chill through me.

"You think you've won, don't you, Cassie?" he spits. "But tell me, how well do you really know your own family? That spotless reputation your father's built? It's as fake as the integrity of this city."

My heart races. "What are you talking about?"

He lets out a harsh laugh. "Ask Daddy dearest about the McGinnis case from '98. Or better yet, why don't you look into your grandfather's dealings with the old Lenape Savings and Loan? The Maddox name isn't as clean as you think."

The words hit me like a physical blow. I struggle to keep my face neutral, but doubt creeps in like a poison. "You're lying," I manage, but my voice wavers.

"Am I?" Pence smirks.

The officer yanks Pence to his feet. "Save the charm for the arraignment."

I watch, stunned, as they lead him away. The adrenaline draining from my veins leaves me hollow and unsteady. My knees wobble, and I catch myself before I fall.

"Cassie?" My father's voice breaks through my daze. He's at my side, a steadying hand on my arm. "You okay, kiddo?"

I look up at him, searching his face for... what? Signs of deception? Guilt? But all I see is concern. Still, Pence's words echo in my mind, sowing seeds of doubt.

"Yeah, Dad," I lie, forcing a smile. "I'm fine. Just... processing everything."

He nods, pride evident in his eyes. "You did good work here. We couldn't have nailed him without you."

His praise should feel like a victory, but instead, it leaves me cold. As we make our way off the roof, I can't shake the feeling that this is far from over. What if Pence wasn't just lashing out? What if there's truth to his accusations?

I file that possibility away, knowing with certainty I will not rest until I uncover the whole truth.

My phone buzzes in my pocket, startling me out of my thoughts. I fish it out, expecting a congratulatory message from Rafi or maybe a follow-up from the precinct. Instead, my blood runs cold as I read the anonymous text:

You're not ready for the truth yet. But you're getting close.

A shiver runs down my spine, and I glance around reflexively, searching for watching eyes. The rooftop is empty now except for my father and me, but I can't shake the feeling of being observed.

"Everything okay?" Dad asks, his brow furrowing.

I swallow hard, debating whether to show him the message. "Yeah, just... a weird text," I say, my voice steadier than I feel.

He leans in, curiosity piqued. "Oh? From who?"

I stare at my phone, the ominous words burning into my retinas. This message, coming on the heels of Pence's cryptic accusation... it can't be a coincidence. But how deep does this rabbit hole go?

"Cassie?" Dad prompts, jolting me back to the present.

I lock my screen, tucking the phone away. "It's nothing," I lie, forcing a smile. "Probably just spam."

Dad nods, seemingly satisfied. He claps me on the shoulder, grinning broadly. "You were brilliant there, you know. The way you baited Pence into that confession? Textbook stuff."

His pride warms me, but it's tinged with an undercurrent of unease. I want to bask in this moment of triumph, to feel like I've finally proven myself. Instead, I'm left wondering if I've just scratched the surface of something far more sinister.

"Thanks, Dad," I manage, my mind racing. "I learned from the best."

As we make our way back inside, I can't help but recall Pence's words about my family. I glance at my father and try to imagine a younger, more ambitious young police officer. The McGinnis Case of '98 echoes in my mind. Was Pence simply trying to throw me off balance, or was he trying to bring my family down with him? I file away the case and my grandfather's alleged dealings with Lenape Savings and Loans for another time. It'll have to wait, as a few loose threads beg to be pulled in this current case.

* * *

The car rumbles to life, carrying us away from the towering Shenandoah Partners building. I stare out the window, watching the sleek skyscrapers of downtown Lenape City blur into a grey haze. My phone feels heavy in my pocket, that mysterious text message burning a hole in my mind.

"You okay, Cassie?" Rafi's voice cuts through my spiraling thoughts. He's twisted around in the front seat, his brow furrowed with concern. "You look like you've seen a ghost."

I force a weak smile. "Just processing everything, I guess. It's been a hell of a day."

Dad chuckles from behind the wheel. "That's an understatement. You should be proud, kiddo. We've been trying to nail Pence for months."

"Yeah," I mumble, my enthusiasm failing to match his. I can feel Rafi's eyes on me, probing, concerned.

"Cassie," he whispers, "what aren't you telling us?"

I hesitate, torn between bringing up Pence's accusations and protecting my father from whatever storm is brewing. The text flashes through my mind again: *You're not ready for the truth yet.* What truth? And who decides when I'm ready?

"It's nothing, really," I lie, hating the way the words taste in my mouth. "Just... wondering what comes next, I guess."

Rafi's eyes narrow. "Uh-huh. And that has nothing to do with why you've been clutching your phone like a lifeline since we left?"

I sigh, realizing I can't hide everything from him. "There's... there might be more to this. I'm not sure yet, but—"

"But you're going to dig deeper," Rafi finishes, a mix of resignation and worry in his voice.

I nod, grateful for his understanding. "I have to, Rafi. This feels bigger than Pence, bigger than Shenandoah Partners. I can't just let it go."

Dad's eyes flick to the rearview mirror, meeting mine. "Whatever it is, Cassie, you don't have to face it alone. I've got your back."

His words should be comforting, but they only intensify the knot in my stomach. How can I trust my father when doubt hangs so heavily on my mind? What's he been hiding from me about my family? The weight of secrets and half-truths presses down on me as we drive through the familiar streets of Lenape City, heading towards a future suddenly fraught with uncertainty.

28

Fractured Loyalties

A sickly, flickering glow illuminates the sea of papers strewn across the desk. I flip through another file, my eyes scanning for any detail we might have missed. The precinct buzzes with muted activity around us, but here at my father's cluttered desk, the tension is palpable.

"We've been at this for over a day and none of this makes sense," I mutter, tossing the file onto the growing discard pile. "Dan Lutman and that other officer took Shayan Easton into custody. We... a lot of us saw it happen... then that IRS agent, James Stanton showed up. How could both officers and an arrestee be missing?"

My father leans back in his creaking chair, his weathered face etched with exhaustion. "Paperwork goes missing all the time, Cassie. Stanton might've pulled jurisdiction and taken her into federal custody. You'd be surprised by how often this happens."

"With no chain of custody?" I ask. "Did they all just disappear?"

Dad pinches the bridge of his nose and exhales slowly. "Contrary to what you think, I'm not informed of every inner working of this precinct. Sometimes, things get rerouted above my pay grade."

"You mean, people get rerouted," I say. "You don't just lose a federal agent, two officers, and a witness without paperwork. Not unless someone wants it that way."

Dad gazes at the window where frost has formed against the evening chill. "Cassie," he says. "The evidence doesn't always line up with what we *think* we know. But that's not the same as not knowing at all."

There's a weight to his words, something unspoken. Understanding clicks into place, steady and unwelcome. Chief Burgess's name hovers on the tip of my tongue, but I swallow it back. Some suspicions are too dangerous to voice out loud.

"We need to bring Albright in," my father continues, his voice taking on that authoritative edge I know all too well. "He's our best lead."

I shake my head, leaning forward. "No, that's exactly what we can't do. Don't you see? Albright's just a piece of this. If we move on him now, we risk tipping off whoever's really pulling the strings."

My father's eyes narrow. "What are you suggesting?"

I lean forward and lock eyes with my father. "Use me as bait. Just like we did with Pence."

The silence that follows is deafening. I can see the war playing out behind my father's eyes—the detective battling with the protective parent. I press on, my words coming faster now.

"Think about it. I've already established a connection through the Shenandoah Partners investigation. If we play this right, we might be able to draw out the real power players."

My father's jaw clenches. "It's too risky."

"And arresting Albright without solid evidence isn't?" I counter, gesturing at the mess of files surrounding us. "We both know there's more going on here than meets the eye. The missing fingerprints, the conveniently misplaced evidence that points to him as a murder suspect. This stinks of a cover-up."

As I speak, I can't help but wonder how deep this corruption really goes. But now isn't the time for doubt.

My father leans forward, his voice low. "Cassie, you don't know what you're walking into here."

"Maybe not," I admit, meeting his gaze. "But I know we won't get to the truth by playing it safe. Sometimes you have to risk everything to uncover what's really going on."

The silence stretches between us, heavy with unspoken fears and shared determination. I can see the moment my father's resolve begins to crack.

"We do this carefully," he finally says, his voice gruff. "Every step planned, every angle covered."

I nod, a mix of relief and anticipation coursing through me. "Of course. We'll make sure we have all our bases covered."

As we begin to hash out the details, I lean back in my chair, studying my father's face. There's a tightness around his eyes that betrays his unease. Why is he so reluctant to pursue Albright? He trusted me with Pence, but now...

"Dad," I start, choosing my words carefully. "What aren't you telling me about Albright?"

He opens his mouth to respond, but the sharp ping of an incoming email cuts him off. Dad turns to his computer, his brow furrowing as he reads.

"What is it?" I ask, leaning forward.

He hesitates before answering. "An anonymous tip. With a photo."

I rise, circling the desk to look over his shoulder. The image is grainy, but I can make out a familiar figure—Gregory Hunter, tied up and gagged.

"Who's that next to him?" I ask, though I already know the answer. I zoom in closer, my pulse quickening. Even in the grainy photo, I recognize Lila's pixie cut. "Where is this?" I demand, my pulse quickening. "When is this?"

Dad shakes his head. "Some abandoned industrial site. Time unknown. Cassie, we can't trust this. It's too convenient. It screams trap."

"Jesus," I breathe, my fingers trembling as I zoom in further on the image. "Dad, we have to move. Now."

My father's hand clasps my wrist, surprisingly gentle. "Hold on, Cassie. We need to think this through."

I whirl on him, disbelief etched across my face. "Think it through? That's Lila in there with Hunter! My best friend, Dad. We don't have time to sit around and debate this!"

As I lock eyes with my father, the noise of the precinct fades to a low hum. His face is a mixture of concern, determination, and something else. Fear?

It's clear he doesn't agree with my plan.

"This all seems too convenient," he says in a hushed voice. "An anonymous tip, a perfectly timed photo—it's textbook manipulation, Cassie. You're not even a police officer. You gave up that path when you intentionally failed out of the academy."

"What does that have to do with saving Lila and Gregory?" I snap, aware that we are attracting attention but not caring in the slightest.

"Maddox," Chief Burgess calls from his office door. My father and I both stand at attention.

"Detective Maddox," Chief Burgess corrects himself, emphasizing the word 'detective.' "I need to speak with you in my office."

"Don't be rash," my father advises, his tone grave. "Wait until I return."

As he walks away to join Chief Burgess, I sink back into my desk chair, heart pounding with anticipation. When the door to Burgess' office closes, the photo of Gregory Hunter and Lila Baker taunts me from the corner of my vision.

"Don't be rash," I mutter to myself sarcastically. "Who does he think he is, telling me what to do?"

I lean over my laptop, typing furiously as I cross-reference the location from the anonymous tip. My eyes widen in realization as everything falls into place.

"Holy shit," I breathe out, leaning in closer to the screen. "This is where the police allegedly found Hunter's body."

This isn't a random location. I lean back in my chair, running a hand through my hair as I consider my next move. Dad's right; this is most likely a trap, but my gut is urging me to take action now rather than waiting and strategizing. I've learned to trust my instincts over the years, and they have rarely failed me. Yet, there's a lingering sense of doubt in the back of my mind—disregarding my father's advice feels like a risky move.

"Damn it," I mutter, closing my eyes briefly. When I open them again, I am resolute. "I have to act now."

I rise from my chair, gathering my jacket and keys as I prepare to leave. My eyes involuntarily drift towards the closed door of Chief Burgess' office, wondering what important matters are being discussed inside. A familiar sense of determination floods through me as I clench my jaw, a habit I inherited from my father. Despite any doubts, I know taking risks can lead to great results. But doing so without a backup plan, that's just stupid.

I snatch a sticky note off Dad's desk and jot down a message.

Forgive me, Dad.

I couldn't wait. See you there.

Cass

* * *

I step out into the afternoon sunlight, fighting against the cold to warm this chilly winter day. My mind races with possibilities for what else I might find at the warehouse. Lila and Hunter are being held hostage—but who took them? And for what purpose?

As I pull out my phone, my fingers hover over Rafi's number. The weight of what I'm about to do settles on my shoulders. "Hey, Raf," I say into the voice memo, trying to keep my tone light. "I've got a lead on a warehouse connected to Shenandoah Partners. I'm heading there now to check it out."

I pause, considering how much to reveal. "Look, I know it's risky, but this could be big. I'll send you the location. If you don't hear from me in an hour, call my dad. I've already left him a message just in case... you know... he hasn't already figured out where I am." I add the address and hit send, hoping I'm just being paranoid.

As I slide into my car, the familiar hum of the engine does little to calm my nerves. Lenape City unfolds around me, the mix of historic buildings and modern skyscrapers a stark reminder of the changes sweeping through our town. I'm lost in thought when my phone buzzes. Uncle Alfred's name flashes on the screen.

"Uncle Al," I answer, trying to sound casual. "What's up?"

"Cassandra, my dear!" His polished voice fills the car. "I wanted to congratulate you on nabbing Thomas Pence. Quite the accomplishment."

I grip the steering wheel tighter. "Thanks. Just doing my job."

"Ah, but it's more than that. You've rid us of a real snake in the grass." He chuckles, but there's an edge to it. "You know, I trusted that weasel for years. We had such high hopes for Lenape City's future."

"I'm sure it's a shock," I reply, carefully neutral.

"Well, these things happen. Not everyone who can afford a country club membership belongs there, if you catch my drift."

I frown, mulling over his words. There's something off about his tone, a falseness that sets my teeth on edge. As I navigate through the city's winding streets, I can't shake the feeling that this conversation is more than just small talk.

"Uncle Alfred," I start, then hesitate. How much should I reveal? "Do you think there might be others involved? People Pence was working with?"

There's a pause on the other end, just a beat too long. "Now, Cassandra, let's not get ahead of ourselves. The system worked, didn't it? Pence is behind bars. Sometimes it's best to let sleeping dogs lie."

I bite my lip, torn between pressing further and playing it safe. In the end, caution wins out. "You're probably right," I say, hating the lie even as it leaves my mouth.

As I end the call, Uncle Alfred's words echo in my mind, mixing with the doubts I've been trying to ignore. What if Pence is right? What if my family is involved in corruption? Already, evidence suggests my uncle isn't exactly clean. But what of my father?

Pushing those thoughts aside, I focus on the road ahead.

* * *

The warehouse stands tall and imposing, casting a dark shadow in the moonlight.

I slow down as I approach the warehouse. Uncle Alfred's words echo in my mind, each one now heavy with unspoken implications. His evasiveness, the calculated pauses—it all points to something sinister lurking beneath the surface.

"Trust the system," I mutter under my breath, mimicking his tone. "Yeah, right!"

I park my car a good distance away from the warehouse behind a cluster of overgrown bushes. As I step out, the wind whips my hair, carrying the scent of rust and stagnant water.

I scan the area, every sense on high alert. The warehouse seems deserted, but appearances can be deceiving. I've learned that lesson the hard way.

"Okay, Cassie," I whisper to myself, "what's the play here?"

My hand instinctively checks my concealed weapon, the Sig, a cool, comforting metal. Uncle Alfred may have friends in high places, but I've got determination and the truth on my side.

As I creep closer to the warehouse, the air feels too still, too aware, like I'm not alone. Every shadow seems to hide a potential threat, every sound a warning. But I push forward, driven by the need to uncover the truth despite the unknown dangers lurking within.

"Time to see what skeletons are hiding in this closet," I mutter, approaching the rusted door.

My heart pounds as I approach the warehouse, each step a battle between caution and curiosity. Dad's warnings echo in my head, but I push them aside. I've come too far to turn back now.

"This could be it," I whisper, then shake it off—Hunter and Lila come first.

I pause at the door, my hand hovering over the handle. The metal feels cold beneath my fingers, a stark reminder of the danger that might lurk inside. I close my eyes for a moment, centering myself.

"You've got this, Cassie," I mutter. "Just like with Pence. One step at a time."

I reach for my Sig, the familiar weight of it grounding me. I check it quickly, more out of habit than necessity.

"Alright, warehouse," I say, a hint of defiance in my voice. "Let's see what secrets you're hiding."

The wind picks up, whipping my hair across my face as I gaze at the imposing structure. Somewhere inside, our next lead awaits. Maybe it's a trap, or maybe I'll rescue my friends and bust this case wide open.

Either way, I'm ready.

I check my phone one last time and share my location with Dad and Rafi, just in case.

I grip the door handle, my resolve solidifying. Whatever's waiting for me on the other side, I'll face it head-on. With one last glance over my shoulder, I push open the door and step into the unknown, the darkness inside swallowing me whole.

29

The Trap

The rusted door creaks open, and I slip inside, my gun a cold comfort in my sweaty palm. Shadows dance across concrete walls, and the musty air tickles my nose. Every step echoes a betrayal in this hollow space.

"Gregory? Lila?" I whisper, my voice barely audible over the pounding of my heart.

Silence answers, broken only by the distant hum of city traffic. I scan the cavernous room, squinting through the gloom. Stacks of crates loom like sentinels, their contents a mystery. A faint scrabbling sound from above makes me freeze.

"Just a rat," I tell myself, but my finger tightens on the trigger.

A floorboard creaks, and I whirl, gun raised. Nothing but shadows. My breath comes in shallow gasps as I force myself to move forward.

"Come on, Cass," I mutter. "You've got this. Think of Lila."

Sweet, trusting Lila. How could I have let her get mixed up in all this? And Gregory—for all his secrets, he doesn't deserve whatever's happening to him.

I approach a metal staircase, its railings rusted and flaking. Up appears to be the only direction to go. My dad's warning echoes in my mind: *Cassie, this screams trap!*

Despite every instinct telling me to turn back, I continue forward. "Alright, Maddox," I whisper to myself. "Time to live up to our name."

With a last glance behind me, I ascend the stairs, each step taking me further into the unknown.

The concrete staircase reverberates my every step, and my muscles tense. Sweat beads on my forehead, and I swipe it away with the back of my hand, never lowering my gun. The air grows thick, oppressive, as if the very walls are closing in.

"This is insane," I mutter, my voice barely a whisper. "What am I even doing here?"

But I know the answer. Lila's face flashes in my mind—her bright smile, now surely twisted in fear. And Gregory, with his guarded eyes, hiding so many secrets. I can't abandon them.

As I reach the third floor, a faint glow catches my eye. A sliver of light escapes from beneath a heavy steel door at the end of the hallway.

My heart pounds so loud I'm sure it'll give me away. I press my back against the wall, inching towards the door.

"Okay, Cassie," I coach myself. "On three. One... two..."

Steadying my nerves, I push the door open, ready for anything.

Except this.

* * *

Gregory and Lila sit bound to chairs, their faces a canvas of bruises. Lila's eyes go wide when she sees me, a mixture of relief and terror.

"Cassie!" she cries out. "It's a—"

"Trap," a cold voice finishes from behind me. "Drop the gun, Ms. Maddox. Now."

A hollow ache settles in my chest. I wasn't fooled. I was reckless.

I freeze, my fingers tightening around the grip of my weapon. The voice behind me is familiar, but it can't be...

"I said drop it," Officer Dan Lutman repeats, his tone icy. I can practically feel the barrel of his gun trained on my back.

Panic claws at the edge of my thoughts. There's no escape. Slowly, I lower my gun to the floor, the metallic clatter echoing in the cavernous room.

"Kick it away," Lutman orders.

I comply, watching my only defense skitter across the concrete. "Dan," I say, fighting to keep my voice steady, "what are you doing?"

He doesn't answer. Instead, a rough hand grabs my shoulder, spinning me around and forcing me to my knees. The cold muzzle of his gun presses against my temple.

"You just couldn't leave the case alone, could you?" Lutman sneers, his face twisted with a malice I've never seen before. "Always playing detective, always digging where you don't belong. But you never were much for subtleties, were you?"

I swallow hard, thinking about our encounter at Crossroads Cafe, trying to mask my fear. The way he tracked me down within an hour of losing me at The Peterson Group. He wasn't tracking down a lead. No, he had inside information. Knew of Shayan's whereabouts and had access to restricted information. He wasn't just doing his job.

"This isn't you, Dan. We're supposed to be on the same side."

He barks out a laugh. "Same side? You're so far out of your depth, Cassie. You have no idea what's really going on here."

Lila and Gregory's faces say it all—pale, tense, silently pleading. By now, my father must've not only seen the note I left for him, but he must already be on his way. I need to keep Lutman talking, buy some time.

"Then enlighten me," I challenge, meeting his gaze. "What am I missing? How long have you been on the take?"

The warehouse door creaks open, and a new figure saunters in. My stomach drops as I recognize the stocky build and gleaming eyes of Chuck Albright. His gun hangs loosely at his side, a stark contrast to the white-knuckled grip Lutman has on his weapon.

"Well done, Lutman," Albright drawls, his voice dripping with mock praise. A smug grin spreads across his round face as he surveys the scene. "Now, let's tie up our loose ends."

Lutman tightens his grip on his pistol, his finger hovering closer to the trigger, his breath quickening. Is he nervous? Good. I file that away, searching for any advantage.

Albright's gaze lands on me, his eyes narrowing. "Cassie Maddox. You've been quite the thorn in our side." He chuckles, a sound that steals my resolve. "But I suppose I should thank you. Your meddling has accelerated our timeline."

"What timeline?" I ask, buying time. My eyes flick to Gregory, whose mustache twitches nervously. He knows something.

Albright begins to pace, clearly relishing his moment in the spotlight. "Oh, it's quite the tale. You see, Thomas Pence and I had a vision for this city. But Carl Peterson? He was in the way."

My blood runs cold.

"But you knew that already," Albright continues, waving his hand dismissively. "A necessary step to take control of The Peterson Group. And Shenandoah Partners? That was our masterstroke."

He gestures grandly, his voice taking on a theatrical quality. "A front for our true operations. Money laundering, asset manipulation—all hidden behind a veneer of urban renewal."

I glance at Lila, seeing the horror dawn on her face. "She didn't know," I say. "Why pull her in now?"

"Ms. Baker was nothing but a pawn in our game," Albright sneers, then turns his calculating eyes to land on Gregory. "You see, we didn't feel Mr. Hunter would be sufficient bait to lure you to the warehouse. We needed someone much closer to you."

Lila yelps as tears stream down her face. Albright strides over to her and tuts at her distress.

"Don't worry, my dear. It'll all be over soon." He turns back to me, a smirk playing on his lips. "You see, Ms. Maddox, we didn't expect your meddling in the minor affair with Ms. Easton. But thanks to Mr. Pence's hasty hiring of you, we have no choice but to… eliminate you all from the equation."

My jaw clenches as I try to process his words. Albright couldn't have orchestrated this alone. As vice president of property acquisitions at Shenandoah Partners, surely there must be someone higher up pulling the strings. Maybe someone unassociated with the company. Who is Albright answering to? Then it hits me—Shayan's words about Albright not being recognized by anyone at the company. She worked closely with Pence and would have known every single one of Shenandoah's executives. No, Albright is a new player to the game, a wild card thrown in to clean up Pence's mess.

Albright chuckles, as if reading my thoughts. "Always the detective, Ms. Maddox. Too bad you won't be around to see your deductions come to light."

"You won't get away with this," I say, more to convince myself that Rafi had already sensed I was in trouble and contacted my father well before the one-hour window I gave him.

Albright laughs, cold and hollow. "My dear, we already have."

The air thickens oppressively, as if someone has sucked out the oxygen. Lutman shifts slightly, ready to shoot at a moment's notice.

I swallow hard, letting fear creep into my voice. "But... how? How did you manage to keep it all hidden for so long?"

Albright's eyes gleam with pride, as if he knew I'd come here alone. He takes a step closer, unable to resist the opportunity to gloat. "Ah, Ms. Maddox. It's all about the details. The right bribes, the perfect paper trail. This..." He gestures toward Gregory and Lila, "trap!"

As he speaks, my eyes dart between Gregory and Lila. Gregory wears a mask of barely contained rage, while Lila's shock has replaced her flow of tears. I need to keep Albright talking; buy us some time.

"And the Old Town Plaza project?" I ask, my voice trembling. "Was that part of your plan too?"

"Oh, that was a stroke of genius," Albright boasts, pacing now. "A legitimate front for our less... savory activities. Who would suspect anything with all that progress and community improvement?"

Despite the cold, a bead of sweat rolls down my back. Dad must be on his way by now. He just needs a little more time, and I need Albright to keep talking.

"But surely someone must have noticed something," I press, fighting to keep my voice steady. "The bank, maybe?"

Albright chuckles. "Lenape Savings and Loan? Please. We have friends in very convenient places."

"So what happens now?" I ask, my mind racing for our next move.

Albright's smile turns predatory. "Now? Now we tie up our loose ends. Starting with you, Ms. Maddox."

My heart pounds. Where's backup? How much longer can I stall?

Albright nods to Lutman, and my blood runs cold. This is it. I squeeze my eyes shut, bracing for the inevitable—

"Enough."

The single word slices through the tension like a knife. My eyes fly open to see James Stanton striding into the warehouse, his own weapon drawn and steady. Relief floods through me, quickly followed by confusion and wariness.

"Stanton," Albright hisses, his earlier bravado evaporating.

I watch, frozen, as Stanton's piercing gaze sweeps the room. His presence seems to suck the air out of the space, leaving everyone holding their breath. Behind me, Lutman lets out a breath, and his resolve to pull the trigger seems to waver.

"The flash drive," Stanton demands, his voice deceptively calm. "The one Shayan Easton stole. Hand it over."

Albright's face contorts with a mix of anger and fear. "I don't—"

"Save it," Stanton cuts him off. "Your incompetence is staggering, Albright. And you," he turns to Lutman, "nothing more than a mindless lackey. Did you really think you could pull this off?"

I feel a flicker of hope, but it's quickly doused by the cold smirk Stanton throws my way. "And you, Ms. Maddox. Did you honestly believe you were clever enough to outplay me?"

My cheeks burn with shame and frustration. How could I have been so naïve? I thought I was making progress, unraveling this web of corruption. But Stanton's clearly been ten steps ahead this whole time.

"I was close," I argue, more to convince myself than him. "I figured out—"

"You figured out exactly what I allowed you to," Stanton interrupts. "A trail of breadcrumbs to keep you busy while the real work happened behind the scenes."

I glance at Gregory and Lila, still bound and silent. Their eyes reflect my growing realization: we're dispensable and unwitting pawns in a much longer game.

Stanton strides forward, snatching the flash drive from Albright's trembling hand. He turns it over, examining it with a satisfied smirk. My stomach churns as I realize how close I came to uncovering the truth, only to have it slip away.

"Better luck next time, Maddox," Stanton says, his voice dripping with condescension. "Maybe stick to lost pets and cheating spouses. Leave the investigations to the professionals."

His words sting, but I force myself to maintain eye contact. I won't give him the satisfaction of seeing me crumble. "This isn't over," I say, my voice steadier than I feel.

Stanton chuckles, already turning away. "Oh, but it is." He melts into the shadows, his footsteps fading until silence engulfs the warehouse once more.

I'm frozen, my mind racing. How could I have misjudged everything so badly? Dad was right; I was in over my head. The thought of facing him after this makes me want to—

The warehouse door bursts open with a deafening crash. "Police! Don't move!"

My father's voice. Relief and dread war within me as chaos erupts. Lutman, caught off guard, swings his gun wildly. It's the opening I've been waiting for.

I drive my elbow into Lutman's ribs with all the pent-up frustration of the day. He grunts, doubling over, and I wrench the gun from his grip. My heart pounds as I level it at him, hands steady despite the adrenaline coursing through me.

"It's over," I say, meeting his shocked gaze. "Your move, Officer Lutman."

The warehouse erupts into a flurry of activity as Dad's team swarms in, their voices echoing off the metal walls. Lutman crumples to the ground, defeated, as two officers roughly cuff him.

"You can't do this!" Chuck Albright shrieks, his face contorted with rage as he's dragged towards the exit. "Stanton! It was Stanton! He's the one you want!"

I watch as Albright's stocky frame thrashes against the officers' grip, his thinning hair wild and his round face flushed. His corporate smooth talk has dissolved into raw, desperate accusations.

"Cassie!" Lila's voice cuts through the chaos.

I turn to see Gregory cutting through Lila's bonds with a pocket knife an officer handed him. The moment she's free, Lila launches herself at me, her pixie cut tickling my chin as she buries her face in my shoulder. I can feel her trembling.

"It's okay," I murmur, wrapping an arm around her. "You're safe now."

Gregory approaches us, his tall frame hunched, eyes darting nervously. "Thank you," he says, his voice barely above a whisper. "I... I didn't think anyone would come."

I nod, a lump forming in my throat. The relief on their faces is palpable, but so is the lingering fear. What horrors did they endure in this place?

"Ms. Maddox," an officer interrupts. "We need to question Officer Lutman. Your presence would be... helpful."

I give Lila's shoulder a reassuring squeeze before following the officer. Lutman sits handcuffed to a chair, his earlier bravado completely deflated.

"Start talking," I say, crossing my arms.

Lutman's eyes flick between me and the officer. "It wasn't supposed to go this far," he mutters. "Albright promised me a cut. Said with my position in the force, we could do great things."

"And kidnapping? That was part of your 'great things'?" I can't keep the disgust from my voice.

He flinches. "Hunter was poking around where he shouldn't. We grabbed him after your little chat at the fountain." Lutman's gaze shifts to Lila. "Baker was... convenient. Drunk at that dive bar on the edge of town. Easy pickings."

My stomach churns at his casual cruelty and my guilt for leaving her there by herself. "Who gave the order?"

Lutman's face goes blank. "I don't know," he says, but there's a flicker in his eyes that makes me doubt his words.

"And Shayan Easton?" I ask, uncertain as to whether I want to hear the answer.

Lutman hangs his head, averting his eyes away from me. That's answer enough for now.

As the officer leads Lutman away, I can't shake the feeling that none of this will lead to the arrest of the mastermind behind this kickback scheme. Somewhere in this city, he has already washed his hands of Albright and all the criminal activity connected to him.

* * *

I lean against the cool brick wall of the warehouse as the adrenaline fades, leaving behind a bone-deep exhaustion and a gnawing sense of unease. Stanton's smug face flashes in my thoughts, and I clench my fists.

"Cassie?" Lila's voice is small, uncertain. She's standing a few feet away, arms wrapped tightly around herself.

I push off the wall, forcing a smile. "Hey, you ready to get out of here?"

She nods, relief flooding her features. As we walk to my car, I can't stop my racing thoughts. Who else is working for my uncle, if he is indeed the mastermind behind this criminal enterprise?

"I can't believe Stanton would..." Lila trails off, her voice cracking.

I unlock the car, my movements mechanical. "I know. I didn't trust him, but to stoop so low."

We slide into our seats, the familiar leather offering little comfort. I grip the steering wheel, knuckles white. "Lila, I'm so sorry. I should have—"

"Don't," she interrupts, reaching over to squeeze my arm. "You saved us, Cass."

I start the engine, the rumble matching the turmoil in my gut. "I barely saved you. But I also pulled you into this mess."

Lila shakes her head. "Working at The Peterson Group, we both know I would've found trouble on my own," she says with a weak laugh.

As we drive through the nighttime streets of Lenape City, the shadows seem deeper, more menacing. I can't shake the feeling we're being watched.

"I'm not letting you out of my sight again," I mutter, half to myself.

Lila snorts. "What, you gonna move in and be my bodyguard?"

I crack a smile despite myself. "No, just your roommate. But I have to warn you, I make a mean pillow fort."

We lapse into silence, the weight of the night settling over us. My mind drifts to my father, his warnings echoing in my head. I grip the wheel tighter. I won't let him down. I won't let myself down.

"We're not done, are we?" Lila asks quietly as we pull up to her apartment.

I meet her gaze, seeing my determination reflected there. "No," I say firmly. "We're just getting started."

30

A New Chapter

I stand in the center of my new office, breathing in the scent of fresh paint and possibility. Just three weeks ago, I was staring down the barrel of a gun, my heart pounding as I faced the consequences of my reckless attempt to save Lila and Hunter. Now, I'm surrounded by half-unpacked boxes and mismatched furniture, the physical manifestation of my dreams finally taking shape.

As I carry a modern and stylish particleboard desk across the room, I am filled with both a sense of accomplishment and annoyance. This office space, Maddox Investigative Services, is mine. But the memory of my father swooping in to save the day—again—leaves a bitter taste in my mouth. I'd been reckless, and that could've cost not just my life but the lives of those I love.

I'm arranging a stack of case files when the door swings open, and Rafi strides in, carrying a large sign under his arm. His grin is infectious, and I feel my mood lifting instantly.

"Special delivery for the most reckless PI in Lenape City," he announces, propping the sign against the wall. 'Maddox Investigative Services' gleams in bold, professional lettering.

I raise an eyebrow. "Reckless? I prefer 'Audacious Risk-Taker.'"

Rafi chuckles, his dark eyes twinkling. "Opposite sides of the same coin.

So, where do you want this beauty?"

I tap my chin, pretending to consider. "Hmm. Maybe we should hang it upside down. You know, to keep things interesting."

He rolls his eyes, but I catch the hint of a smile. "Always the rebel, Cass. But I was thinking more along the lines of, you know, actually helping people find your office."

As we debate the merits of various sign placements, I can't help but notice how at ease I feel around Rafi. His presence grounds me, reminding me that I'm not alone in this venture.

"What about here?" I suggest, gesturing to the wall beside the door. Our fingers brush as we lift the sign together, and I feel a familiar flutter in my stomach. I push it aside, focusing on the task at hand.

"Perfect," Rafi declares, stepping back to admire our handiwork. "Now it's official. Cassie Maddox, Private Investigator extraordinaire."

I laugh, but there's an underlying current of uncertainty in my voice. "Let's hope I can live up to that title."

Rafi's expression softens. "Hey," he says, resting a hand on my shoulder. "You've got this. And I've got your back, always."

I meet his gaze, warmth spreading through my chest. "Thanks, Rafi. I couldn't do this without you."

For a moment, we stand there, the air charged with unspoken possibilities. Then, clearing my throat, I turn back to the mountain of boxes. "Now, want to help me unpack the rest of this stuff? I promise there's pizza in it for you."

Rafi grins, already rolling up his sleeves. "You had me at pizza. Let's do this, partner."

As we settle into a rhythm of unpacking and organizing, I can't shake the feeling that this—Rafi, the office, my newfound independence—is the start of something big. Something that's uniquely mine, even if the path here wasn't as smooth as I'd hoped. And for now, that's enough.

The ding of the elevator interrupts our unpacking rhythm. I glance up just as my parents step into the office, their expressions a mix of pride and concern that I've come to know all too well.

"Oh, honey, it's wonderful!" Mom exclaims, her eyes sparkling as she takes in the space. Without missing a beat, she makes a beeline for an unpainted wall, pulling a roller and paint tray from her oversized bag. "This cream color will brighten things up nicely."

Dad, meanwhile, prowls the perimeter, his detective's gaze cataloging every detail. I brace myself for the inevitable lecture.

"Cassie," he starts, his tone measured but firm. "I know you're excited about this venture, but remember what we talked about. Stay safe, far from danger. Don't take on anything outside your purview or beyond your capabilities." His eyes lock onto mine. "We can't have another warehouse incident."

I swallow hard, the memory of cold steel against my temple still fresh. "I know, Dad. I've learned my lesson."

But even as I say it, a part of me bristles at the reminder of my dependence. I clear my throat, changing the subject. "Hey, did you ever track down that flash drive Stanton took from Albright?"

Dad's expression tightens almost imperceptibly. He opens his mouth to respond, but Mom's voice cuts through.

"Rafi, dear, that Ficus would look much better by the window. Natural light, you know."

Rafi, bless him, doesn't miss a beat. "Actually, Mrs. Maddox, I was thinking it might work better here. It is our office, after all."

I hide a smile at his subtle assertion of our partnership, grateful for the momentary distraction. But as I turn back to Dad, I can see the wheels turning behind his eyes. There's more to this flash drive situation than he's letting on, and I'm determined to find out what.

"Dad?" I prompt, keeping my voice low. "The flash drive?"

He sighs, running a hand through his salt-and-pepper hair. "It's... complicated, Cassie. There are jurisdictional issues at play. Let's just say it's being handled at a higher level now."

I nod, processing this. The investigator in me itches to dig deeper, but I know pushing too hard right now will only reinforce Dad's concerns about my judgment. Instead, I file the information away for later, already formulating plans to do some digging of my own.

As I watch my parents and Rafi navigate the space—Mom directing, Dad observing, Rafi asserting his place—I'm struck by the strange juxtaposition of my old life and new. I'm caught between the safety net of family and the exhilarating unknown of independence. It's terrifying and thrilling all at once, and I wouldn't have it any other way.

Dad leans in closer, his voice dropping to a whisper. "Listen, Cassie. Stanton's still in the wind, but it's the IRS's problem now." His eyes lock onto mine, concern etched in the lines of his face. "Just... don't sleep too far from that Sig of yours, okay?"

My nerves buzz, but I nod, trying to project confidence. "Got it, Dad. I'll be careful."

As we step back, I catch Mom eyeing a spot on the wall critically. "You know, sweetie," she calls out, paintbrush in hand, "this shade of beige is awfully drab. Have you considered something with a bit more life?"

I can't help but roll my eyes. "Mom, it's an office, not an art gallery."

Dad chimes in, his detective's gaze sweeping the room. "Speaking of which, are you sure about this location? It's a bit exposed. Have you considered—"

"Oh, for heaven's sake, Dylan," Mom interrupts, shooting him a playful glare. "Let the girl breathe. This isn't one of your stakeouts."

I stifle a laugh, caught between amusement and exasperation. It's so typical—Dad seeing potential threats everywhere, Mom trying to brighten up the world. And me? Stuck in the middle, as always. It's a wonder they lasted until my ninth birthday.

"Hey, guys," Rafi's voice cuts through the familial banter. "Where should I put this Ficus? I was thinking right here in the center—"

"Absolutely not!" Mom exclaims, abandoning her paint job to rush over. "That'll block the whole flow of the room. No, no, it needs to go in that corner by the window."

As Rafi opens his mouth to object, probably to remind her that this is our office, I catch his eye and give a subtle shake of my head. Sometimes, it's easier to just let Hurricane Julia have her way.

I watch them all—my overprotective father, my well-meaning but overbearing mother, and Rafi, my partner in this new adventure. The tension between my desire for independence and the comfort of family support pulls at me. But looking around at this space—our space—I know I've made the right choice. It won't be easy, but nothing worth doing ever is.

I turn to the wall behind my desk, carefully lifting a framed newspaper article. "From Shadows to Spotlight: How Cassie Maddox Exposed a Citywide Conspiracy," the headline screams. My fingers trace the edge of the frame as I hang it, a small smile tugging at my lips.

"Can't believe they used that picture," I mutter, studying my face staring back at me. It's strange seeing myself through someone else's lens. The woman in the photo looks determined, almost fierce. Is that really how others see me?

My mind drifts back to the warehouse, the cold press of a gun against my temple. The fear, the adrenaline, the moment my life could have ended. But it didn't. I solved the case, exposed the truth. I saved Lila and Hunter and proved myself.

"You okay, honey?" Mom's voice breaks through my reverie.

I nod, turning back to face my family. "Yeah, just... processing, I guess. It's been a wild ride."

Dad steps closer, his eyes flickering between me and the article. "You did good, Cass. Just remember—"

"I know, Dad," I interrupt, gentler than I mean to. "Stay safe, stay smart. I promise."

The office door swings open unexpectedly, and I instinctively tense. But it's not a threat that walks in—it's Mel Albright. The tall, athletic blonde looks out of place in our cluttered office, her usual confidence replaced by something... fragile.

"Mel?" I ask, surprised. "What are you doing here?"

She offers a shaky smile. "I, uh... I saw the article. Wanted to say congrats on taking down Uncle Chuck. That's... that's pretty badass, Cassie."

There's more to her visit than a simple congratulation—I can feel it in my gut. Whatever's brought Mel here, it's serious. I glance at my parents, silently willing them to take the hint.

"We should get going," Mom says, as if reading my mind. "Lots more unpacking to do at home."

As they gather their things to leave, I can't shake the feeling that this moment—Mel showing up here, now—is the start of something big. Something that might test everything I've learned about being a PI, about trust, about myself.

* * *

I pull a chair up. "Mel, why don't you have a seat? Tell me what's really going on."

Mel sinks into the chair across from me, her long fingers twisting nervously in her lap. I lean forward, trying to project calm and openness. Rafi, ever-present and perceptive, quietly positions himself nearby, ready to offer support or technical expertise if needed.

"It's... it's about my scholarship," Mel begins, her voice a mixture of fear and determination. "To Penamore College. Something's not right, Cassie."

I feel my eyebrows knit together. "What do you mean, not right?"

Mel takes a shaky breath. "At first, I was thrilled. I mean, Penamore? It's a dream come true. I'll be able to play lacrosse there, just like we talked about those summers ago. But then... things started feeling off."

As she speaks, I can see the conflict in her eyes. This isn't just about a scholarship; there's something deeper, more insidious at play.

"Go on," I encourage gently, my mind already racing with possibilities.

"It's like... there are strings attached. Expectations." Mel's voice drops to almost a whisper. "I'm a good lacrosse player, sure, but my grades? They're okay, not Penamore-level. And now there are these... people. Important people. They keep hinting that I owe them, that I need to play along."

My stomach tightens. This sounds disturbingly familiar—the hallmarks of corruption I've seen before in Lenape City. But targeting a high school senior? That's a new low.

"Play along with what, exactly?" I ask, trying to keep my voice neutral.

Mel shakes her head, frustration evident. "That's just it—I don't know the details. But it feels wrong, Cassie. Like I'm being set up as some kind of... I don't know, pawn? In a game I don't understand."

I glance at Rafi, seeing my concern mirrored in his face. This isn't just about a questionable scholarship anymore. This has the potential to blow wide open into something much bigger, much more dangerous.

"Mel," I say carefully, "I need you to know that if we dig into this, it could get complicated. There might be powerful people involved who don't want their methods exposed."

She nods, a flicker of that familiar determination in her eyes. "I know. But I can't just ignore it. If I stay quiet, I feel like I'm part of whatever this is. And if it comes out later... my whole future could be ruined."

I lean back, considering. This case could be exactly what Maddox Investigative Services needs to establish itself. But more importantly, Mel needs help. She's caught in a web she didn't choose, and I know all too well how that feels.

"Okay," I say finally. "We'll look into it. But Mel, promise me something. No heroics, no confronting anyone on your own. This stays between us for now. Deal?"

Mel's relief is palpable. "Deal. Thank you, Cassie. I didn't know who else to turn to."

As she speaks, I can't shake a nagging feeling. This case feels bigger than just one scholarship. There's a shadow looming over Lenape City, and I have a sinking suspicion we're about to step right into the middle of it.

I lean forward, my elbows on the desk. "Mel, I need you to think carefully. Is there anyone specific you suspect might be involved in this scheme? Any names or connections you've noticed?"

Mel hesitates, her eyes darting to the floor. I can see the internal struggle playing out on her face. Finally, she looks up, her voice barely above a whisper. "I... I think your uncle might be involved. Alfred Maddox."

The name hits me like a punch to the gut. I let out a humorless laugh. "Well, isn't that just perfect? Seems like everyone in Lenape City's got a crooked uncle these days."

Mel's eyes widen in surprise. "You... you're not shocked?"

I shake my head, running a hand through my hair. "Let's just say I'm aware that my dear Uncle Alfred's business dealings aren't always on the up-and-up. Though I never imagined he'd be mixed up in something like this."

The links are clear now, even if I'd rather not acknowledge them. The Genesee Country Club, my uncle's pride and joy, takes on a more sinister air. How many deals did people make on those perfectly manicured greens?

"Cassie?" Mel's voice pulls me back to the present. She looks uncertain, maybe even a little scared. "I'm sorry, I shouldn't have—"

"No," I cut her off, my voice firm. "You did the right thing by coming to me. And I promise you, Mel, we're going to sort this out."

I stand up, walking around the desk to place a hand on her shoulder. "I know how scary this must be for you. But you're not alone in this, okay? We'll figure it out together."

Mel nods, some of the tension leaving her shoulders. "Thank you. I just... I don't want to ruin my future, you know? But I also can't live with myself if I don't do something about this."

"I get it," I say softly, thinking of my own past struggles. "Sometimes doing the right thing feels like the hardest path. But in the end, it's worth it. Trust me on that."

As I watch Mel's face, a mix of fear and determination, I feel a renewed sense of purpose. This case isn't just about exposing corruption; it's about protecting someone caught in the crossfire of scandal. And maybe, just maybe, it's a chance to finally step out of my father's shadow and prove what I'm capable of.

"We've got this, Mel," I say, injecting confidence into my voice. "One step at a time, we'll unravel this thing. Just remember, you're doing the right thing."

I guide Mel towards the door, my mind already racing with possibilities. "I'll start digging into this right away," I assure her, opening the door. "And Mel? You're brave for coming forward. Remember that."

She gives me a small smile, some of her usual confidence returning. "Thanks, Cassie. I... I'm glad I came to you."

As I watch Mel's retreating figure, my thoughts turn to my uncle Alfred.

Where exactly is he running this scheme from? And what's his angle? The questions swirl in my head, a familiar mix of curiosity and apprehension.

* * *

I turn back to the office, catching Rafi's eye. He raises an eyebrow, silently asking if I'm okay.

"Well," I say, leaning against my desk, "looks like we've got our work cut out for us."

Rafi nods, his expression serious. "You sure you don't want a break before we go chasing down your uncle?"

I can't help but let out a short, humorless laugh. "Breaks are for those six feet under, Raf." My gaze drifts to the framed article on the wall—'From Shadows to Spotlight: How Cassie Maddox Exposed a Citywide Conspiracy.'

"You know," I muse, tracing the edge of the frame with my finger, "part of me wants to dive headfirst into this. Like before. But..."

"But you're not making that mistake again," Rafi finishes, his voice gentle but firm.

I nod, turning back to him. "Exactly. We do this smart. We do this carefully. And we definitely don't go anywhere near warehouses with armed goons. Got it?"

Rafi grins. "Speak for yourself, boss. So, where do we start?"

"We start with what we know. And what we don't know. Time to put those research skills of yours to work, partner."

As I settle into my chair, I can't help but feel a mix of excitement and trepidation. This case could be big. But I'm not the same impulsive investigator I was before. This time, I've got backup. This time, I'm ready.

I lean forward, resting my elbows on the desk. "Hey, Rafi? Those files from our recent investigation—you still have them, right?"

Rafi's fingers fly across his keyboard as he responds, "Of course. Delete nothing, remember? It's my personal motto."

I can't help but smile. "Right, how could I forget? Pull up the list of names associated with The Genesee Country Club, will you?"

As Rafi works his tech magic, I watch him. The way his brow furrows in concentration, the slight tilt of his head as he scans the screen. It hits me then, a realization that settles deep in my chest.

"You know," I say. "I couldn't do this without you. Or Lila, for that matter."

Rafi glances up, surprise flickering across his face. "Where's this coming from, Cass?"

I shrug, feeling vulnerable. "Just... thinking. About how I rushed in last time, trying to prove myself. But I need you guys. And I want to be a better friend to both of you."

A warm smile spreads across Rafi's face. "Hey, that's what partners are for, right?"

I nod, returning his smile before turning my attention to the screen. "Alright, let's see what we've got on The Genesee Country Club. Time to find out just how squeaky clean—or dirty—Uncle Alfred really is."

As we dive into the background check, I can feel the familiar thrill of a new investigation taking hold. But this time, it's tempered with caution and gratitude for the people by my side. Whatever we uncover about Alfred Maddox and this admissions scheme, I know we'll face it together.

THE END

Continue the Series

Don't Miss Cassie Maddox's Next Case

Book 2: Dynasty of Deceit – Now Available for Preorder

Cassie Maddox thought her last case nearly broke her. But when suspicious financial records lead straight to Ignite Global—her uncle Alfred's influential nonprofit—Cassie is dragged into a scandal far darker than she expected.

Forged applications. Hidden donors. A college admissions pipeline built on lies.

And Alfred isn't the mastermind... he's the pawn of someone far more powerful.

As Cassie and forensic analyst Rafi Alvi dig deeper, the conspiracy expands to Lenape City's elite. Loyalties fracture, old wounds reopen, and Cassie's relationships—with Rafi, with Lila, and with her father—are pushed to the brink as the truth closes in.

☞ Preorder Dynasty of Deceit now and continue Cassie's next explosive investigation.

https://www.amazon.com/dp/B0G4SZKGJK

Cassie Maddox survived her first case.

This time, the enemy is home.

Spotify Playlist

1. **"Bad Guy" - Billie Eilish***For the layers of deception and manipulation Cassie uncovers throughout her investigation.*
2. **"Seven Nation Army" - The White Stripes***A powerful anthem for Cassie's determination as she digs deeper into the conspiracy.*
3. **"Creep" - Radiohead***Reflects Cassie's moments of self-doubt and her struggle to prove herself.*
4. **"Believer" - Imagine Dragons***Symbolizing Cassie's resilience and refusal to back down despite the danger.*
5. **"Somebody's Watching Me" - Rockwell***For the constant surveillance and the feeling that Cassie is being followed or monitored.*
6. **"Smooth Criminal" - Michael Jackson***Perfectly matches the clever and calculated schemes of Thomas Pence and Chuck Albright.*
7. **"Rolling in the Deep" - Adele***Cassie's emotional turmoil as she uncovers personal betrayals and navigates strained relationships.*
8. **"Boulevard of Broken Dreams" - Green Day***Represents Cassie's isolated journey as she steps into dangerous territory on her own.*
9. **"Power" - Kanye West***Captures the greed and corruption driving Shenandoah Partners and The Peterson Group.*
10. **"Control" - Halsey***Reflects Cassie's inner conflict and determination to take charge of her destiny.*
11. **"Ain't No Rest for the Wicked" - Cage the Elephant***Highlights the relentless pursuit of money and power among the conspirators.*
12. **"Run the World (Girls)" - Beyoncé***Celebrates Cassie's strength, resourcefulness, and ability to navigate a male-dominated world.*

Optional Bonus Tracks

- **"The Chain" - Fleetwood Mac** (For the theme of fractured loyalties.)
- **"Dirty Little Secret" - The All-American Rejects** (Hinting at Alfred Maddox's potential schemes.)
- **"You Don't Own Me" - Grace feat. G-Eazy** (Cassie's independence and fight for agency.)

Book Club Guide

Introduction

Shadows of Deceit by Timothy R. Baldwin is a gripping mystery-thriller about private investigator Cassie Maddox, who becomes entangled in a dangerous web of corruption, financial crime, and betrayal in Lenape City. As she navigates her investigation, Cassie faces strained family relationships, personal risks, and moral dilemmas that test her resolve and ingenuity.

Discussion Questions

Themes and Plot

1. What did you think of the central mystery surrounding Shenandoah Partners and The Peterson Group? Did the twists surprise you?
2. How does the theme of family loyalty versus personal ambition play out in Cassie's relationship with her father and uncle?
3. The story tackles themes of corruption and power. How did the portrayal of corporate greed resonate with current events or real-world scandals?

Characters

1. Cassie is portrayed as both resourceful and vulnerable. How did her character development shape your connection to her?
2. Detective Dylan Maddox plays a complex role in the story. How do his actions influence Cassie's choices?
3. What are your thoughts on the antagonists, especially Thomas Pence and Chuck Albright? Were they convincing as villains?

Writing and Structure

1. How did the author use pacing and tension to keep you engaged? Were there any moments where you couldn't put the book down?
2. What role did the setting of Lenape City play in establishing the story's atmosphere?
3. Did the alternating moments of lightheartedness (e.g., Cassie's interactions with Lila) and intense danger enhance your experience of the story?

Moral Dilemmas and Choices

1. Cassie often debates the ethics of withholding information, especially from her father and Trudy Hunter. Do you agree with her choices?
2. The story hints at a larger conspiracy involving Alfred Maddox. How do you interpret Cassie's decision to pursue this lead in future investigations?
3. How would you have handled Cassie's final choice to align herself with her father and Gregory Hunter despite her initial misgivings?

Activities and Extras

1. **Soundtrack Challenge**

Discuss the *Shadows of Deceit* Spotify playlist. Which songs resonated most with the story or specific characters? Would you add any tracks?

1. **Role Play: The Next Lead**

Imagine you're Cassie at the end of the book. What would be your first move in uncovering Alfred Maddox's potential involvement in the college admissions scandal?

1. **Favorite Scene Discussion**

Share your favorite scene and why it stood out. Was it a tense confrontation, a lighthearted moment with Lila, or a key revelation?

Recommended Pairings

If you enjoyed *Shadows of Deceit*, consider reading:

1. **The Girl with the Dragon Tattoo by Stieg Larsson**: A dark, investigative thriller with complex family dynamics.
2. ***Big Little Lies* by Liane Moriarty**: A layered exploration of secrets and moral dilemmas.
3. ***The Firm* by John Grisham**: A legal thriller focused on corporate corruption and personal stakes.
4. **Any of these excellent thrillers from Indies United Publishing House https://www.indiesunited.net/thrillers**

Final Thoughts

What do you think Cassie Maddox's future holds? Would you want to read a sequel, and if so, what loose ends or characters would you want explored further?

Cocktail Pairings

"The Lenape Noir"

Inspired by the dark, mysterious, and gritty tone of *Shadows of Deceit*, this cocktail balances intrigue and boldness with a hint of sweetness to reflect Cassie's sharp wit and occasional lighthearted moments with Lila.

Ingredients:

- 2 oz bourbon (symbolizing the strong foundation of Cassie's determination)
- 1 oz black cherry liqueur (a nod to the shadowy secrets of Lenape City)
- ½ oz fresh lemon juice (for Cassie's sharp, investigative edge)
- ½ oz simple syrup (to balance the bitterness with a touch of sweetness)
- 2 dashes of aromatic bitters (representing the complexities of betrayal and family ties)
- Garnish: Luxardo cherry and a twist of lemon

Instructions:

1. Fill a shaker with ice and combine bourbon, black cherry liqueur, lemon juice, simple syrup, and bitters.
2. Shake well until chilled.
3. Strain into a rocks glass over a large ice cube.
4. Garnish with a Luxardo cherry skewered with a lemon twist.

"The Phantom Beat"

This vibrant cocktail matches the energy of Phantom Beats, the nightclub where Cassie and Lila share moments of joy and levity amidst the tension of the investigation.

Ingredients:

- 1 ½ oz vodka (Lila's bold and carefree spirit)
- 1 oz blue curaçao (a playful nod to the neon lights of Phantom Beats)
- ½ oz pineapple juice (for a tropical twist, reflecting the warmth of friendship)
- ½ oz lime juice (adding a zesty edge to Cassie's analytical mind)
- Splash of club soda (for a bubbly, celebratory touch)

- Garnish: Edible glitter rim or a neon swizzle stick

Instructions:

1. Rim a highball glass with edible glitter for a fun, glowing effect.
2. Fill the glass with ice and pour in vodka, blue curaçao, pineapple juice, and lime juice.
3. Stir gently, then top with a splash of club soda.
4. Garnish with a neon swizzle stick or a slice of pineapple.

Mocktail Option: "Shayan's Secret"

A non-alcoholic alternative inspired by the mysterious Shayan Easton and her stolen flash drive. This drink hides its complexity behind a smooth, refreshing exterior.

Ingredients:

- 2 oz pomegranate juice (for the deep, hidden layers of the story)
- 1 oz fresh orange juice (adding warmth and brightness to the mix)
- ½ oz grenadine (representing the hints of danger and suspense)
- Splash of sparkling water (for a light, crisp finish)
- Garnish: Pomegranate seeds

Instructions:

1. Combine pomegranate juice, orange juice, and grenadine in a shaker with ice.
2. Shake well and strain into a coupe glass.
3. Top with sparkling water and garnish with a few floating pomegranate seeds.

About the Author

Tim, a seasoned educator with over 15 years of teaching experience across multiple grade levels in English and Drama, has established himself as a dedicated writer with a diverse academic background. He holds a B.S. in Theatre from Towson University, an M.A.T. from Notre Dame of Maryland University, and an M.A. in Creative Writing and Literature from Fairleigh Dickinson University.

Originally from Syracuse, New York, Tim currently resides in Maryland, where he imparts his passion for English, Creative Writing, Film, and Theatre to high school students. His journey into writing began earnestly in 2014, spurred by the encouragement of his own students.

Tim's love for storytelling stems from his upbringing, where his mother's dedication to reading to him and his siblings laid the foundation for his literary pursuits. Tim embarked on his writing endeavors, influenced by authors such as C. S. Lewis, J. R. R. Tolkien, Piers Anthony, and others in the mystery, thriller, and fantasy genres.

Since his debut publication in 2019, Tim has rapidly expanded his literary footprint, amassing a wealth of published works. Beyond writing, Tim enjoys indulging in his diverse interests, including reading, teaching, camping, savoring cigars, shooting, and attending live music concerts.

Tim is also grateful for the support he's received from the editors, authors, and publisher at **Indies United Publishing House**. So, if you're looking for your next great read—or a vibrant community where authors and readers connect—visit Indies United Publishing House. It's where diverse voices, fresh stories, and passionate indie authors come together to celebrate creativity in every genre.

You can connect with me on:

- https://linktr.ee/timothyrbaldwin
- https://x.com/timothyrbaldwin
- https://www.facebook.com/TimothyRBaldwin
- https://www.instagram.com/timothyrbaldwin
- https://www.tiktok.com/@timbaldwin.author
- https://www.indiesunited.net

Also by Timothy R. Baldwin

Timothy R. Baldwin writes crime fiction rooted in classic noir tradition and sharpened by modern stakes. His stories favor tight pacing, sharp dialogue, and investigators who learn—often the hard way—that truth comes at a cost.

His *Cassie Maddox Mystery* series follows a private investigator navigating corruption, loyalty, and consequence as each case pushes further into personal and professional gray zones. In *Dynasty of Deceit*, familiar faces return, and readers may recognize Marcus, Alissa, Janice, and Nate stepping back into the orbit—connections that reward those who have followed Baldwin's work across titles.

Baldwin is also the author of the *Kahale & Claude Mystery Series*, where teamwork, curiosity, and fast-moving puzzles drive a younger cast of sleuths through layered mysteries. Across series and standalones, his books are linked by character, theme, and an evolving world.

Readers who want to follow these threads—and discover where they began—will find more cases, familiar names, and new angles in the "Also By" section.

Dynasty of Deceit

A FAMILY OF POWER. A CITY OF MASKS.

A SECRET THAT SHATTERS THEM BOTH.

Power corrupts. Family deceives. And in Lenape City, the truth is the most dangerous currency of all.

Private investigator Cassie Maddox wants nothing to do with another high-profile case—not after the last one nearly broke her. But when suspicious financial records point straight to Ignite Global, her uncle Alfred's prestigious nonprofit, Cassie is pulled into a scandal far bigger and darker than anything she's faced before.

Forged applications. Hidden donors. A college admissions pipeline built on lies.

And at the center of it all? A family dynasty willing to sacrifice anyone to stay on top.

As Cassie and forensic analyst Rafi Alvi dig deeper, the conspiracy widens to include Lenape City's elite: politicians, power players, and the people who shape the city from behind closed doors. Every answer uncovers another lie. Every lead exposes another betrayal. And when Cassie realizes Alfred isn't the mastermind—but the pawn of someone far more powerful—she's forced to confront a legacy she never asked for.

Loyalties are tested. Friendships crack under pressure. And someone in the shadows is watching Cassie rise...with plans of their own.

Fast-paced, twist-packed, and emotionally charged, DYNASTY OF DECEIT pushes Cassie Maddox to the edge as she battles corruption, family secrets, and the price of exposing the truth. Perfect for fans of Tana French, Karin Slaughter, and Michael Connelly, this second installment in the Cassie Maddox series delivers a gripping blend of noir tension and explosive revelations.

Cassie Maddox survived her first case.

This time, the enemy is home.